THE
ONES
WE LOVE

THE
ONES
WE LOVE

A NOVEL

ANNA SNOEKSTRA

DUTTON

An imprint of Penguin Random House LLC
1745 Broadway, New York, NY 10019
penguinrandomhouse.com

Book design by Katy Riegel

LIBRARY OF CONGRESS CATALOGING-IN-PUBLICATION DATA
Names: Snoekstra, Anna, author.
Title: The ones we love: a novel / Anna Snoekstra.
Description: New York : Dutton, an imprint of Penguin Random House, 2025.
Identifiers: LCCN 2024031398 (print) | LCCN 2024031399 (ebook) |
ISBN 9780593475720 (hardcover) | ISBN 9780593475737 (ebook)
Subjects: LCGFT: Thrillers (Fiction) | Novels. Classification: LCC PR9619.4.S6255
O54 2025 (print) | LCC PR9619.4.S6255 (ebook) | DDC 823/.92—dc23/eng/20240708
LC record available at https://lccn.loc.gov/2024031398
LC ebook record available at https://lccn.loc.gov/2024031399

Printed in the United States of America

1st Printing

The authorized representative in the EU for product safety and compliance is
Penguin Random House Ireland, Morrison Chambers, 32 Nassau Street,
Dublin D02 YH68, Ireland, https://eu-contact.penguin.ie.

For Sadie and Marlow

THE
ONES
WE LOVE

PROLOGUE

Janus watched his wife remove her makeup. She swiped a cloth across the ball of each eyelid, once, twice, three times, then rubbed her lips ungracefully, like her mouth was a doorknob that needed polishing, not the thing she used to speak and sing and kiss. His wife, the ex–ballet dancer; his wife, with her shoulder muscles, her protruding spine, reptilian against the cotton of her T-shirt. She was all bone and muscle and strength. Not like him, with his writer's physique of bad posture, twig arms, and caffeine bloat.

He was watching Kay from the bed through the half-open door of the ensuite. He lay with his laptop on his belly. In front of him, his last typed sentence: *The carpet is a mess of red blood and sinew.* He tried to think of another word for sinew.

His wife had only come back from work ten minutes ago, and she said hello but didn't peck him as she passed. She went straight into the bathroom to brush her teeth and remove her makeup. It was unusual for her to wear makeup at all at work—she always said that she'd only sweat it off anyway. She was a Pilates teacher now, the ballet career ending with the birth of their daughter.

Kay lathered cleanser between her fingers and rubbed her skin clean, then cupped her hands under the tap and threw water onto her face. She looked up at her reflection. She didn't move, only stared into her own eyes with an unreadable expression. It was a private moment, sure, but nothing was ever truly private in a marriage. Janus could always read his wife's face. He'd seen every version of her: glittering onstage, panting through labor, internalizing at the dinner table, beaming at school plays. But this expression, this strange blank look she was giving herself as water dripped from her chin, wasn't one he'd seen before. He couldn't read it. Then her eyes slid across and met his in the mirror, and whatever she was thinking was gone. She smiled at him, the muscles of her cheeks tightening.

Red blood and sinew. He could try *muscle* instead of *sinew.* Or *gristle* or *tissue.* Or he could delete the sentence entirely. Instead he closed his laptop. It would be tomorrow's problem.

"Has Casper called you? He hasn't called me," Kay said, rubbing on hand cream and coming out of the bathroom. They did this every night. Taking stock of their children was as much a routine as the hand cream.

"No. But that's not a bad thing. He's more likely to call if he's hating it."

"True."

"He'll be back on Saturday, he'll tell us about it then."

She pulled open the sheet, slipped in next to him. "I just hope he's making friends," she said, and riding on those words he smelled alcohol on her breath underneath the mask of toothpaste.

She turned onto her side to switch off her lamp. "Olivia's out late again."

"We did promise we'd trust her." He put the laptop onto the floor next to the bed. The skin of his stomach was cold without its hot machine weight.

"Easier said than done. But I'm glad she's doing that internship, it's good for her," Kay said, but she didn't turn back to face him.

"She's okay. She's getting there." He switched his light off too. He should have tried to finish that section. How could he call himself a writer if he couldn't even get through a paragraph without then spending an hour scrolling *Fangoria* or the *New York Times Book Review*?

He reached over and rested a hand on her waist and tried not to think about the scene or another word for sinew; tried not to worry about the deadline or the knowledge that he'd moved his whole family across the world for this. Instead he focused on the swell and release of his wife's rib cage under his hand as she breathed, and stared over her shoulder to the palm tree outside which he could see through the gap in the blinds. He would always look at that tree when he had trouble sleeping; having it right there by his window felt like a triumph. It was such an emblem for this city, a representation of dreams realized. But tonight, in the glistening smog, it looked strange, almost gothic. It was too still, not a breath of breeze in the air. And one frond was dangling, hanging on by a tendril.

He couldn't sleep. The problems with his career scrolled through his brain as he stared into the dark. But he must have drifted off eventually. He must have. Because some time later, he woke with a jerk and the sky outside was warming and the hanging frond was gone, and he could hear something from downstairs. The noise, it sounded animal. But the constriction of his throat, the ice-pick prickle of his skin, all his body's senses told him that the awful sound downstairs was coming from a person.

ONE

Olivia and Leilani sat in the corner, away from the DJ and the dancing. They were posing, really, and trying not to stare at the B-list celebrities or the too-young models doing lines with indie-sleaze soft boys. Liv licked the salt from the rim of her margarita, sucked on the lime. Next to her, Leilani was vaping cherry vanilla and leaning back, her legs crossed at just the right angle, bronzed and long in her snakeskin heels.

"There he is." Leilani's breath warm on her ear, tilting her head toward a guy in a black suit.

"Dior?" Liv asked.

"Raf Simons."

Liv could guess the designer of a dress from a city block away, but she was still working on her familiarity with menswear.

"He's hotter in person." Leilani looked like she wanted to eat him.

"You're after a new job, remember? Not a hookup."

"Couldn't hurt."

It was the Los Angeles Designer Showcase closing-night gala, and they weren't really meant to be here. Leilani had swiped the invitation from her boss's desk. She'd said he wouldn't notice; he wasn't noticing much of anything at the moment. She expected he'd be back in rehab by the end of the month, which was why she was after a new position.

For the past six days, Liv had been interning at the showcase backstage, stripping thousand-dollar outfits from models and then redressing them before the bridge of the song finished. It was where she'd met Leilani, a model turned PA. They'd been going out every night after wraps, bonding over free drink cards at the festival pop-up bar downtown. They'd talk about guys and bitch about the designers. Leilani would wrap her arm around Liv's shoulders, rest her cheek on her head, and say, *You're fucking great, Liv, I'm so glad I met you*, and Liv would beam. She'd moved to the US from Australia with her family a few months ago, and this was her first real friend. The move was meant to be a fresh start, and after flunking out of fashion school and then getting into partying, she needed one. But it had been hard going back to living with her parents at twenty-two, after years of living with friends. She'd started staying at Leilani's every other night. It was nice to reclaim a bit of independence, to wake up late and make coffee together on the stovetop and not have anyone breathing down her neck.

They were on a two-drink maximum for this party. Even though she'd be staying at Leilani's, she still had no intention of getting the slightest bit messy. She was going to meet people and network and be seen so that when she applied for an apprenticeship, she wouldn't be just another desperate, hopeful nobody. She looked perfect—she knew that. She'd driven over to Leilani's place with a bag of clothes, but ended up wearing something of Leilani's from her modeling days: a romper in a thick blue satin that shone like the ocean. She hadn't thought it would fit her, but in fact, it was snug on her curves and looked sexy and expensive. They'd taken caffeine pills so they'd still be clearheaded when the party turned to dregs and everyone started opening up about their last failed relationship and the hole inside them that felt so big. It was going to be a great night.

"We should mingle." Leilani snapped up onto her heels. She reached out to Liv. "Come on."

↓

EVERYTHING HURT. LIV'S brain kick-drummed inside her skull. Her stomach buckled. She turned over on the couch, retching. Leilani would kill her if she puked on her floor, so she swallowed the bile back down.

Her eyelids smarted as she blinked them open against the late-afternoon sun pouring into the room. Liv startled. She wasn't looking down at Leilani's scratched wooden floorboards, but at gray carpet. She wasn't in Leilani's living room. She wasn't lying on the pink crushed-velvet vintage couch.

A Japanese Godzilla movie poster on the wall. Blue jersey bedsheets. She was home, in her brother's room.

She pushed herself up, and her head felt like it was splitting in two. The room spun.

She remembered the gala. The margarita. Leilani's cherry vanilla. They'd been sitting on the couches, they went to network, and then . . . complete blackness, like a cloak had been thrown over her memory. Somehow it was Friday afternoon already.

She looked around for her brother, but there was no one else there. Swim camp, she remembered. It was early June, and Casper was at swim camp.

She forced her feet out from under the sheets and scrunched her eyes shut against the swinging room, and just that, just scrunching shut her eyelids, brought on sharp pain. This was more than a hangover. She stepped onto the carpet, pressed her heels down hard, trying to steady herself. When she felt like she could stand, she opened her eyes back up. Her knees were pink and gray, slightly bruised. She must have fallen last night. And the short romper in shiny blue was gone. Now she was just wearing her white tank top and underwear.

Liv pushed off the bed, skittered the ten steps to the bathroom across the hall, pulled up the toilet lid, and threw up into the bowl. She spat twice and then flushed it down. Her limbs trembled as she stood; her back and neck were slick with sweat. Turning the tap on, she filled her mouth with water and spat again into the bathroom sink. Then she drank straight from the faucet, guzzling the water down.

When she straightened, she was met by her own reflection.

Something had happened.

There were blotchy red marks on one side of her neck and her eye was swollen up and something purple was peeping out of the neckline of her top. She pulled the fabric down. There was a huge bruise on her chest above her breasts, purple turning to a crimson red in the middle. She touched it with her finger, and it seared hot with pain.

She left the bathroom and headed past her parents' room toward the stairs. But she stopped and took a step back into their doorway. Her mother was sitting on the double bed in the near dark, the blinds closed against the sun. She looked frozen there, hands in her lap, spine stick-straight, face blank.

"Mum?"

Her mother turned to her, but her expression didn't waver.

"What happened? I was meant to stay at—" Liv started coughing as she was about to finish the sentence, but she forced herself to stop; otherwise she'd be sick again.

"We can't ever talk about it."

"Did I puke somewhere? God, I'm sorry."

Her mum didn't respond right away; she just stared. Liv had never seen her face so pale. Her mother's skin was bloodless, corpse-like.

"We have to pretend it never happened. Okay? That's the safest way. Promise me."

"What?"

Her mother got annoyed with her sometimes, or disappointed. But this strange coldness was something else. This wasn't normal.

"Don't talk about it. Not to your friends back home. Not even to me and your dad. Thank God Casper's at swim camp. One day later and he would've been here . . . but he can never know. Promise me, all right? Not a word."

Liv had no idea what to say. She needed some ibuprofen. Her head hurt.

"Olivia, promise me."

"Mum, I—"

"This isn't a conversation. Not after what we've done for you." Her voice was brittle. Thin glass ready to shatter.

"Okay, okay. Fine, I won't," Liv said. She couldn't deal with this right now, not with the thumping pain behind her eyes and her stomach still roiling. Liv turned away and went down the stairs. She needed to take something for her head and then go to her room and find her phone, call Leilani and ask her what the hell had happened. Running her hand down the handrail to steady herself, her palm slid over something gritty on the wood. It was a small wine-red smear. Dried blood.

Her room was next to the garage. It was small, meant to be a study, but it afforded a shred of privacy since it wasn't on the same level as the rest of her family. She was about to turn toward it, but she heard vacuuming. Her dad must be home. He'd tell her what was going on.

In the lounge room he was holding the vacuum in his hand, but he wasn't moving. He was standing there suctioning one square of carpet.

"Dad?"

He jumped, like she'd yelled. "Oh, Liv, how are you, honey? You okay?"

"Not really. I can't . . . Last night is a bit blurry. Did I . . ." She wanted to ask what happened, but her mum had just told her not to.

"Am I okay?" she said instead. Meaning: *How bad was it?* Meaning: *How upset with me are you?*

"You're okay. Go back to bed," he said. But he didn't meet her eyes. He started moving the vacuum then, even though the floor was spotless around him.

She turned away and headed for her bedroom. But something was different. There was a bolt drilled into her door, fastened closed with a padlock.

TWO

They had arrived in America at night. LAX shone with white lights as they waited outside for a cab. Kay could still remember the swell of anticipation she'd felt standing in that line. Even at ten p.m. in January, it was warm. The air stank of exhaust and the smoke from huddles of tired travelers sucking on their first cigarettes after long flights. While her husband, Janus, was explaining to Olivia the plot of the movie he'd watched on the plane, Kay had put her arm around Casper. He'd hugged her back for a moment even though they were sweaty and disheveled from the journey and he'd become prickly about hugging his mum in public. Casper hadn't wanted to come, but now even he was buzzing; his eyes were big and shiny. Somehow Janus's little horror novel had become a big deal, making it all the way to a producer's desk in Hollywood. It was an opportunity none of them had expected. A new beginning for them all.

As their cab sped down the freeway, they passed convertibles with their tops down, women's long hair flickering in the black night. The cab's headlights bounced off a town of tents set up on the verge. The road signs were dirty, foretelling turnoffs for Beverly Hills, for Studio City, for Sunset Boulevard. Endless lines of palm trees stood tall in air that gleamed with pollution. No one had spoken on that cab ride, the possibility of this new place stretching out for each of them. That was only five short months ago.

Now it was a Sunday and Kay was dawdling on her dog walk. Casper had returned from swim camp yesterday, and she and Janus had news that he wasn't going to like. She'd meant to head straight back after the dog park, but had gone to the café instead to get a takeaway, anything to put off going home. She took the first sip of her coffee and shivered. She hated Americanos. So bitter. She preferred milk in her coffee, soft creamy lattes. Warm, not hot. But she wouldn't let herself have an indulgence like that. It had only been two days.

Kay untied Ginger's leash from the post, catching a snippet of conversation as two women passed her.

"She just never seemed violent to me."

"Do you think she'll be arrested?"

Kay stiffened. The rest of their conversation was cut off as they went into the café. She wanted to follow them, ask them who they'd been speaking about—was it about her family, was it about her daughter? But of course she couldn't do that.

She set her spine straight and headed home. Their house was on Maltman Avenue in Silver Lake, a long, steep street on the side of a hill. The Spanish-colonial-style houses were painted in salmon pinks, baby blues, and yellows. There were palm trees the whole way up. Even residential streets like theirs had palm trees.

"Wait up, Kay!"

It was their next-door neighbor Esperanza, who everyone called Rani. She was coming down her driveway with her dog, a staghound, Rufus. Ginger threw herself to the ground and rolled onto her back at Rani's feet.

"Yes, I see you there, Ginger, baby," Rani said, bending down to rub the spot where the Jack Russell's pink belly showed through her fur. Rani was one of those women who seemed effortlessly beautiful. All dark curls, silky scarves, and kind eyes.

"Going home?" Rani asked.

"Yes, we've already been to the park," Kay said, looking up at her house.

"Did you hear about what happened?"

"No," Kay said, trying to keep her face blank.

"You know those robberies we've been having?"

Kay relaxed. This had nothing to do with her, or her family.

"They arrested them?" she asked.

"Not exactly. You know Jessie Nguyen? She lives on Baxter Street."

"Vaguely." Kay had seen her looking sleep-deprived with her two little kids at the park.

"Apparently she was keeping a pipe filled with cement by the front door. The guy was trying to get into her garage at dawn, and so she whacked him over the head with it."

"Wow."

"Yeah. Didn't want him near her kids."

"Fair enough, I guess. She probably did us all a favor."

Kay pulled her keys out of her pocket. She had to keep moving. She couldn't put off talking to Casper all day. She said goodbye to Rani and went up the path. It was a small house, some might call it poky, but she had loved it straightaway. Big arched windows that let in the light, rose-colored tiles in the bathroom, the kitchen in sage green that opened out to the little dining room so you could talk while you cooked. It was the kind of house that had suffered from decades of being a rental. The stucco walls needed a fresh coat of paint; the tiles had cracks; the air-conditioning unit was broken. Still, to Kay, it had been charming. Now she'd be happy to never see the place again.

A sick ripple started in her gut and came up through her chest, burned in her throat. She tried to swallow. Couldn't. She paused at the doorway, keys held up to the door. She knew what she had to do: go through the door; be the mum, the wife, the normal woman.

Pretend nothing had happened.

Still, she couldn't make herself put the key in the lock.

"You all right, Kay?" Rani was farther up the street, turning back to look at her.

"Fine!" Kay pushed the key into the lock. Turned it. Opened the door. Stepped inside.

"No coffee for me?"

Janus was in the kitchen, already dressed and shaven. Even freshly showered, the man looked disheveled. His T-shirt was overwashed. His orange hair spiked up at odd angles. His glasses were smudged.

"Sorry," she said. "You were in bed when I left."

"It's okay."

After only two days, it was amazing how good they were at play-acting.

"Anyway, I told Cas we needed to talk, and he hasn't let it go. He's been at me about it all morning."

She quietened her tone. "Have you done her place yet?"

"Not yet. But I will. Don't worry."

For a moment they stood looking at each other, the horror pulsing in the air between them, then he faked a smile and she turned away.

Kay went into the lounge, where their son, Casper, was sitting. He had one skinny-jeaned leg folded over the other, his dark curly hair in his eyes, his arms crossed.

"What's going on?" he said. "Dad's being all weird and elusive."

"Everything is fine," Kay told him, sitting down on the couch. "Don't worry."

He leaned his head back and groaned. Sometimes she looked at her children and wondered how they'd become so big, so full of personality.

"I *am* worried. Last time we did this was when you said we were moving here. Where are we going now? El Salvador?"

"El Salvador?" Now she smiled. "Why El Salvador?"

"I don't know! Why LA?"

"You know why, Dad's career."

"Yeah, okay," he said and looked at her through his hair, and she knew just what he was thinking: *What career?*

She'd read somewhere that a fetus's DNA stayed in their mother's blood for decades after birth. That made sense to her. She had made each of her children, but equally both of them had remade her entirely. When she looked at Casper, she could feel it. His cells still existed in her veins.

Janus came back in, and behind him, their daughter, Olivia. Somehow, with her hair buzzed down to an inch, she was even more striking. All high cheekbones and big dreamy eyes. Kay had never dared cut her own hair any shorter than shoulder length. She noticed that Liv was dressed up. She'd barely been out of her pajamas these last couple of days, but now she had on a hot-pink top and a short red skirt.

Liv smiled at her in that new, searching way of hers. Kay turned away, trying not to let any emotion show on her face. Maybe it had been long enough that Olivia's cells had left her body. She didn't understand her daughter at all anymore.

"So what is it?" Casper said.

Kay looked at Janus, but he said nothing. He was waiting for Kay to break the news. It was always up to her. Since they'd moved, she'd felt frustration toward him simmer, but since this weekend, it had been dialed all the way up to boiling-hot rage.

She let the silence fill the room, but Janus kept on looking at her expectantly.

"What's going on?" Liv said.

"Mum and Dad have decided to talk to us via ESP. It's not working."

Liv snorted a laugh.

"Where are you going anyway?" he asked her. "I thought you'd decided to become one of those women who never leaves their—I mean *my*—bedroom and then gets really massive and then dies and we have to get a crane to lift you out and all the neighbors come and watch."

She looked at him, one eyebrow raised. "God, you've only been back a day and you're already such a pleasure, aren't you?"

"I live to please."

"In answer to your question, I'm going out."

"Where?

"Shopping."

"You have no money."

"Window shopping."

"Can I come?"

"No, you're too annoying."

Casper crossed his arms across his chest. "I don't care anyway, I need to pack."

"Casper," Kay said, "that's what we need to talk to you about."

She looked at Janus. He shifted uncomfortably. The anger pulsed behind her eyes. She gave in.

"We've changed our minds about your trip."

"What!?" Casper said. "We planned this ages ago!"

"We're struggling a little financially," she said. "And we want to keep you close right now. You're too young to go by yourself."

"Hang on, hang on." Casper was sitting forward now. "Can't we talk about this? It's just back home. And I'll be staying with James, and you know his parents."

"We're sorry, Cas. We should never have agreed in the first place." Janus's eyes were on his lap.

"But I don't want to stay here! What am I going to do for the rest of the summer?" Casper said.

"He'll be fine." Olivia sat down next to her brother. "Fifteen isn't that young and he knows Melbourne. Plus, he's such a nerd, as if he'll get up to anything."

"Exactly," Casper said. "I'm a massive nerd. I'm boring!"

"We trust you, it's not that," Kay said. "And we really didn't want to disappoint you."

"You have your job here," Janus said.

"I only get like one shift a week at the café. And Liv was going to take over helping Hélène while I was gone."

"Yeah, easy," Olivia said.

"It's not up for discussion!" Kay said, and her voice was too loud and too sharp. They both looked at her, surprised. She wasn't the type of mother who yelled.

"So Liv and I are meant to keep sharing a room?" Casper said.

"The landlords are going to sort out the mold in Liv's room soon," Kay said.

"The padlock is kind of overkill," Olivia murmured.

"It's a legal thing. Insurance. Mold spores can be really dangerous," Janus said, but even to Kay it sounded flimsy.

Casper looked Kay right in the eye. "I don't want to stay here, Mum. I want to go home."

"Sorry, Cas," she said. And she was. She was so, so sorry.

"We just want you close right now," Janus said.

"Why though?" Casper asked. "What's changed? You've both been so weird since I've been back. I only went away for a week, what happened?"

"Nothing," she said.

"Well, great. This is perfect." Casper stood up and stomped up the stairs.

Olivia stood up too, slinging her bag back over her shoulder.

"Can I take the car for a couple of hours?"

Kay glared at her. She had no idea how Olivia could even hold her head up.

"No," Kay said.

"What? But I only want to go to Melrose, just to walk around and try on clothes and hang out. I'm not going to be meeting up with anyone or drinking or anything like that."

"You can take the bus."

Olivia just looked at her. Then she turned and left the house silently, her shoulders high like she was keeping in a sob.

Kay and Janus sat in silence for a moment.

"Have you started Liv's room?" he asked.

"Working on it," she said. "It's . . . more complicated than I thought it would be."

"Okay," he said. Then Janus got up and left the room without another word.

She waited until she was sure he was gone, then took the note out of her pocket. She'd found it in the mailbox when she'd gotten home late last night. It was the real reason why she'd insisted that they cancel Casper's trip. She unfolded it. There were two short sentences scrawled across in black ink: *I saw. My silence will cost you.*

Kay ripped the note up again and again until it was confetti in her hands.

THREE

At work that afternoon, Casper took his frustration out on the dishes: scouring off smears of sauce and beans with all his strength, turning the shooting water jet up to boiling hot and banging the dishes into the tray so hard that he actually broke one plate clean in half. He started on the coffee mugs, enjoying the clunk-whack of ceramic on ceramic.

It was stinking hot in the kitchen at Café Sabrosa. It was always hot in LA. Always clammy and sticky and dirty and gross. With the oven and stovetops behind him and the steam from the boiling water, he was drenched in itchy sweat under his T-shirt.

"Still feeling angry, I see," Carlos said from behind him. Casper hadn't noticed him coming into the kitchen. He had a dishrag on his shoulder and a stack of new dirty plates in his hands. Carlos was his boss, but he was actually a cool guy. He chatted to him as much as the other staff, even though Casper was just the dish pig.

"I'm fine."

Casper forced himself not to slam down the next cup.

"A lot of people share bedrooms," Carlos said. He'd realized that Casper was upset as soon as he'd walked in for his shift. Casper had let Carlos believe it was because of the sharing-a-room thing, when really it was the staying-in-LA-for-the-summer thing. He didn't want Carlos to think he didn't like the job. He did. Short-term.

"Yeah," Casper said, "but not with a sibling of the other sex. I mean, that's different, I reckon."

"It is," Xav the cook yelled over the sound of simmering onions. "I don't know how they do it in Australia, but—"

"Stop!" Casper said. "Whatever lame xenophobic incest joke you are about to make, just don't."

"I didn't say nothing 'bout incest!"

"I shared with my brother when we were little," Carlos went on. "When he moved out, I didn't know how to sleep on my own. Used to call him and beg him to come back."

"I didn't know you had a brother," Xav butted in.

"He's not around anymore."

Casper wasn't sure what that meant exactly, that his brother was dead or just living in a different state, and it wasn't like there was a tactful way to ask, so he just said, "It's only for a couple of weeks until they fix the mold."

"You really believe that?" Xav called. "They probably want to put the other room on Airbnb."

"Just shut the hell up, okay? Do you think that you can manage that?"

"Table eight is all done," Carlos said before Xav could reply. "Do you want to take off after you've done these? Your friend is out there."

"Okay. Thanks."

Casper didn't smash any more dishes. He did them quickly, loaded the glass washer, and forced himself to be nice to Xav so he could ask him to make him a breakfast burrito.

That was one thing he did like about LA. The breakfast burritos.

Tye was sitting at the table under the community noticeboard, which was crammed with postcards and ads for handymen and pictures of fat babies. Tye's notebook and iPad were in front of him, and his headphones were on. He'd stopped halfway through cleaning his glasses on his black T-shirt and was squinting at something on his screen.

"If you put them back on, you could probably see that better," Casper said, sitting down across from him.

"Casper!" Tye pushed his thick glasses back on and beamed at him. "They announced Agustín Delgado's new film, and it's a drama about some kid who has lost his shoes, can you believe that?"

"Is that good?" It was hard to tell sometimes.

Tye looked at him like he was insane. "If you know how to make people cry in a space movie, why would you go back to making dramas? About shoes?"

Tye had a lot of opinions about genre movies. He liked thrillers the most, especially '90s crime ones starring Denzel Washington. He wanted to be a director and kept saying he'd be the first Black director under twenty-five to win a Saturn Award. Originally, he'd said eighteen, but Casper had gotten him up to twenty-five. Considering they were the biggest genre-movie awards in the world, twenty-five seemed like a safer bet.

Casper placed a large takeaway mochaccino in front of him, and Tye's eyes lit up. The guy lived off these ridiculous American coffees with towers of cream on them. So much caffeine and sugar—that was probably why he was always so excited by everything. In Australia everyone had plain milk in their coffees.

A text came through on Casper's phone. It was from Hélène, an older French lady who lived down the street. She'd had a hip replacement a few months ago, so she sometimes paid Casper to do stuff for her like pick up groceries or mow her front lawn. *I called in an order at Sabrosa, can you drop it by on your way home?*

Sure, he replied.

Merci infiniment. Just leave it by the door, I'll be taking a bath.

"Should we walk?" he said to Tye.

"Yeah, sounds good."

They made their way out of the café, grabbing the bag for Hélène from under the heat lamps. Outside, the bleached daylight baked the sidewalk. Casper unpeeled the foil from his burrito and took a huge bite. He closed his eyes when he chewed. Scrambled eggs, lemony guac, creamy pinto beans, cheese. Xav was an asshole, but he really could cook.

"One day I'm going to film you eating a burrito. The way you close your eyes . . . you make it seem romantic."

Casper opened his eyes. "Okay, no, definitely not."

"It's art."

"Everything is art to you."

"Casper." Tye always said his full name, not *Cas* like everyone called him back home. And he'd elongate the *r* in that American way. *Casperrrrr.* "You seem grumpy."

"How can you tell?"

"Your eyes get all clouded over when you're pissed about something. Is it Liv? The room-sharing?"

"Don't tell anyone about that. I'm getting enough *Flowers in the Attic* jokes at work as it is."

"Who am I going to tell? Anyway, you're leaving next week."

He shrugged. "Yeah, about that. They canceled my flights."

"What?"

"Mum told me this morning. Apparently they've decided they don't want me to go home for the summer."

His voice hitched on the final word. *Home.* Tye looked at him and Casper wished he hadn't told him. He took another bite of his burrito, not that he could taste it anymore. He didn't want Tye to see him upset; then he'd probably never want to hang out. He was glad they were walking so he had an excuse not to look at him.

"Why can't you go?"

"Don't know," he said between mouthfuls. "Just another part of my parents' personality transplant."

"What do you mean?"

"They've been so weird since I got back this weekend. Mum is next-level pissed off and Liv is like the walking dead and Dad is . . . Sorry. I'm talking too much. How are you doing? How's your short film script?"

"Oh, no, don't change the subject," Tye said. "You know I like a mystery. Something weird happened, don't you want to figure it out?"

"This isn't like a proper mystery! There's no detective. There's no crime."

"Still . . . there could be something. Like . . . I don't know . . . an affair. Drugs! You guys love meth in Australia, right?"

"It's not meth."

"What about a gambling addiction or—"

"No, I don't think it's anything like that. It's not them . . . It's something to do with Liv. I'm sure of that. She has bruises."

"Bruises? Like . . . bad ones?"

"Yeah, pretty nasty. And I saw a really bad one on her chest she was trying to cover up. Apparently she went out on Thursday night and got really drunk or something." He was about to mention the padlock on Liv's bedroom door, but stopped himself. It sounded so weird.

"That's not good. Someone must have hurt her."

"I know, right? I was so worried she'd been attacked at first. Like maybe she had her drink spiked? But she said that she hadn't, that she'd know if that had happened."

He didn't know why he'd brought any of this up. It freaked him out.

"Do you believe her?"

He shrugged. "Yeah. I mean . . . if she'd been attacked or something, then why would my parents be so mad at her? Plus, she seems so ashamed of herself. She just said she drank too much and Mum and Dad had to look after her and now they're pissed off about it. That's the only thing that makes sense."

But really, none of it made sense.

"But she didn't say how she got her bruises?"

"She says she was too drunk to remember and that Mum and Dad don't want to talk about it."

"Doesn't she want to know though?"

He groaned. "That's my sister for you. She's literally the most avoidant person I know. If something seems like it's going to be confrontational or make her feel bad about herself, she'll just ignore it."

Plus, he knew Liv had gone through a bad phase with going out too much last year. But he wouldn't mention that to Tye; he might look at it as confirmation of his meth theory.

"But you believe that something big happened. And that they're hiding it from you?"

"Yeah. I do."

"Well, we should try and figure it out. We should . . . I don't know, call the people she went out with Thursday night or—"

Casper held up his hands. "No, no, I'm not doing that! This is not going to be some teen mystery-club bullshit. Whatever issues they have, it's their problem."

"I guess," Tye said. "Although it sounds like it's kind of your problem too."

"Whatever. I don't even care. They'll figure it out."

He left the food by Hélène's door and they kept walking.

"Anyway, your short film. How's it going?"

"Screenplay is good. I still think you should act in it."

"I don't know why you think I'm an actor."

"I don't think it, I feel it. I see it!"

He and Tye had first met in media class. Starting a new school in a new country midway through freshman year wasn't ideal, and Casper had struggled to connect with anyone. He'd joined the swim team in an attempt to be social—he'd been part of the team back home—but somehow even the smell of chlorine, the familiar strokes, the echoing banter of the changing room, all felt wrong and different. It didn't help that in the US they swam on the right side instead of the left, and he kept getting mixed up and accidently swimming into the lane line. He and Tye had been paired up in media for a film assignment, something he'd never had much interest in before. Casper agreed to let Tye film him performing Morpheus's speech from one of the crappy *Matrix* sequels. *This is Zion and we are not afraid!* He thought they were just mucking around, but Tye got this funny look on his face. He said that Casper had "it," whatever that meant. Ever since, it seemed they'd just wind up hanging out without even planning it—it helped that Tye was a total caffeine addict and came to Sabrosa every other day.

Now he let Tye tell him his ideas for his "epic" short film. He tried to keep his eyes focused, but really he was thinking about that day he'd come back from swim camp. How his mum's face was so pale he could see the thin blue veins in her temples. How he'd noticed his dad put his hands in his pockets to stop them from shaking.

Something had happened while he'd been away, something big. And he was the only member of his family who didn't know what it was.

They stopped in front of his house.

"Maybe you're right," Casper said. "Maybe we should try and figure out what's going on. With my family."

He looked quickly at Tye, hoping he wouldn't think it was weird
he'd said the word *we*, but Tye was beaming.

"Really?"

Casper scrunched up the foil into a ball in his hand. "Why not?
Otherwise it's going to be a really long summer."

FOUR

Liv caked a fresh layer of concealer over the bruise on her neck. There was something vaguely anti-feminist about using makeup to cover bruises, but she didn't want to deal with anyone's questions. At first, she'd hated touching the tender, mottled flesh. Her black eye was basically healed, and her neck had turned from red to a black maroon to the green-gray of old guacamole, but at least the lighter colors were easier to conceal. The one on her chest was still too dark to cover up, which meant wearing high-neck tops in the middle of summer. At least her makeup skills had improved. She'd found a You-Tube tutorial from a part-time drag artist, part-time cage fighter who boasted about turning their face from crime scene to beauty queen in half an hour.

The whole makeover was probably overkill for babysitting her rich neighbors' six-year-old, but she was happy for a reason to get out of the house. It had become like a prison. A boring, domestic, un-air-conditioned prison where her cellmate was a sarcastic teenage boy and her warden was an uptight Pilates teacher. It had been a couple of days, but she was still mad about the way her mother had looked at her on Sunday, the expression of disgust on her face, how easily she'd shut her down. The way her eyes had traveled up Liv's body, Liv knew that she was looking at her legs and seeing the fat that she would blast off if Liv ever went to one of her fitness classes. But she never would. She was sick of the body-shame bullshit. She used to wish she'd inherited her mum's petite dancer's frame, but now she was glad she hadn't. She liked her soft bits.

She headed downstairs and straight out the front door. She crossed the grass, which was crispy under her feet on their side, and green and springy once she crossed the property line. She let herself into the neighbors' place using the spare key they kept out for her under a potted plant. They were always out back by the pool and never heard her knock, so she didn't even bother anymore. She'd been baby-sitting for Rani and Brian for three months now. They paid cash, which was awesome, although she'd need another job if she was going to move out. And she needed to move out.

She opened the door to fridge-like AC. Being rich in a city like this meant the luxury of not having to worry about sweat stains. She had resented Brian and Rani's wealth to begin with—she always disliked wealthy people on principle. And it wasn't hard to see them as some gross cliché: a wealthy white guy who edged on arrogant and his younger Latina wife who gave up her art career when she married him. But it became hard to keep judging them when they were always so straightforwardly kind to her.

"Liv!" Their six-year-old daughter, Maria, came running through the open glass doors into the kitchen. She propelled herself into Liv, knocking the wind out of her chest. Liv stifled a yelp—her bruise was still so sore. She grabbed Maria, grimacing, and pulled her up on her hip. The little girl was barefoot and soggy in her green bathing suit, chlorine dripping from her dark curls.

"Whoa, you're almost too big to carry like this."

"Not yet!"

They went out to the backyard, and she set Maria down onto her feet.

"Will you come in the pool with me?" she asked.

"Nah, it's going to get dark soon. Why don't you go get cleaned up and we can do something fun?"

Maria crossed her arms and Liv tickled her.

"How about some marshmallows, all right? How does that sound? We'll put them in the microwave and see what happens."

Maria squealed and ran back inside.

"Mommy! Liv said I can have marshmallows for dinner!"

Brian was down by the fence line, drinking what looked like a gin and tonic with a thin slice of cucumber instead of lime. She headed over to him.

"Hey, Olivia." He shook the ice in his glass. "You should try this gin once you've put Maria down."

"Thanks."

Olivia liked how Brian always treated her like an equal, despite her being a babysitter and him being a rich dick in a suit. Square jaw, ash-blond hair, broad shoulders, he was like the stereotype of the all-American man without the firearms and the racism.

He was an entertainment agent, but Liv had seen him home in the middle of the day recently when she'd looked out her window. She wasn't sure if that meant he wasn't working right now or what, but he only ever seemed to be home when his wife wasn't, which made Liv think that she might not know. It was none of Liv's business anyway.

"Ginger! Stop it! No digging! Bad dog! Back inside!"

Her father's voice was loud from next door. Brian raised his eyebrows at her. She could smell tobacco wafting over the fence. Sometime this week her dad had started secretly smoking again.

Rani came out through the back patio doors behind Liv. She looked beautiful, dressed in a green jumpsuit that had wide-leg pants and a contrasting fuchsia scarf.

"Gucci?" Liv asked.

"Spring/Summer 2018," Rani said. "I guess that's probably considered dated now."

"No, it's a knockout."

One of her favorite parts of babysitting was seeing what Rani would wear out to the exclusive restaurants they went to. That, and the free rein she got over their fridge and medicine cabinet.

"I don't think my husband agrees with you."

Brian came up to her, throwing an arm around her shoulders and kissing her cheek with a smacking sound. "I do," he said, "but you know I like you in dresses better."

She shrugged him off, smiling. "You're so old-fashioned."

He held up his hands. "I can't help it. I can't get past a beautiful woman in a beautiful dress."

Rani hesitated, like she was actually considering getting changed.

"Don't listen to him," Liv said. "You look great. So, where are you going? Somewhere really fancy?"

LATER SHE SAT on the carpet letting Maria give her a makeover. Maria's room was small and sweet. She had framed illustrations of rabbits above her little bed, and a thick downy comforter. In the corner hovered a half-deflated foil balloon in the shape of the number 6. It was pitch black outside and probably close to her bedtime, which meant Maria kept insisting that there was just one more thing that she needed to do to make Liv beautiful. She'd applied some horrible dark blue lipstick to Liv's mouth and some cheap kid-glitter in circles on her cheeks. Luckily, Maria didn't even attempt eye makeup, which was good because although the bruise was almost faded, her eye was still tender. Liv knew Maria's real ambition was to make her look as silly as possible, even though she kept saying "Stunning, stunning" the whole way through. Liv wondered if Rani ever let Maria give her a ridiculous makeover. Liv's own mother definitely hadn't when she was a kid.

With Maria distracted, Liv had time to pull out her phone. She typed a DM to Leilani: *Hey girl, everything okay? Hoping you can tell me just how bad I was on Thursday. Miss you!* She deleted the last two words, added an *x*, then hit send. How many unanswered messages took you over the line from repentant friend to *Ingrid Goes West*? This was the fourth she'd sent in the last five days with no response. Since Friday, she'd been shame spiraling. She knew she must have been an absolute mess for this kind of fallout from both her parents as well as her friend. A vomit-in-the-hair, wet-your-pants kind of mess. Just thinking about it made her ears turn hot.

"I think it's bedtime," she told Maria.

"Almost done. This would be much easier if you had longer hair." She took a silver curly ribbon from the basket of wrapping paper.

"Okay, well, whatever magic you are doing, you only have five more minutes."

"Why do you have makeup on your neck, Liv?" Maria said, rubbing at it.

"Just for fun," Liv said, trying to pull away. But Maria wrapped her arms around her head to keep her there.

Liv's running theory was that she'd fallen down the stairs. That would explain her injuries and that small smear of dried blood on the handrail, which had disappeared by the next day. Her mother was still furious. Her dad was barely looking at her. She couldn't pretend she didn't know why. She'd promised them it would never happen again.

The last time was a month before they moved here. In fact, it was a big part of the reason she'd decided to come along for this fresh start. She'd been thrilled when she got accepted into fashion school and ecstatic when she moved into a crumbling house share with some friends. For a while there, she was having fun and doing well in her course and delighting in this new shiny life that she'd built for herself. She aced the first year of her degree, attempted to watch every Jean-Luc Godard film with her housemates, managed to juggle night shifts in a bar with studying, had her first adult relationship (with one of the regulars at the bar—it fizzled at three months) and her first real heartbreak (with her manager at the bar, and the courtship only existed for fifteen minutes at a time in the underground keg room that stank of sulfur). Then everything started to slip. At first, she had just been going out after her shifts ended and arriving to class hungover. Then she was missing class entirely because she was coming down from whatever pill or tab she'd done the night before. She failed her second year of school, the assignments stacking up too quickly at the end of the semester, but she didn't tell her parents. She was entirely focused on her job at the bar and her friends and the good time she was having and who was going to meet her at what club after her shift ended and which house party they'd finish up at. It was exhilarating to be able to do what she wanted, to mess up, to make bad choices, without anyone judging her, worrying about her, watching her. When her mother called, she often didn't even answer.

It was so much fun, until it wasn't. Until it was being fired from the bar for coming down on shift by the manager who she still wished would love her. Or unexpected panic attacks. Or a twisting stomach that seemed allergic to any food she ate. But that was all daytime stuff. When she was out, it was great music and fizzy blood.

She'd met the guy at a house party. He was a friend of a friend. She'd seen him around before, thought he was cute in that dirty-jeaned, home-done-tattoo sort of way. They'd texted all week. It was just before Christmas and all her roommates had gone away or back home for the holiday. He said he'd come over and make her tea. She'd thought he'd meant magic mushroom tea, which she'd had before and not really enjoyed, but she was into him enough that she'd agreed. But he'd boiled a saucepan of water on their grime-encrusted stovetop and put in a clear medical patch. *Fentanyl tea*, he'd said, eyes sparking. *It's amazing.* An hour later the guy had gone and she'd called her parents hyperventilating. They'd come straight to her house, and despite her eyelids drooping and her short sharp breaths and the all-consuming panic that she was going to die, she still noticed her dad look down and see the used condom on the carpet next to her mattress. Her parents had taken her to emergency to get her stomach pumped, but it was that moment that always replayed in her head, that look on her dad's face. She told them that she was sorry and that she was failing uni and that she would do better, but she really, desperately didn't want to talk about any of it.

She'd stayed with them over Christmas and started really looking at what her life had become. She could see the path she was on. The fentanyl incident had scared her. So, when her parents had offered her the chance to come with them on this move, she'd said yes. And she'd been so good since then, not touching drugs, not even weed, and never having more than a couple of drinks on those nights out with Leilani. She hadn't been to a real party until the gala, and then straightaway she had messed things up again. It was humiliating. Really, she wasn't sure if she wanted to know the details of what had happened. She didn't need more ammunition to feel like a complete deadshit. She'd always had such clear focus on her dream of being a fashion designer. She wasn't sure how it had become so muddied.

Maria yanked a chunk of her hair.

"Careful!" Liv said. "That's attached to my head, you know."

"It's okay," Maria said, patting the spot she'd pulled like Liv was a cat. "You know, Mommy and Daddy have a safe in their room that is filled with magical jewels."

"Is that right?"

"Yeah. It's in their wardrobe. Mommy says it has emeralds and rubies inside. I can show you if you like?"

"No, you can't," Liv said, "because it's bedtime, missy!"

"I'm almost finished. You need another ribbon."

"Last one."

"Why don't you have long hair? Like a girl?"

"I like it this way," she said. "Hey, Maria, tell me, what are you going to be when you grow up?"

"A hairdresser."

"Really?"

"No. Umm . . . a doctor."

"Those are pretty different."

"What are you going to be when you grow up, Liv?"

"I'm already grown up! Now I'm just going to the bathroom and then it's story time," she said, standing up.

"Don't look in the mirror, okay? I'm not finished yet."

She went around into Rani and Brian's room to use their ensuite. She had made it a habit to use Rani's fancy Chanel moisturizer, every dollop of which was probably more than they paid her by the hour, but the tube was gone. She must be all out. She rummaged through their meds. Xanax, atenolol, Ambien, Stay Awake. She took that bottle out and shook a few caffeine pills into her palm. She'd taken a couple of them before, and Rani and Brian hadn't said anything—

they had so many meds in here they probably hadn't noticed. They were a nice, legal way of staying up late when she was out without drinking or proper drugs, although she was fooling herself to think she would be invited out again anytime soon.

Outside, she heard a sound. It was the front gate squealing open and then banging closed. They must be home early. She stuffed the pills into her pocket, arranged the meds back as she'd found them, and clicked the door shut.

"Bedtime," she said as she got back into Maria's room.

"Not yet!"

"I think your parents are home, so come on. Pick a story. Otherwise we might both get in trouble."

"Okaaay," Maria groaned, hopping up into bed.

"The giraffe book again?"

She heard a shuffle from outside. The doorknob jiggling, but not the jingle of keys. Then there was a knock. Maria looked up at her, stricken.

"Maybe your parents forgot their keys," she said. She went over to the window, which looked down onto the front of the house, and peered through the edge of the curtain.

There was a man out there. He was standing by the front door in the shadows. He knocked again, but it was louder this time, more like banging.

She dropped down under the window.

"What's wrong?" Maria's eyes were wide. "Isn't it Mommy and Daddy?"

Oh God. This was her actual worst nightmare. Scenes from stupid horror movies reeled through her head. *Have you checked the children?*

"Um," she said, "I think . . . umm, they must have the wrong house."

The knocking came again.

"Shouldn't we answer it when someone knocks?"

"No," she said, "no, let's just leave it. Come on, lie down and I'll read the book for you. How do I look? Did you make me beautiful?"

"Yeah." Maria's eyes darted back to the window.

"It's a silly person who has come to the wrong house."

Liv went over to the window and looked out. The man was gone.

"He's gone now. He's just—" But then she saw movement from the side. The man took a running jump at the side fence. Rufus started barking from the backyard. Her hands went to her pockets. But she had a skirt on and the pockets were sewn shut. Her phone was downstairs.

"Stay here."

"Liv!"

Abruptly, Rufus stopped barking. The silence was worse.

"Stay here, okay? It's okay. Just don't come out."

She went out of the room and shut the door tight behind her.

The house was dark. They'd been sitting up in Maria's room for over an hour as the sun went down. The hallway was shadowy and gray. She didn't want to go downstairs, with all the big windows that looked out onto the backyard. But she needed her phone. Her parents were only a hundred meters away.

She got to the stairs. They were pitch black. But she knew her way around the house well enough not to need the light.

"Liv?" Maria called from her room, voice high.

"Stay in bed!"

She reached the bottom landing and looked out. There, through the back windows, she could see the shape of the man. She had to be quick.

She rushed over to the kitchen. She swore she'd left her phone on the counter when she reheated the dinner that Rani had left them.

But it wasn't there. It must have been on the dining room table, which was right in front of the glass door that opened out to the patio.

The click of the back door handle. The slide of the patio door opening. She hadn't locked it. Hadn't even thought about it. It had still felt like day when they'd gone upstairs.

She hid behind the cabinets. The floorboard squeaked under his foot. If he kept walking, he'd see her. You had to pass the kitchen to reach the stairs. And she couldn't let him reach the stairs.

She grabbed the closest thing she could find, the saucepan, from where she'd left it on the drying rack. She had the element of surprise at least. He took another step closer. She raised the makeshift weapon over her head. He took another step. Element of surprise. She had to use it.

She jumped out.

"Get the bloody hell out of here!" she yelled.

He screamed, jumped back.

"Get out!" she yelled again.

"What!?"

In the light from the kitchen she could see he was younger than she'd thought, not much older than her.

"Back off!" she said. "The cops said they're five minutes away. No, one minute! They aren't putting the sirens on so they can surprise you! This place is surrounded! They called a SWAT team!"

"Who are you?" he said.

That wasn't the response she was expecting. She noticed Rufus was right behind him.

"Get him!" she yelled. Rufus looked at her, tail wagging.

"What's going on?" the guy said. He seemed confused. His eyes darted up to the saucepan. He didn't look much like a robber. He was wearing wire-frame glasses and a blue button-up shirt, the sleeves rolled up above the elbows. But you never knew in LA. This was a dangerous city. Anyone could be a criminal.

Then she heard a sound from the stairs.

"Go back to bed!" she yelled. But Maria was running down toward them. She barreled past her, and Liv thought she was making a run for it out through the open back door, but she threw herself against the guy instead. He smiled and rested a hand on the back of her head.

Liv lowered the saucepan.

"Umm . . . Maria, do you know him?"

"I'm Austin. I'm her brother," he said. He had a nice voice.

"No," she said, shaking her head. "No, Rani and Brian don't have another kid."

"Um, yes, they do." He pointed at a family portrait.

She'd noticed the photo before. It was a couple of years old. Maria was still a baby in it. She had seen the older guy smiling from next to her, and thought he must have been a good-looking cousin or something. But up close, she could see that, though his dark hair wasn't long, the ends were beginning to curl like Maria's. He had Brian's razor-sharp jawline, Rani's warm eyes, his skin light brown, a shade somewhere between his parents. He was looking at her like she was some escaped mental patient.

"¿Qué le pasa a esta chica?" Austin said to Maria.

"Ella es sólo australiana," Maria said, pressing her chin on his stomach and looking up at him.

"Oh," she said. She had no idea what they were saying. "Well, hi! I didn't know you were coming."

He pushed his glasses up the bridge of his nose. "I was planning to come tomorrow. But my last class was called off, so I thought I may as well arrive early and surprise them." He laughed then. "I guess I did that."

"You're at uni or something?" she asked, leaning on the cabinet. Was it too late to act casual?

"Oh, college, yeah. Berkeley. Third year."

"Cool," she said.

"And . . . um, who are you?" he asked.

"Liv's my babysitter!" Maria said, unwrapping herself from his waist and grinning at the two of them. "Don't you think she's beautiful?"

"Maria!" she said, her cheeks reddening. She rubbed a hand through her hair to press it down. It rustled. She caught her reflection in the oven door. Glitter cheek circles. Blue smeared lipstick. Curly Christmas ribbons.

"Yeah," he said, grinning. "Yeah, she looks nice."

THE NEXT MORNING Liv got up early and went down to Café Sabrosa, the Mexican American café at the end of their street where Casper worked. She was going to sit down and figure her life out. She ordered an iced Americano with oat milk at the counter.

"To go?" the tattooed barista asked.

"No, I'll have it here."

The barista winked at her, and she rolled her eyes back at him. Who winked at people anymore? This wasn't the '90s.

"How's the internship?" Carlos asked, coming in from the kitchen. Carlos had a little pug, and on his off days she'd see him at the dog park. He was a thick-shouldered man, always in white T-shirts no matter the weather, and had dimples when he smiled.

"It finished last week."

"And now you can make it longer-term? Is that what you said?"

"Yeah, sort of, an apprenticeship. But you have to put a portfolio in and stuff. I think I might just get a regular job."

He grinned. "Where's your ambition gone?"

"I don't know. I keep asking myself the same thing."

"You're in LA now, you've got to hustle. You can't sit around waiting for them to come to you."

"Yeah, I know."

She thanked him and took her coffee outside. She loved the garden part of Sabrosa. It was so relaxed, with long bench seating around the sides, little individual tables, and Astroturf on the ground. The walls were wooden trellises with different plants climbing up them, and there was a shade cloth strung up for the back tables. It wasn't hot yet, but the sun was starting to glare down. It was warm across her shoulders through the fabric of her top. She sat in the back corner, pulled out her phone, and opened up the apprenticeship application again. It would be an amazing opportunity to see how a design house really worked, to meet fashion workers, help in fittings, and hone her CAD skills. This could be a real step back on track toward becoming a designer. But getting it was such a long shot, and she hadn't given herself enough time to put together a decent application anyway. Maybe she should just be focusing on the problem in front of her: moving out and getting her shit together. That was why she'd worn this outfit: black turtleneck, black tailored pants, men's work shoes. She was a little warm—LA was pretty much hot all the time—but she felt good in this. Like Jean Seberg in *Breathless*. Sleek. Effortless. Employable. She was going to hand out résumés today, find a decent job.

She took a sip of her coffee through the cold metal straw, spying on what everyone else was doing. There were only a few people around; most of them were on their laptops tapping away at screenplays. It seemed like everyone in this city was trying to get into the film industry, just like her dad.

Film runner? she wrote down on an empty sheet of paper. She could do that, right? Go and get people coffees and stuff. But she didn't know how to even apply for something like that.

Waitress? She'd tried working in cafés back in Melbourne, but her hands always shook when she carried coffees, and the saucer would end up filled with milk.

She didn't want to be a waitress again. She wanted to work in fashion.

Seamstress? Stylist?

A shadow fell over her table.

"Hi."

She looked up. It was the last person she wanted to see: Austin.

"Oh," she said, praying that her cheeks weren't going to heat up. "Hi, how are you doing?"

He laughed and sat down at the table next to hers. That wasn't an invitation. Did he think it was? He was wearing a black T-shirt today, and his hair was damp.

"I'm doing fine," he said, "despite almost being murdered by a glitter-faced lunatic in my own home last night."

"Glitter-faced, you say?" She stared at the ice bobbing in her drink. "Bizarre. Is that a new fashion trend for murderers these days?"

"Could be," he said. "Once someone has a face covered in glitter, you don't notice much else."

She could faintly smell his shampoo.

"Then it works, I guess. A distraction tactic."

"That must have been the plan."

She forced herself to look at him. Grinning at her, he took a sip of his coffee from his reusable takeaway cup. There was nothing hotter than a guy who cared about the environment. But that thought wasn't helpful.

"Is Maria okay?"

"Okay?" he said. "She loved it. She wanted to stay up to tell Mom and Dad—it was impossible to get her to sleep."

"She was scared though," she said, "at first. I feel bad."

He shrugged. "She's tougher than she looks." He was leaning back against the trellis, smiling at her like he expected her to keep entertaining him.

"So, you must have a really busy day. Just back from Berkeley and all that. Must have lots of people to catch up with."

He kept smiling at her. "Are you telling me to go away?"

"No," she said. "You do what you want. I probably have to go soon though."

"To work?"

"Yep."

She pulled at the neckline of her top, trying to cool herself down.

"Where are you working?" he asked.

"Well, I was doing an internship at the Designer Showcase."

"But you're looking for a job?"

"Huh?"

"Film runner, waitress, seamstress—"

He was reading from her page. She snapped the notebook shut.

"No. That's . . . a poem."

He looked at her a second longer. "Okay. Well, it's beautiful. Very lyrical."

He stood up, which was good because now she was both embarrassed and annoyed.

"See you later, then," he said.

She looked up at him, about to say goodbye. But then she saw her mother inside the café talking to Carlos. It was bad enough trying to interact with her at home; she didn't want to have to deal with her here too. Liv shifted over so Austin was blocking the sight line. She smiled at him.

"What are you up to today?" she asked.

He looked surprised. "Going to hang with my mom when she's back from dropping off Maria. We're going to Malibu—she knows a gallerist there and I've been trying to convince her to visit them for ages."

"That's nice. You must miss your mother heaps when you're away. She's awesome, I love her."

She looked around him. Her mum was still at the counter, tipping her head back and laughing. She hadn't seen her laugh like that in ages.

"I mean, not *love*," Liv said. "*Love* sounds weird. It's not like I want your mother to be my mother. Well, actually, maybe I do a little bit. I mean, your family is, like, idyllic, even more now with you in the mix. But I mean . . . you know?"

"I don't know if I do," he said. A crease had formed between his eyebrows. Now he was looking at her again like she actually might be slightly mad.

"No, no, I mean . . ." She looked around him again—her mum was still laughing, with one hand on Carlos's arm. "What the hell? Is she flirting?"

"Huh?" He went to turn around.

"No, no, don't move," she said. She took a breath, looked at him properly. "My mum's in there. I don't want to talk to her."

"Oh." His face relaxed. "Why don't you want to talk to her?"

"I can't bear her at the moment."

"Why?"

"She's angry at me. But . . . I mean, don't look, but she's talking to Carlos, and she has her hand on his arm, which seems kind of flirty."

"Some people are just touchy," he said, "but now I really want to look."

"Don't!"

But he'd already looked.

"It's on the line," he said. "Borderline flirting. But it doesn't necessarily mean anything. Middle-aged people are human too."

"Yeah, right. If that was your mum in there flirting with some other guy, you wouldn't say that."

"My mom wouldn't risk it."

"Oh, I see." She was properly annoyed now. "So my mum is some hussy willing to risk her family, but your mum is an angel. I mean, your mum *is* an angel. She's awesome, but—"

"I'm going to go."

She was annoyed, but also aware she was being very rude.

"No, don't. Just one second. I'm sorry, I'm not usually like this with people. I'm usually really nice and forgettable."

"It's all good," he said, and turned away. She ducked down as low as she could as he went back inside.

He lingered by the door for a second, blocking the view. She wasn't sure if her mum was still there or not. He stood looking through the various sugar packets and silver jugs of cream and milk.

Then he gave her a thumbs-up behind his back and walked out of the café. Her mum was gone as well; it was only Carlos inside now behind the register.

She took a breath, then looked back at the list. But she didn't want to spend the day job-hunting. She opened her phone again and looked at the apprenticeship application. It was due on Friday, and they wanted a written essay as well as a portfolio of designs. If she'd given herself time, she could have nailed this. If she hadn't been going out after the festival every night with Leilani, she could have already applied. She'd told herself she was networking, but really she knew she was just slipping back into old ways. It didn't take much. But chances like this were the reason she was here. Not to work crappy jobs and definitely not to get distracted partying again. This was meant to be her fresh start, her chance to get back on the path she'd always seen her life taking. There were way fewer opportunities in Melbourne, and because of the scarcity, the competition was fierce. The apprenticeship here was also a paid position, so if she got it, she could move out.

Maybe it was time to start banking on herself again. She also needed to stop being so avoidant. There was no point texting Leilani another time, so instead she dialed her number. Maybe being more direct would help. She'd find out what she'd done at the party once and for all. But the phone rang and rang and no one answered.

FIVE

Casper sat on the backyard step, the morning glare in his eyes. It was going to be another scorcher today. Liv had rushed out first thing dressed like a mime for some reason, like it wasn't forecast to be about a million degrees again. Casper was finding it hard to gather enough motivation to get going himself. He'd have to wear shorts. He hated wearing shorts. His legs were so skinny and pasty, and the hair grew unevenly on his knees. Once he was eighteen, he was going to move someplace where it was freezing cold all the time and everyone always wore long pants. The sun glinted off something wedged in the gap between the wooden slats of the steps. A silver hair clip. Casper pulled it out and fiddled with the prongs.

The last four days had dragged. He should have been packing for his trip home. Instead he was stuck in this *Twilight Zone* version of his family. His mother was almost never home, and when she was, she was distracted. She used to find small ways to get close to him, sitting next to him on the couch or touching his shoulder as she passed. He'd usually shrug her off. Maybe he shouldn't have. He missed it.

His dad had gotten even more scattered and nervy. If he wasn't at the library, he'd spend most evenings here in their crappy backyard, sitting on the cracked plastic outdoor dining set smoking when he thought no one was around, or talking to the neighbor, or squatting down next to the wilting avocado plants. He'd gotten into gardening all of a sudden, probably an excuse not to be in the house.

His mum had said they were moving here as a family, like it was going to be an adventure. But it was the most boring adventure he'd ever had. Back home, they used to have this tradition of watching old monster movies and ordering pizza on a Friday night. His dad would make popcorn in a frying pan and add sprinkles so it would turn rainbow, while he, Liv, and his mum would pick the movie. His mother liked the really corny ones like *Bride of Frankenstein*, while he preferred the original black-and-white series of Godzilla films—the one with Mothra was his favorite. Liv liked the 1980s ones like *The Blob*, but he had a feeling it was more about the mullets than the monsters for her, and his dad always went for the classics. They hadn't done this once since they moved here. Not once. And now things had gotten suddenly more fractured and he didn't have anywhere to escape to.

His phone buzzed, a text from Hélène: *It's going to be too hot for gardening today. Reschedule?*

Are you sure? he wrote, disappointed. Not because he wanted the money; he just liked talking to Hélène, even though she was an old lady. He knew that sometimes the work she had him do was a pretext for company, and the truth was he needed it too. He liked getting her advice, hearing her thoughts about love and living. Was it depressing that his second-best friend here was over eighty? Probably, but he didn't care.

I don't want you to roast, she replied. *Everything okay?*

Casper got up and went back inside, getting out of the sun. He threw himself into one of the kitchen chairs. His dad was standing at the bench, staring at the toaster with vacant eyes. The toast popped, but he didn't even react.

His mother came in from walking Ginger. He watched as she unhooked her leash, balancing her phone and a takeaway coffee from Sabrosa. He flicked the metal comb of the clip, wondering if he could just come out and ask her straight-out what was going on.

She turned to him, and for once she seemed to be really looking at him, but then her gaze fell. "What's that?"

"What?" he asked.

She was glaring at the hair clip in his hand.

"This?" Casper held the clip up.

"Is this some kind of joke?"

She looked angry. Furious, in fact. Her eyes were darting between the clip and his dad. The question, he realized, wasn't for him.

"A joke?" his dad asked. He wasn't looking at the toaster anymore; he was staring wide-eyed at the clip as well. "Why would I do that?"

"What's the problem?" Casper asked. "It's just a hair clip . . . It's broken anyway."

He held it up: Two prongs of the comb bit had been snapped off. His mum was still glaring at his dad. Casper watched his dad's Adam's apple dip as he swallowed, and then his hand came over his mouth like he might burst into tears.

"It's probably Liv's," Casper said, knowing as he did that her hair was too short for that.

"It's not." His dad's voice sounded strangled.

"Janus!"

His mum walked over and snatched the clip out of Casper's hand. She took a long quiet breath, and then she smiled at him, but it wasn't right. He could see all her teeth.

"Go get ready for school, sweetheart," she said.

"It's summer break. Remember?"

"I know," she said.

"Are you okay?" he asked, but she'd already turned away. She either didn't hear him, or she was ignoring him, because she went straight up the stairs without another word, the clip in her hand.

"WELL, IT'S PRETTY obvious, isn't it?" Tye said. Casper had DMed him on a whim, and Tye had replied straightaway and asked if he wanted to meet at the park. They'd bought fruit cups from the street vendor who was always set up with a rainbow umbrella, and now they sat under a tree eating ice-cold diced watermelon, mango, and jicama with chili and lime juice.

"Obvious? What's obvious? That my parents have completely gone off the deep end?"

"No . . ." Tye raised his eyebrows at him. "I mean . . . do you really want to know what I think? You might not like it."

"Come on!"

"Okay, well . . . I mean, your parents are fighting, then you find a hair clip . . . a woman's hair clip . . . and it makes your mom really angry at your dad."

"Wait . . ." Casper laughed. "No, that's not it. No way."

"What isn't?"

"You think Dad had an affair or something, right?"

Tye shrugged his shoulders. "It makes sense."

"Nah, I'm sure it's got something to do with Liv."

"Maybe Olivia is the one who saw him with the other woman. Maybe he had her over while your mom was at work and she dropped her hair clip and then Olivia came home and walked in on it."

Casper ate the final slice of mango. The icy tang of it with the sour lime and chili seasoning was so perfect. He hated LA, but they sure did know how to make good hot-weather food. He'd eat this every day if he could.

He leaned back onto his elbows and properly entertained this theory. His dad and another woman? He couldn't picture it. His father just didn't seem like the type. He always was a bit subservient to his mum. But then again, maybe that was a reason to do it. And their dynamic *had* changed since his dad's book had been published a year ago. Even before they'd moved, he was always at the library, and when he was at home, his writing was all he ever wanted to talk about. That had remained the case since they'd gotten to LA. It got pretty boring after a while. Casper had noticed that his mum seemed to be doing her best to support him, but every time he brought up his book, her jaw tensed. That was the side of his mother that irritated him: She pandered to his dad sometimes. Why couldn't she just be honest and tell him that it was more interesting cleaning the toilet than listening to him blab on about character arcs?

"I guess he did grow a bit of an ego when his book came out," Casper said.

"Yeah . . . maybe he wanted a woman who would stroke it a little more."

"Oh my God, you're going to make me vomit!"

"Stroke his ego, I meant."

"I know, but please never use the word *stroke* in relation to my dad. It creates . . . an image."

"Noted. No more visual language. But talk me through his movements. What does he do all day?"

"He just writes in the Silver Lake public library. He cycles there."

"Is he into fitness?"

Casper scoffed. "No. But Mum takes the car to work, and unlike everyone else in this city, we just have the one. It was never an issue back home. Anyway, he usually heads out by about . . . maybe ten? And then he's always home in the evening, hanging around and try-ing to get someone to watch *Seinfeld* with him."

"So if there's another woman, it would be a daytime situation."

"I guess."

Tye started shoveling down his fruit.

"What are you doing?"

Tye swallowed, little red beads of the chili seasoning on his lips. He got to his feet. "We've got to get moving. We have to follow him."

THEY TOOK CASPER'S bike, him cycling with Tye dinking on the back. They wouldn't want to ride on the main road like this, but the library was only ten minutes away, so they could stay on the footpath. It wasn't like anyone walked around here anyway. They waited at the end of the street, just around the corner from the house, for his dad to leave, and as soon as the garage door opened, they followed from a few blocks back. Casper expected him to turn left onto Glendale—that was the way to the library—but instead he veered right before the turnoff. They stopped at the bottom of the hill and watched him park his bike outside a diner. They waited until he went inside, then walked Casper's bike up the hill. Sweat crept down Casper's neck. He was almost afraid to see who his father was meeting. But at least he'd have an answer; he'd know for sure what happened last weekend, why he was suddenly stuck here all summer. Maybe if everything was out in the open, he could talk them out of canceling his trip. It was winter in Melbourne. Everyone would be wearing trousers and all his friends would be there and he'd get to go back to being who he really was for a few months.

They made their way up to the building, and then snuck around to the parking lot near the big window. There was a huge bougainvillea bush there that provided some shade.

His dad was sitting in the back corner, the same vacant expression in his eyes which he'd had that morning when he was looking at the toaster. Watching him out like this in public, Casper couldn't shake how pale and strange he looked. His expression was haunted and unfamiliar. He didn't look anything like Casper's annoying, geeky father.

But then the waitress came over and he snapped out of it and looked just like his dad again.

"He's totally meeting someone," Tye whispered.

"You think?" Casper said. For a second he'd forgotten Tye was even there. Maybe he shouldn't be involving him in his family issues like this.

"Look at the way he keeps adjusting his top button," Tye said.

But no one came. They lurked under the bougainvillea bush, the sun making the little flowers glow like pink paper lanterns. Casper almost relaxed, even though this whole thing was stupid and he was sweating like mad and he shouldn't even be here. His dad was just sipping his coffee and looking awkward and normal now. Maybe everything was fine. Maybe there was no secret at all. But then a brand-new Tesla pulled into a spot next to him and Tye, and a woman with glossy hair and expensive trainers emerged. When she went inside, his father's face lit up.

CASPER WHEELED HIS bike back into the garage. He'd dropped Tye back at his apartment, and they'd agreed to catch a free movie the next day. Casper should have been happy to have plans, but his brain was still processing seeing his dad with that woman. There was no way he was a cheater, even though that was exactly what it looked like.

He dumped his bike against the washing machine. The thud made something rustle from behind it. A tiny bit of orange plastic was sticking out. Casper squeezed around the side and pulled it free. It was a Home Depot bag. He put it on top of the machine and opened it. Inside was a knife, a claw hammer, and a pair of gloves. There was also a receipt. It was from three days ago. He had no idea who in his family would have bought this stuff, and why. Maybe it was something to do with his dad's new gardening hobby? But then, that didn't explain why the bag was hidden.

He put it back exactly where he found it and went inside. The kitchen and living room were silent and empty, but there was the faint sound of movement coming from above. He went up the stairs. The door of his parents' room was open, but the light was off and the blinds were drawn.

In his room, Liv was sitting on her bed, which his parents had squeezed in here while he was away, her laptop on her knees. "Hey," she said.

He went in and threw himself down on his bed. "Hi."

Liv was staring at the computer, looking at some boring fashion website. She was back in her pajamas, he noticed. The mime outfit was crumpled on the floor.

He pulled out his phone, thinking about texting Tye about the Home Depot bag. But he didn't. It wasn't just what was inside the bag, but the fact it was hidden. A mystery was one thing, but he didn't want Tye to think his family were a bunch of psychos. Maybe another woman wasn't such a bad scenario after all.

"Hey, do you reckon Dad would ever have an affair?"

He'd been hoping for shock, but Liv didn't even look up. "He hasn't got the stamina."

"I mean . . . it's possible though, right? That he has stuff going on we don't know about."

"I guess."

He watched her staring at the screen. She was so flat.

"Are you okay?" he asked her.

"Fine."

"Are you sure?"

"Yeah. I just . . . I don't know. I was going to apply for this thing, but . . . I probably don't even have a shot anymore."

Finally, she was opening up to him. "Does it have something to do with last weekend?"

Her eyes snapped back to the screen.

"What happened?" he pushed.

"Nothing."

"Liv—"

"Stop asking. It's annoying."

"Fine, but if you're going to wear the same pajamas every day, you should probably wash them."

She ignored that, but she shouldn't. She was going to reek soon. That bruise on her chest peeked out from the T-shirt. It looked terrible.

He was sweating all over his sheets and the room was hot and airless. He rolled over and faced the wall. There was no point in even talking to her. And stalking his dad had just confused things more. His sister had been in some kind of fight, his father was meeting rich mystery women, there was a creepy bag of stuff hidden in the laundry, and he didn't even have his own bedroom to process all this in. It was a mess. Most of all he kept thinking of the way his father had looked sitting at that table with those vacant eyes. He didn't look like his dad in that moment. He looked like a stranger.

SIX

All day, Janus had felt that edgy prickle of being watched. That sense of movement just outside his field of vision. The itch of eyes boring into him. It was all in his mind, he was certain. He'd been feeling it on and off all week, but today it was stronger. He locked up his bike outside the library and resisted the urge to turn around and scan for followers. It was just simple paranoia; he had to stop entertaining it.

He walked up the stairs, passing a homeless man by the entrance. The library itself was full of the unhoused and screenwriters. At first Janus had found it enchanting: two different types of people sharing the space together. He'd thought up some great metaphor about how the power of stories and reading broke down boundaries. He couldn't quite remember it anymore. For all he knew, half those homeless men were failed screenwriters.

Janus sat himself down at his favorite table by the window. He stared out, trying to force himself to shake off his bad mood by sheer will. He had work to do at the library, lots of work. And then, this afternoon, the other task loomed: the dark shadow of the thing that he had been trying with increasing desperation not to think about. Instead he let his mind return to the morning and the disastrous experience with Maggie at the diner. It hadn't gone well at all.

HE'D ARRIVED THERE early—that was his first mistake. It had given him time to get anxious, start overthinking things. He'd sat waiting, surrounded by people on Tinder dates. Six of them at least, all stiff backs and bad eye contact. Their conversations had been a weird mix of self-promotion and flirtation. He tried not to listen, but they all talked so loudly.

"I just like myself sober. My skin is clearer now. It wasn't ever, like, an addiction or anything."

"I realized that CrossFit was good for my body but bad for my mind."

"I really wanted to get into sleep-deprivation therapy, but my ex kept saying that it was literally torture."

"The dream is to be in nature, hills and sky and all that stuff."

When did dating become so much like a job interview? It had been ten thirty on a Wednesday in LA and none of them were at work. Clearly, the dream for all of them was movies. Though who was he to talk?

"I already love myself," the woman next to him told her date, "but I'm looking for someone to share that love with, you know?"

He had stolen a glance at them. She was more beautiful than her date, with her perfect clavicles and lovely hair swooping over one shoulder. The man, in contrast, looked pink. Was he sunburned or embarrassed? Janus could imagine what would happen. They'd sleep together after brunch. Move in together. The man wouldn't be able to believe his luck. He'd keep waiting for her to leave, but instead she'd get pregnant, she'd marry him, they'd have a picture-perfect family together, and then, out of nowhere, everything would change, and she would no longer look him in the eye . . .

"Refill?" The waitress had been doing the rounds with a jug of coffee.

"Yes, please."

That had been his second mistake. Too much caffeine only added to his anxiety, but he'd accepted another coffee anyway.

"Ready to order?"

"I'm waiting for someone."

He had looked at the door and fiddled with his top button. When it was done up, it was too tight around his neck, but when it was undone, he worried it made him look too relaxed. Plus, a little bit of his orange chest hair was visible, and he'd never forgotten that time when Lisa Telfer had asked if he was hiding a ginger cat under his shirt in year eleven.

"Good morning!"

He stood to kiss his producer's cheek, and she sat down across from him. He did his top button back up. He was a little scared of Maggie, if he was completely honest with himself. She was in her fifties and always casual in jeans and sneakers, but you felt it. Power rolled off her.

"How is my favorite Aussie novelist today?"

"I'm great, really good. Feeling great about the draft, really really good. I'm, you know, excited for next steps." Janus had sent her the new draft of his adaptation of his novel last week. He was sure he'd gotten it right this time. This one was perfect. He'd nailed the story; he could see the film playing out in his head as he read it. Yes, they were at a diner and not the usual flashy restaurants where they'd gone for their previous meetings. But this place was nice enough, and Maggie would order them a feast, and mimosas too, because why not! She'd list all the inspired choices he'd made like she did when she first read the book and wanted to option it. They'd be a little tipsy, and she would tell him about the casting they'd done that he wasn't really meant to know about yet.

The waitress came over.

"Anything from the menu?"

"No, no," Maggie said, sliding it off the table and handing it to her. "We're just having coffee."

He'd felt himself start to sweat, even though the diner was air-conditioned.

"You don't think it's ready?" he'd asked.

"No," she said, and the fact there was no fluff, no praise, made his skin prickle. He swallowed.

"The whole way through reading it, I kept asking myself," she went on, "'Where is the blood? Where are the corpses?' This script could be a family drama the way you've written it."

He shook his head. "No, no, but the horror is intellectual, you know? It's in the protagonist's mentality. That's what I was trying to convey."

Maggie just looked tired.

"Janus, it's about a lake monster."

"Well, yes. But no. It's about family, it's about, you know, it's . . ." He was having trouble articulating himself. That hot swell of anxiety expanding in his chest. "It's a metaphor," he choked out. "The lake monster is a metaphor for . . . for . . ."

Maggie didn't jump in; she just watched him stammer. He'd looked around, trying to regain his composure, and he had caught sight of something in the window. The sun was glaring, and he squinted to see, but for a second he'd seen movement. The tips of two heads darting out of sight as soon as he'd looked up. He was paranoid. So paranoid that now he was seeing things.

"Janus?"

He looked back at Maggie. "Yes?"

"You were talking about metaphors. But I'm having trouble following you. We really want to see this film get made, we do. We're still excited about it. But we were meant to have a draft a month ago."

"But I've sent you a draft. I've sent you two."

"I mean a usable draft. I see what you've written as more . . . embryonic."

She took a sip of her coffee and looked at him over the rim of the cup.

"It's just . . . I mean . . ." He had to get his shit together. He was embarrassing himself. He was meant to be a writer, and he couldn't even seem to construct a sentence. He took a breath, started over. "I want to make sure I'm expressing the interiority that made the novel so—"

"Films use a different language than novels, you must know that. You have to write in images. This is meant to be horror, so show me something horrifying."

He had swallowed and then nodded, his eyes darting back to the window, but no one was there.

JANUS HAD NEVER expected his novel to even get published, let alone do so well. It had just been about the character for him, about his protagonist, Angela. She'd come to him fully formed, had possessed him with her story. It had never been about success or money. At least that was what he'd always used to say in interviews.

In reality, he'd spent many sleepless nights imagining what he'd say in award speeches (he'd make self-effacing jokes, but also quote Hemingway) and what he'd do with a big advance payout (a hybrid car, a foot in the door of the stock market). The stuff about Angela was true too, but he wasn't interested in being one of those writers who did it just for the love of words; he wanted to actually get published. So, when an editor at a midsize Australian publisher replied to one of the submission emails he'd sent out, he only feigned shock. When the publishing contract came through, with an advance that wasn't quite big enough for any of the material things he'd envisioned, he swallowed his pride and accepted, knowing that just seeing his book on a shelf in a store would be more than enough. Everything else was just silly fantasy. Nighttime daydreaming. Pipe dreams.

On the day he signed the contract, Kay had made a big deal of it. She'd secretly hired a screen and projector, and when he'd gotten home from his accounting job, their suburban backyard had been transformed into an outdoor cinema. They'd watched the movie which had first inspired his book, *Creature from the Black Lagoon*. Even Liv had come and smiled and laughed, and they'd all ignored the black circles under her eyes. When his novel was published, he had a small launch at the local bookstore. He drank his cheap wine and thanked his friends and family for coming, since it was only friends and family who had come.

It happened slowly: A review came out on a well-known horror blog. He was asked to be on a few genre podcasts. His publisher called to say the book was coming out in the UK, then the US, then in German and Spanish and Korean translations. And somehow, three months after its release, his book became a bestseller. And when the first royalty check came, he found he'd already paid off the advance; in fact, he'd made enough for a hybrid car after all. A secondhand one, but still. And then the phone call came. The call that changed everything.

When his editor had told him a producer from California was going to give him a ring, he hadn't bothered to get excited. It was too unlikely that it would come to anything; it was probably some wannabe graduate or maybe even a swindle. But he'd been wrong. Maggie made movies, real movies, movies that won Oscars. She told him about her vision for the project, that she just loved this book, she adored it, and she knew it could be a big movie. He said if it was going to be a film, he'd want to write the script himself; this story was his baby. He didn't want some hack Hollywood screenwriter ironing out all the nuance, all the literary integrity, and turning it into some slasher featuring a washed-up ex–teen star with large breasts. Maggie had agreed. When the contract came through, the figures astounded him. If this was what Hollywood money was like, he could quit his job, live his dream, *and* make his family rich. He could knock out the script in a month, get in some writing rooms, and by the end of the year have enough saved for a whole fleet of hybrid cars. He could achieve the impossible dream he'd long given up on, something he knew not to even mention to his parents as a boy: to be able to support his family as a full-time writer.

But it had been six months, and two drafts, and the studio still clearly wasn't happy with the script, and his signing payment was all but spent on their big move. Maggie seemed to think he'd gone soft. Maybe she was right.

THE AIR-CONDITIONING IN the library smelled like sweat. Janus took out his laptop. He had to find that magic again, when all this was just a pipe dream rather than a slow-motion crushing of his soul. He needed to find his character, find Angela, and let her possess him again. She was a flawed protagonist, that was for sure, but she was headstrong. She never let fear stop her doing anything. Every barrier he'd thrown at her, she'd found her way through. He could make it through this.

He opened the file called TheKindandUnkindGirls_final_Final. He re-saved it as TheKindandUnkindGirls_final_Final_FINAL. He scrolled straight to a crime scene. Blood and death and corpses. He could do this.

INT. CINEMA—NIGHT
The run-down cinema is dark and empty, the screen blank. The seats are broken, the carpet is stained, and exposed insulation hangs from the walls. Angela uses her phone torch to shine her way down the aisle.

    ANGELA
    Billy? Are you here?

She keeps walking when, SUDDENLY, she trips. Her phone spins out of her grasp, shining frenzied lights around the cinema. She grabs it and shines it on what made her trip, then rears back in horror.

Billy is facedown on the carpet, between the seats, his feet poking out onto the aisle. His clothes are splattered with green mud, and the carpet is a mess of red blood and sinew.

    ANGELA
    Billy!

Angela turns the corpse over. Billy's face is white. So white, and it hasn't been long. Already it doesn't look like him anymore. There's blood on her hands. It's sticky. It smells like coins.

Old coins.

Like when he'd emptied his childhood piggy bank. That smell, it was like it was stuck in the back of his nostrils. He could smell it now. He could feel the warmth of the sticky blood on his fingers.

THE HOMELESS MAN was still sitting out front as Janus left the library, lighting a cigarette as soon as he was outside. Janus had quit over twenty years ago, when Olivia was born, but God, it felt good to start again. He walked down the stairs, smiling at the homeless man as he passed, and the man smiled back. Janus went cold. The man was wearing dirty clothes, but his teeth were perfect. Janus had watched a crime documentary once where they said the best way to spot an undercover cop was their teeth. Janus turned back to look at the man. His skin was bad and his hair was overgrown. But those teeth.

The guy turned to him. "What are you looking at?"

"Nothing. Sorry. No, nothing."

"Spare a dollar?"

Janus dropped his cigarette and pulled his wallet out of the back of his jeans. His hand was shaking. He had almost thirty dollars in small bills. Not much of a bribe, but still, he held it out to him.

"Thanks, man," the guy said, meeting his eye. If this guy was a cop and knew what they'd done, he'd be looking at Janus with contempt, maybe even disgust, but he wasn't. A furrow formed on the guy's brow.

"You all right, man?"

"Fine," Janus said. "Totally, completely fine."

SEVEN

Kay stood in the staff changing room, sweat slipping down her face. The afternoon reformer Pilates class she'd just finished instructing was meant to be for beginners. If she had managed to work up a sweat herself, then she'd probably pushed them too hard. But if her muscles weren't crying out and the music wasn't blasting, she'd start thinking too much. Near the beginning of class she'd let her mind wander and then she realized that she'd gone quiet and left them in a high plank for almost five minutes. There was too much she didn't want to think about. Especially what she was looking down at now as she unzipped her bag. The hair clip. Its two broken prongs glinted under the fluorescents.

Where's the other clip?

Maybe she only had one?

No, there were two in her hair, I'm sure.

Does it matter?

It's evidence.

If they'd missed this, what else might they have missed?

She zipped her handbag back up and headed for the showers. Stripping off, she turned the cold tap on full and stepped under it. The shock of icy water hit her face-first, then streamed down her body. She clenched her muscles, stood unmoving underneath the stream. But still, she could hear the echo of Janus's voice.

I can't do it, Kay, he'd said. *I just can't.*

In the car on her way home, Kay inched forward. LA traffic was a joke. She spent most of her life on the 101, staring at the bumper in front of her as she crawled from home to her work at the Downtown Pilates studio and back. She used to listen to podcasts while she waited in traffic; she'd liked the excuse to take a break, learn about some obscure topic she'd never thought to think about.

She'd taken an Uber on Saturday, her brain a foggy mess, but today she was back to driving herself. She couldn't focus on the words of the presenters anymore; she kept turning the volume up, but still she'd lose the thread of conversation. She tried music, but it was exasperating. Her thoughts were too loud. Attempting to drown them out only made them louder. She switched that off too and drove in silence.

She had to deal with Olivia's room. That was most important. But it had been impossible to find a moment in the house alone earlier in the week with Olivia moping around and Casper constantly watching. She'd always loved how astute he was, how emotionally attuned, but now it was making things difficult.

And she had to check the mail. She'd started checking it every chance she got, not that anyone else in the family ever looked. There'd been no further notes since Saturday. Not yet. She still hadn't mentioned the first one to Janus. She'd been the one to convince him that they could control the situation. If she told him about the note, she knew how he'd react. He'd freak out. He'd say, *Someone knows. Someone saw.* And he'd be right. Someone had seen. Someone knew exactly what had happened, someone who lived on their street. Maybe even someone Kay knew. And now they were preparing to blackmail her while keeping up appearances that everything was normal. Panic was a reasonable response but not a helpful one; it would just be another thing for her to manage.

Sometimes, even before these nightmarish last few days, this whole existence she was living was like some absurd hallucination. It was impossible that this was her real life. Traffic jams and loneliness weren't what she had imagined when she agreed to move here. She hadn't wanted to when Janus had first brought the idea up. But she'd allowed herself to be convinced.

Kay had met Janus in the theater bar when she'd still been dancing with the Australian Ballet. She'd ordered a drink, her hair lacquered back with hair spray, her stage makeup heavy on her skin. His gaze tickled her cheek, but she'd held her face forward; she hadn't wanted to speak to anyone. She hadn't eaten all day, and then, in the half hour before the performance began, she'd downed a Valium and a can of Diet Pepsi. That was her preshow ritual, the lack of food keeping her light, the Valium controlling her nerves and caffeine giving her enough buzz that she wouldn't faint. She usually tried not to speak to anyone afterward until she was at least one vodka in, but the person next to her started attempting to introduce himself. She turned to him then, intending to tell him to go away. But as soon as she saw him, she stopped. He wasn't the usual kind of guy who'd try to chat her up in a bar. He was wearing a boring suit and ugly tie; he looked like an accountant, but his eyes were a glowing bottle green. Once he had her attention, he began to babble about how his friend was dating one of the ensemble and dragged him along, how ballet wasn't his thing but he'd been just blown away by her performance, transported to another realm. As he spoke, she was struck with an unexpected but powerful bolt of desire, not to kiss him but to hug him, to hold his body tight against hers. He was adorable.

For years, that sudden urge to pull Janus close would hit her often. At mundane times, like when he was doing the dishes, his hands scrubbing in the hot soapy water, or when he was telling her about the lunchbox politics at work (it turned out he really was an accountant) or when he came home from the office late with a bottle of wine in a brown paper bag, his orange hair all fuzzy from the wind. Kay's mother had barely touched her growing up, so loving affection had always felt uncomfortable. Now it came easily: a hand resting on his shoulder as she passed, or her head in his lap on the sofa, or their ankles hooking together in the middle of the night.

Before they decided to move, she hadn't experienced one of those powerful pangs of softness toward him in a long while. He'd been so distracted by his novel, his bottle green eyes only seemed to brighten when he spoke about his writing, which he did often and in asinine detail. He would talk about the character from his book like she was a real person, like she was a woman he was infatuated by rather than someone he'd invented.

Bit by bit, her husband turned into someone else in front of her, someone with an ego, someone who was no longer content with his job, with their home, any of it. She'd been such an ambitious person when she'd met him, but his calm and steady approach to life seduced her. Maybe it was okay to teach fitness part-time rather than retraining as a choreographer like she'd originally planned. It meant she'd always be able to be there when the kids finished school. And she loved their house on their quiet street; she loved the idea of creating a real home, a rock-solid family, giving her kids the childhood that she'd always craved. But Janus didn't seem to want that anymore, and Olivia had moved out and was barely answering her calls, and Casper was starting to drift away too. One night she bought a bottle of red wine and let Janus try and convince her. He described what their life in America might be like, how it could be an adventure all four of them went on together, and she'd reached for his hand without having to think about it.

Now, on the 101, Kay's car was filling with the stink of exhaust. Her window was open, but she didn't close it. Instead she envisioned the black fumes she was breathing soaking into the spongy membranes of her lungs, turning them gray and heavy.

She craned her neck out the window, trying to see around the traffic to whatever was holding everyone up. But all she could see were more cars. The time on the dash was 4:07. She needed to be home in fifteen minutes if she was going to have time to do Olivia's room, cook dinner, and then leave again before Janus got back from the library. She'd leave a cheery little note on the oven door: *Cannelloni! Help yourself xx.*

Her family would presume she'd gone back to work for a late class. They never asked, so she never had to lie.

She closed her eyes, breathing the exhaust from the old bomb in front of her, and took herself away from it all, to the life she'd begun to dream of: A hotel room by the beach somewhere. Her phone off. No one trying to contact her. Lying naked in crisp white sheets. Soft sunlight creeping through mesh curtains. The sound of the shower running in the bathroom.

A horn blared from behind. She opened her eyes. The traffic was moving.

↓

AT HOME, SHE idled in the driveway and hopped out to check the letter box. Nothing. Not even a bill. Thank goodness.

She parked the car in the garage and came into the house. It was silent. Perhaps she finally had her opportunity. She'd already bought the stuff she needed for Olivia's room at the hardware store and hid-

den it behind the washing machine, so she went back into the garage
and put the supplies into her gym bag.

She went back in through the internal door and straight to Olivia's room, unlocking the padlock with the little key. She had been
dreading doing this, but knowing it was still there had loomed over
her for days. It would be unpleasant, but it had to be done.

"Mum?"

Casper's voice. She looked up. He was standing at the top of the
stairs, staring down at her, his brow furrowed.

"What are you doing?"

"Nothing," she said. "I was just about to make dinner."

She straightened her spine, lifted her chin, shot him a fake smile,
and made her way toward the kitchen, zipping her bag back up and
putting it on the stand by the front door as she passed. She heard his
footsteps coming down the stairs after her, so she busied herself
pulling ingredients out of the fridge. Spinach, ricotta, passata, eggs.
From the cupboard she got out cannelloni shells, a baking dish, a
mixing bowl.

He came in behind her and didn't say anything as he made himself a bowl of cereal.

"How are you doing?" she asked.

"Fine."

He never offered much to her anymore. It had started before they
moved here. She'd used to know everything about him, every time
a kid was mean to him at school, or if he'd stubbed his toe or fallen
off the monkey bars. He'd always tell her what he wished for when
he blew out his birthday candles. She watched her son sit at the table
and bend over his phone, all gangly limbs and Adam's apple and unruly hair.

He looked up. "Mum?"

"Yeah."

"Have you tried a peanut butter and jelly sandwich?"

She smiled. "No."

"You always hear about it in the movies and stuff. They say 'PB and J.' When I was at swim camp, they thought it was nuts I hadn't had it, so one of the guys made me one."

She leaned onto the kitchen bench. "What was it like?"

"Disgusting. It was like an inch of peanut butter and an inch of jam on really sweet white bread. I spat it out and they all laughed and I couldn't figure out whether it was some sort of really pathetic hazing or whether that actually is what they taste like."

Kay smiled at her boy. "I'll have to try one. So how was it at camp?"

He raised an eyebrow. "They played 'The Star-Spangled Banner' every single day. And everyone sang. I'm definitely quitting swimming as soon as school goes back."

She laughed, but really she wished she could give him a hug and tell him everything here felt strange and different to her too. But since he'd become a teenager, he'd gotten prickly at her touch, and she'd found her own stiffness returning. The awkwardness around affection that she'd grown up with and that she'd thought she'd shaken off had been creeping back in, and since Friday it was tenfold. She hated it. She'd thought she'd become the kind of woman warmth came easily to, but the shock had brought her back to the person she used to be. She didn't like that person.

"Mum?" he said again.

"Yes?"

"What were you doing at Liv's door? I thought we weren't meant to go in there—isn't that why they put that lock on?"

"Oh, I was . . . just going to check on the mold. See if it had gotten worse. I thought maybe I could fix it myself."

"Aren't the landlords going to pay someone to do that? You'll breathe it in."

"I thought I might give it a try. You know . . . get Liv back in her own room. I know you don't like sharing."

She turned away from him, taking the colander to the sink.

"But I mean . . . if they put a padlock on the door, isn't it because it's dangerous to go in? Apparently mold spores can get in your lungs and make you really sick."

"I thought you wanted your room back?" she asked him over her shoulder as she washed the spinach. He was looking at her intently. He wasn't buying it. She looked away, massaging her jaw. She'd been clenching it lately without realizing, and she'd started getting tension headaches.

"I'm kind of . . . I don't know . . . worried about Liv," he said.

Her head snapped back around. "Why? Has she done something?"

He was staring up at her from behind his phone. "No, why do you say that?"

She turned it back around on him. "Why are you worried about her?"

"She's so . . . I don't know. Distant."

Kay tried to make her smile reassuring. "Your sister would never hurt you. She loves you."

His brow crinkled up. "I never thought she was going to hurt me, nothing like that at all. I just thought . . . she seems sad. She doesn't even talk about it, but I saw her bruises. She must have been really wasted to get hurt like that and I think that—"

"It'll take a while to adjust to sharing, but you'll get used to it."

He stared at her, a crease between his eyebrows that he was far too young to have. She leaned down to preheat the oven, trying to remember the Fahrenheit conversion for the recipe.

"Have you got any plans tonight, honey?"

"Nope."

He was looking back down at his phone now, but his eyes weren't moving; he wasn't reading. She added the spinach to the bowl with the ricotta, stirred it together, and then took an egg from the carton.

"Mum?"

She knew it was going to be serious from his tone.

"Hmm?" She didn't look at him.

"What's going on? Like between you and Dad and Liv."

"Nothing."

"I feel like something has happened."

Janus's face, shiny with panicked sweat. *I can't do it.*

"What do you mean?"

"You don't seem to care that she's hurt. And Dad seems . . . secretive. I've been getting some weird vibes."

Casper was staring at her. How stupid to think he wouldn't notice anything was wrong. How stupid to think she could protect him from this.

His eyes flicked down to her hands. She had crushed the egg, the phlegmy yoke dribbling between her fingers.

She threw it in the bin, rinsed her hand.

"You've always been sensitive, my love. Everything's fine."

He turned away from her, picked up his bowl, and put it in the sink.

"Where are you going?"

"Got to have a shower, I stink."

She considered abandoning her plans, asking if he wanted to go out to eat. She could ask him now if he wanted to check out Koreatown, but she knew he'd just keep going on with the inquisition, and she couldn't face it.

"Well, make sure you have some of this when it's done. You need a proper dinner."

"I've eaten." He tipped his chin toward the dregs of cereal in the bowl in the sink.

"Real food, Casper."

"I've eaten cereal for dinner every night this week. I don't really like those meals you leave."

"Why?"

"They taste like pandering," he said under his breath.

"What?" she asked, though she'd heard him.

"I just like cereal."

He headed out of the room without looking at her again. She wanted to call out to him. To wrap her arms around him and tell him not to worry, that she had it under control, that he was better off not knowing, that some secrets were meant to stay buried.

Instead she cracked two eggs into the bowl and started mixing. She had to get out of there soon if she was going to avoid her husband.

EIGHT

Janus wasn't the kind of guy who broke into homes. He'd hardly had a delinquent childhood. The worst crime he'd ever committed in his youth was to steal a copy of *Misery* from the public library. He'd cut out the barcode with a pair of paper scissors and put the book in the bottom of his school backpack, and when he read it in bed that night, the delight had turned to guilt, which had turned to horror, and he'd had nightmares of vengeful librarians cutting off his feet for weeks. He still felt a flush of shame every time anyone mentioned Stephen King.

He stood by the front door. If anyone walked by, they'd think he was knocking. He tried the handle. Locked. Of course it was locked. He looked down the street. No one was passing. Not a car, nor someone walking their dog, nor a jogger out for a run. The street was quiet except for the sound of a lawn mower somewhere a few houses up and the faintest sound of talk radio coming from an open window somewhere. Now, he had to do it now, before someone did come by. He ducked around the side of her place and straight through the gate.

Already, sweat was pouring down the back of his neck. He wasn't built for this, not for breaking and entering, not for any of it.

The first window looked into the living room. He pulled on the blue doctor's gloves he'd gotten from the pharmacy, then pushed the glass, hoping that she'd left it unlocked. No such luck. He ventured farther down the side. The sun beat down onto his head. He should have brought a hat. It would have served a double purpose: hide his most identifying feature, his orange hair, and stop him feeling like he was going to throw up from the heat. Second window, a small one to the bathroom. Locked. He hadn't been completely foolish, he had brought along a screwdriver, but what was he going to do with it? There were no visible screws.

Kay was going to be furious with him. But what was he meant to do, break a window? That would totally defeat the purpose.

He reached the small back courtyard. Thank God the fence was tall. There were thick, overgrown bushes all along the fence line at the side and back, and a washing line draped in clothes. The clothes on it were so dry they looked crispy. He'd have to bring those inside, clear away the buildup of mail and packages by the door too.

There was a sliding glass door that entered into the kitchen. He tried it. Locked. He couldn't go home without having done this. Kay had told him that she'd deal with Liv's room and he'd do this, and then it would be over.

In his novel, Angela wouldn't give up. In fact, she'd been faced with a similar problem. When she was looking for her ex-boyfriend Billy, before she found his body in the cinema, she'd broken into his trailer. When he'd written that scene, Janus had researched breaking into houses, and he'd picked a sliding door because the locks were so flimsy. It had worked like a charm for Angela. But in the end he'd had to delete that scene because he hadn't realized trailers didn't even have sliding doors.

Janus knelt down and pried the screwdriver under the door. In the scene he'd cut, Angela had used a fire poker, but hopefully this would work too. He levered the screwdriver at the same time as he pulled the handle and, just like in his novel, that was it. Easy.

He pulled the door wide, stood up, and stepped in.

Her place had a smell. Maybe it was her perfume? Or maybe her detergent? It was slightly floral, sweet, with an undertone of decay. He slid the door shut again behind him. The sound of the lawn mower and talk radio and the faraway growl of the freeway he hadn't even noticed were all silenced. It was cold in here compared to the garden.

He was in her kitchen, linoleum beneath his shoes. There was a sink to his right, a few dirty dishes on the side. A square laminate dining table, two chairs neatly tucked underneath. There was a woolen throw on the couch, a paperback lying open on the wooden coffee table, and, next to it, a vase of dying tulips. The source of the smell, he realized. They had probably been a deep plum color, but now looked gothic. They were splayed at odd angles, the petals split and pulling back, yellowing around the edges.

There was a door to the left, probably to her bedroom and bathroom. But he couldn't deal with her bedroom yet. It was too intimate.

She had a beautiful home. He could tell how much care had been put into each object. The way the stripes in the throw matched the cushions. The coasters on the coffee table—there wasn't one ring on its wooden surface. The framed photographs on the mantel. But he wouldn't look at those. He couldn't. He was breathing too fast. He had to control himself. He wouldn't write Angela as standing in a room and not doing anything. There might be room for an interior crisis of morality in a novel but not in a script. He'd write her taking a breath and then getting started. So that's exactly what he did.

First, the flowers. He took them out of the vase and threw them into her kitchen bin. Then he emptied the moldy water in the sink.

He found a sponge and some detergent and set about washing out the vase, and when he was finished with that, he went on to her dishes. A bit of hot water slipped underneath his hospital gloves, making the plastic stick to his hands. He stacked the dishes by the sink and took out a clean tea towel and dried them and the vase and then put them all back in the cupboard. He looked around. Everything was spotless, clean, neat. Done.

He wiped down the kitchen table, then went to the lounge. He shook out the throw and then neatly folded it up and put it on one arm of the couch. He picked up her book—it was Natalia Ginzburg's *The Dry Heart*—but he couldn't bring himself to close it, to press the pages back together and lose the place she'd been up to. He folded down the corner of the page instead.

There was a bathrobe thrown on the edge of the chair. He picked that up too. It was pale green terry toweling, so similar to the one Kay used to have that he couldn't move. He just held it in his hands, like if he smelled it, he would smell his wife's scent. She'd worn her robe for months after Olivia was born. As the time passed, it accrued grime: stains down the front, gray along the hem. He'd begged her to let him wash it, but she refused to take it off except for when she showered, which was less and less. At first when he'd gone back to work, he'd been sure she would step up, that she just needed some time alone with Olivia for her maternal instinct to kick in. But every day he'd come back to find both of them crying. Olivia screaming purple-faced in her bassinet, and Kay in a ball on the couch. *She won't stop*, she kept saying. *She hates me. She hates me.*

No matter what he said, he couldn't convince his wife she was a good mother, that it was colic, that she was doing her best. After three weeks of it, he took more time off work. For two months, he was Olivia's full-time carer. He bathed her, fed her, and did laps of their suburb while she cried and cried. Kay was like a ghost haunting their apartment. This pale-faced woman who barely spoke and never went outside and locked herself in the bathroom sometimes, which terrified him for reasons he never was able to say out loud. Eventually he convinced her to go to a doctor, to get some pills, to start eating again. Eventually some color came back into her face and Olivia stopped crying and Kay would hold her close to her chest. Once Kay had gotten better, she started doing everything at home, like she was trying to make up for something. Janus was terrified when Kay had gotten pregnant again seven years later, but he needn't have been. She and Casper bonded immediately, becoming inseparable. His daughter didn't remember her infancy, but sometimes Janus felt bad for her, like somehow those early months had left a mark on her and her mother's relationship, a mark that Olivia herself could never understand.

A noise from out front. Janus dropped the robe. It was probably a delivery person, UPS or FedEx or something. They'd knock on the door and then they'd leave. But no one knocked on the door. Instead, very faintly, he heard the sound of the side gate opening and closing. He dove down onto the floor, hiding from view behind the couch. They wouldn't be able to see him from the window. But this was bad; this was really bad. His head was light, his vision too bright. He tried to take a breath, but he couldn't. This person, whoever they were, was coming around the back. He'd left the sliding door unlocked. They would walk straight in, and what could he do, what good reason could he give for being here, hiding behind her couch?

He pressed his head into the couch and waited for it: the whoosh of the door sliding open, the sound of the world coming back in. He had to think quick. He was a storyteller; he should be able to come up with a reason to be here. Something, anything, quickly. But his head was just empty, buzzing panic.

The door didn't open. The person should have reached it by now.

In fact, they should have reached it seconds ago. He waited. Nothing. Were they standing out there, on the other side of the glass, looking in? He had to look around the couch and see. But no, perhaps it was better to wait. He listened. But there wasn't a sound. Not a throat clearing, a foot crunching against the earth, nothing. Maybe he'd imagined the sound of the gate? It had been very faint. He had to do something. He couldn't hide here forever.

Slowly, he inched to the side. He crawled along the floorboards; then he peered out from the side. He was so sure he'd see someone on the other side of the glass that the absence of anyone was more shocking. Her back courtyard was empty, only her strung-up clothes hanging lifeless on the line. He'd imagined the sound.

He needed to get up, back onto his feet, and go into her bedroom, finish what he'd come here to do. But he couldn't. This was so wrong. He shouldn't be here. He wasn't the kind of person to be able to do this. He just wasn't. He had to get out of here.

He got to his feet and went straight to the door, sliding it open. He stepped back outside; the relief of being out of her paused rooms was overwhelming. He pulled the door shut, wondering if he should try and find a way to relock it.

Then, in the corner of his eye, he saw a glint of sunlight. Something was there that hadn't been there before. Trying not to move, he looked over to the glint. It was a reflection from glass, coming from the bushes near the fence. The light was bright in his eyes but, squinting, he could see that there was something there, behind it. A shape in the shadows. There was a figure crouching low on the earth, behind an overgrown bush.

Janus ran. Back down the side, through the gate, slamming it shut behind him, out onto the road and down the street. He had to put as much space between himself and her place as possible. Not that it mattered now. Someone had been there. Someone had seen him.

NINE

Kay heard Yolanda's laugh from outside Sabrosa as she was pushing open the heavy glass door. It was a great laugh, bright and infectious. But it was the last thing she wanted to hear. Kay didn't want to have to make small talk. To sit and laugh and pretend. She had rushed out of the house, leaving the oven on a timer, in time to avoid Janus. Usually as she walked down to Sabrosa, her mood lifted. All day it felt like she was waiting to get here, to this very moment of anticipation, of unclenching. But as she'd made her way down the street, she kept remembering the way her son used to look at her, that huge adoring baby grin. She was his world. In the kitchen this afternoon, he'd looked at her with such disappointment. No, more than that. He'd looked at her like her dishonesty was a betrayal.

Kay headed through the open door of the café and out to the courtyard. Yolanda, a woman in her early thirties who Kay sometimes chatted to at the dog park, was sitting with Rani at a circular wooden table in the full late-afternoon sun.

"Kay!" Yolanda waved her over. "Are you here for dinner?"

"Just a drink."

"You're meeting someone?" Rani asked.

"No," she said, maybe too quickly. "No, only me."

"Well, join us! I had an absolutely heavenly burrito and Rani has just popped in to order takeout, but I'm trying to convince her to have a margarita with me."

"I only have ten minutes," Rani interjected.

"The perfect amount of time for a margarita."

Kay pulled out a wooden chair and sat down. It occurred to her that it was possible it was one of these women who was blackmailing her. Yolanda lived in an apartment block in the street behind. You could see into Kay's house from the second-story balconies. And Rani was right next door. Kay tried to smile naturally.

"You all right, Kay?"

"Yes, just a long day."

She looked around for a reason to change the subject. Yolanda's dirty plate was still on the table, smears of hot sauce across the porcelain; the white pages of a screenplay were underneath.

"New role?" Kay asked.

"Audition. It's for a pilot. Terribly written—they seem to keep getting worse and worse. It's going to be hard to say the dialogue with a straight face, I swear. My character seems to think everything is 'on fleek.'"

Carlos came in from the kitchen, a patch of sweat on his white T-shirt. "Chardonnay, Kay?"

"Yes, please."

"Do you still have that Cloud Break? We'll have a bottle," Yolanda said. "Three glasses."

"Okay, fine. But I'm just having one," Rani said.

"Rani was telling me about Liv's little stunt last night."

Rani grinned. "The saucepan really put it over the edge."

Kay stiffened. What stunt?

Yolanda tipped her head back and laughed. "The makeup! I wish I could have seen it."

"What did she do?" Kay's voice was harsh.

"She thought my son was an intruder when she was over babysitting. Panicked a bit, poor soul."

"Nothing serious, don't stress." Yolanda was looking at her, head cocked to one side.

Kay plastered on a smile. "That'll be my daughter. Always overreacting."

Carlos came back with a bottle of wine sweating into a bucket of ice and three glasses.

"Slight delay on your takeout, Rani," he said. "It'll be about fifteen."

"No te preocupes," she said, and Carlos headed back into the kitchen.

Kay took out the bottle and started pouring it into their glasses as Rani took a furtive look at her watch.

"I saw that," Yolanda said. "I'm sure Brian can deal with waiting another five minutes for his fajitas."

Brian. Maybe it was him? No one was that upbeat and friendly all the time. Or could he and Rani be in on it together?

"It's for the whole family," Rani said. "A feast to welcome Austin home. Brian wanted me to cook, but I can't beat the food here."

"That's a nice thing to do for your son," Kay said, but she made a mental note. Rani's son had arrived in the same twenty-four hours as the blackmail letter. Possibly a coincidence, but who knew?

Kay took a sip of her wine. That first sip was always the best, when the alcohol hit her empty stomach. She never ate dinner anymore;

she liked this feeling too much, of all her worries taking a step backward.

"You know, I think that's the reason I can't commit," Yolanda said, sipping at her own wine. "I don't want to answer to anyone, you know? I don't want to be on the clock."

Kay wished Rani and Yolanda would go away. She didn't want friends; it was too difficult to watch what she said. She'd prefer to drink her wine without having to fake it.

"I mean," Yolanda continued, "I know I've got a way to go with acting regardless. A long way to go. But if I settled down, if I thought about, God, don't make me say it . . . kids . . . then straightaway the compromises would start, you know? Then the sacrifices."

Rani had been fiddling with her silk scarf, but now she looked at Yolanda straight on.

"You think I gave up my art practice because I got married?"

"I didn't say that."

Kay laughed. "Yeah, you kind of did."

Yolanda laughed too. "You're right, I sort of did, didn't I? But what about you, Kay? You were like, what, a famous ballet dancer in Australia, right?"

"Who told you that?"

Yolanda tipped her head toward the kitchen. Carlos.

Kay took another sip of wine and felt her jaw unclench. Maybe she didn't have to be careful. As long as they stayed in the past. She'd been thinking about her past more and more lately. Like it was some sort of mystery. As though, if she could solve it, she could figure out how she got to the life she was living now.

"Actually, giving up dance was probably the bravest thing I ever did."

"Really?"

"Yeah. For a while ballet was my life, you know? 'Ballet is every-thing,' that was our mantra. I started when I was six, left high school at sixteen to board at the Academy. When you've made it your whole life, it's a really hard thing to see your way out of. I got pretty wild for a while just to have an escape."

"Oh, now this is juicy. Wild how?"

"How else? Clubs, men, booze, pills. Ballet is so regimented, you know? I remember when me and my friends used to hit the clubs, how fun it was to get on the dance floor, knowing everyone was watch-ing us."

She can still remember it. Waiting for the shots to hit her blood-stream, or the pill to drop. The flashing lights, the sticky floor, danc-ing with your heartbeat without having to remember to breathe.

"But then you had a kid?"

"Olivia."

"And was it worth it?" Yolanda asked. "Giving up your passion."

It was a hard question to answer neatly, but Rani saved her.

"Marriage and family . . . I don't know, it changes you. Don't you think? I've heard people say that marriage is a process of sanding down your edges."

"That's exactly it," Yolanda said. "I like my edges as they are."

But Kay was focused on Rani. "It's true. But no matter what you do, it never seems like enough, don't you think? You always feel like you should be better."

She thought of Casper's face, his look of betrayal. This huge gap that had appeared between them, between her and all of her family. No, not a gap, a chasm.

Rani held Kay's eye. "It's an awful way to feel."

Something about Rani's stillness, her ability to listen, made Kay want to confide in her. She'd have to be careful of that.

"I used to have this problem, years ago now, where I would lose my balance," Rani said, staring into her wineglass. "Faint, I guess. For no reason at all. I'd be walking around completely normally, and then it would be like I'd been knocked over. I'd suddenly be on the ground. I went to the doctor, got checked for vertigo. For low blood pressure."

"How scary," Kay said.

"It started getting better on its own. I just had to accept it, you know? Be okay with not being the perfect mom and wife I wanted to be. I used to worry that my family thought I was losing it. The doctor was insinuating it was psychological."

"That's so patronizing," Kay said.

"More than patronizing." Yolanda leaned back in her chair. "I bet if you were a white man, they wouldn't have treated you like that."

Rani put down her glass and smiled. "It's true. I'm either passionate or I'm crazy."

Yolanda took a swig. "Well, I'm either sassy or angry."

"What about me? I guess I'm either nice and"—Kay thought of Casper—"pandering. Or I'm a bitch."

"Oh, I think we can all be bitches," Yolanda said. "It's the worst thing for a woman to be, right? Selfish. But why does wanting things make us selfish? This is exactly it. Why I'll never have kids."

"No, it's your husband that will make you feel like that," Rani said, which surprised Kay. She'd always thought her and Brian's marriage was rock-solid. But maybe no marriage was without its cracks. "He'll make you feel like you have to be forever accommodating. But isn't that what we're always taught? That you have to crawl around making sure everyone likes you."

"God, you're right." Kay said. It was exactly what she'd been doing that day. Crawling around the house to make sure she still appeared accommodating. And to who? Casper didn't even eat her food. It wasn't for Olivia. So it was for Janus, who she was so angry with she could barely even breathe.

She raised her glass. "Let's cheers. To not appeasing. To doing what we want."

"Oh, I like this. Cheers to being selfish bitches," Yolanda said, and the three women clinked their glasses together.

TEN

Janus sat alone at their outside table, a plate of steaming cannelloni in front of him. He'd rushed home. All he'd wanted was to see Kay, to throw his arms around his wife and pull her to him and have her hug him back, tight and warm and unreserved. But the house had been silent except for the low hum of the oven. It had filled the already warm kitchen with stifling, heavy heat. Janus had brought his dinner outside, but he couldn't bring himself to take a bite. Instead he lit a cigarette. He'd thought that prickle of eyes he'd felt all day had been paranoia. At the café, outside the library, on his bike. But that figure in the courtyard had been solid, hiding, watching him, waiting for him to come out. That wasn't imagined. It was real. Too real.

"Hi, Janus." Brian popped up from over the fence. He held a beer in each hand.

"Savior," Janus said, standing up to take one from him.

Brian was an alpha type, with wide shoulders and a big jaw. He was a talent agent for teen heartthrobs and pop stars. That was this city for you; even the jocks were in the creative industry.

"So I finished your book," Brian said, leaning onto the wood.

"You did? Thoughts?"

"Loved it. Best thing I've read in a long time."

People had used to say this to Janus often. He'd gotten used to it. In fact, he'd started to crave it when he introduced himself, and always said his full name in case it was recognized.

"It was great, man. Honestly, that twist in the end—" Brian let out a low whistle. "You killed it. And you didn't study writing?"

"Nope." He'd had this conversation before, and he loved it every single time. "I'm self-taught." Janus took a sip of his beer. "Back when I was an accountant, I'd write on the train on the way to work and on weekends."

"That must have been a slog."

"It was brilliant. Happiest time of my life."

And it was. He had loved their little house. Loved sitting on the train for an hour, writing freehand in his one-dollar exercise book as the sun climbed. He loved typing up everything in his pajamas on a Saturday morning, hearing the kids' voices as they came and went. Kay bringing him a coffee and reading bits over his shoulder. Now, when he mentioned his writing, her eyes glazed over. It had been that way for months. He took another drag of his cigarette.

"It's a great concept. I can see why you got so much buzz. I mean, it's like a warped high school reunion, right? She goes home when her high school friend is killed near the lake, and then her old boyfriend is murdered in the cinema, then another friend, and it's like . . . what the fuck is going on? Is she being targeted or is it a coincidence? And when she figures out the crime scenes are the places where she spent her happiest moments with each of the victims, it's like, whoa . . . inspired!"

There was nothing Janus enjoyed more than other people describing his own book back to him.

"It's meant to be a comment on nostalgia, and how toxic it can be."

"Toxic nostalgia, I totally got that."

"The lake monster is a metaphor for all the memories that don't fit with the version of our pasts that we want to believe." Why had that been so hard for him to say this morning? Thinking about it made him shiver with humiliation.

"That's fascinating," Brian said, and it seemed like he actually meant it. Janus took another sip of beer. It was cold and crisp, and maybe he had imagined the figure; maybe there hadn't been anyone there. It wouldn't even make sense. Why would someone hide like that? Do nothing, not even confront him?

"Are you writing another?"

"Too much work to do on the adaptation right now."

His book had been a bestseller in Australia, but not here in the States. He wasn't even a small fish in a big pond here; he was a goldfish in the ocean.

He shifted in his chair. The cracked plastic outdoor furniture was always pinching his bum. This wasn't what he'd imagined his Los Angeles life to look like. Where were the groups of bare-breasted out-of-work models sunning themselves on tiny balconies? Perhaps he'd watched too many Raymond Chandler adaptations. But what about the transcendent sear of Joan Didion's Santa Ana winds? Or did those come later in the year? Then again, he also wouldn't describe it as the "plastic asshole of the world" like Faulkner so famously had. More so, it was just a grimy, sprawling city that promised dreams on a sharpened knife's edge.

"Is that your dog?"

Janus looked around. He could hear the scraping of Ginger's claws against the back door.

"I'll take her for a walk later."

"She's still trying to tunnel to Mexico?"

"Yeah, she wants to kill my avocado plants."

"Wrong season for those anyway, man. You should have planted in spring."

The door swung open and Casper came through. Janus dropped his cigarette and kicked some dirt over it. Casper met his eye with an unreadable expression.

"You're home," he said.

"Hi, Cas, how was your day?"

But Casper just looked at him. "Where have you been?"

"Me? The library."

"Really? And how was that? Productive?"

Janus laughed. His son was talking to him like he was the dad and Janus was somehow in trouble. "It was fine. Why?"

Casper crossed his arms. "So you spent literally all day just sitting in the library?"

Maybe his son was trying to take an interest. "Well, actually, I also met with my producer to chat about the script, the new draft I sent in last week, remember?"

Casper nodded and then pressed the heels of his hands into his forehead.

"She said it's really close," Janus went on, aware of Brian's presence. "Just a few little tweaks and then—"

But Casper cut him off with a groan, then turned around and went back inside, Ginger making her escape before the screen door slapped shut behind him.

Janus looked toward Brian. There was no way his family would behave so rudely to him. He couldn't help but notice the faint smirk that Brian tried to cover by finishing the last of his beer.

"Teenagers, right?" Janus said.

"Right. Although I'm in the sweet spot now. One kid still a child, the other in college making something of himself. I should probably go, actually. We're going to have a nice dinner to welcome Austin home. Have a good night, man," Brian said, and bobbed back down into his own yard.

Of course Ginger went straight for the avo plants. Janus grabbed her under his arm and grabbed his plate with his other hand. The red sauce was now congealing on the pasty cannelloni shells. Ginger whined at him as he brought her back inside.

"Yeah, yeah, I know. I'll take you out front in a minute."

He put her back on the floor and went to the kitchen bin, which was overflowing. He used the heel of his shoe to push it down, and then scraped his plate into it. Some sauce missed, and he watched the red goop trail down the side of the bin. He'd been kidding himself when he'd imagined coming home to Kay's embrace. When was the last time they'd held each other? When was the last time they'd all had dinner together like Brian's family?

Olivia came downstairs rubbing her eyes.

"Hey, Dad," she said. "How'd your meeting go?"

"Great. Really good. One more draft to go."

"I thought that this was the last one?"

"It's a complicated industry," Janus said, sitting down at the table. "Your mum made us dinner."

"That's all right, I'll make my own."

She went into the kitchen and boiled the kettle, taking out a packet of dry noodles from the cupboard.

"That stuff is filled with MSG," Janus told her.

"Not if you use your own sauces rather than the dehydrated stuff it comes with. If you add a fried egg and some fresh veggies it's really healthy. We literally bought a whole box of mee goreng in my old house and I had it every night for dinner. It costs like two dollars a meal. It's awesome."

"But there's a dinner already made for you in the oven."

She began thinly slicing a carrot like he hadn't said anything. He watched her for a moment, the delicate way she used her hands, her focus. He wondered when it would stop. When he'd be able to look at his beautiful girl again and not see what she had done. But the truth was, things hadn't been the same with his daughter since the night she'd OD'd and they'd had to take her to emergency. He hadn't known how to speak to her about it. He didn't even know where to begin. So when he went into her hospital room, and she'd looked so small and pale in the bed, when she'd begun to cry as soon as she saw them and promised that she'd do better, that she didn't want to talk about it, he'd given her a hug and left it at that. He'd decided that it was okay for some things to go unspoken. But the silence between them had festered and grown.

Ginger whined at him again.

"I should take Ginger out." He stood up.

"Dad?"

"Yeah?"

"When are you and Mum going to forgive me?"

He looked at her now. "Oh, honey, we already have. It's not about . . . anger or forgiveness or anything like that. We know you didn't mean it to happen."

"It's like you're both punishing me." She had her eyes on the chopping board.

"That's not it at all. It's just . . . a lot."

She looked up at him. "It wasn't like I meant for that to happen. And I already said I was sorry. And I am sorry. I really am. Why can't Mum just get over it?"

He staggered. "Just get over it?" he repeated.

"Yeah."

He stared at her. His little girl. His angel.

"How can you be so callous?" he said.

"God, Dad, that's a bit dramatic."

He had to get out. He couldn't even look at her right now. He silently left the room, clipped the leash onto Ginger, and went out the front. He was exhausted. His brain and body couldn't do anything more today.

Ginger pulled, trying to get him to go up to the park.

"Sorry," he told her. "I can't face it."

She cocked her head at him. He pointed to the grass. "Pee-pee here."

The fronds of the palm tree rustled in the warm night breeze above him. Tiny moths fizzed around the streetlight. It was daytime in Australia, daytime on their street in Melbourne. He was on the other side of the world. He was writing full-time; this was supposed to be his dream life.

A figure strode up the street toward him. In the dark, all he could see was a silhouette. He swallowed; they were walking fast, straight toward him. Had someone been watching the house, waiting for him to emerge? And then the streetlight beamed over her face, and he saw it was Rani. She smiled at him when she saw him, turning onto the path to her front door. She was clutching two stuffed-full paper bags.

"Off for a walk?" she asked.

"Yep," he said, even though he had no intention of it. "How's your night going?"

"Good, good. Just had a nice glass of wine with your wife actually. I imagine she'll be home soon."

"My wife?"

"Down at Sabrosa. I would have stayed if I wasn't bringing dinner back."

Janus tried to set his face in a decidedly unsurprised expression. He'd assumed she was at work.

"Our son is home for the week," she went on. "Austin."

What was with Americans' fixation on naming their children after their own cities? Imagine naming a child Ballarat? Or Wangaratta?
Then again, Sydney was a name. But it seemed only Americans used
it. He'd never met a Sydney in Sydney.

"Okay, well, I'll see you later," Rani said. He hadn't replied, he
realized. He'd just been standing there. He'd been doing that more
and more lately. He was so used to being alone he was becoming terrible at socializing.

"Bye!" he said. "Have a wonderful meal!"

She went into her house, and Janus imagined the dinner going on
next door. Beautiful Rani taking the food out of the bags, Brian laying the table. The kids bouncing around.

What Olivia had done was only the tipping point. If he was honest with himself, things hadn't been right with his family in months.
But now the silence had a stranglehold over all of them. He and Kay
had done what they'd done for Olivia, but at what cost? His family
was his heart and he wanted to protect them, but this didn't feel like
protection. It felt like he was losing them.

ELEVEN

There were only a few people left in the courtyard at Sabrosa now. An older couple finishing up their meals. Three girls in their twenties drinking mojitos, using their straws to squash the limes and mint. A man alone with a laptop, the light of the screen bright now. Heat hung heavy in the air, and Kay ran her finger over the condensation on her fresh glass of wine. Carlos had delivered a second bottle to the table without her having to ask. This was the ritual that had evolved between them. She'd drink alone first. Reading news articles on her phone and working her way through her body, which she'd had clenched all day, letting her jaw relax first, then the tight tendons of her neck, then the muscles of her stomach.

Once her blood was buzzing and the diners were thinning, Carlos would join her. It had started innocently. She'd come here once a week at most, just to unwind. She'd used to order a gin and tonic or two. She and Carlos would have a chat, about politics usually—there was always so much to say, and Janus never kept up with it. If it wasn't connected to writing, he was no longer interested. With her whole family moving to this new country along with her, she hadn't expected to be so lonely.

Then, on Saturday, less than forty-eight hours after her whole life had been turned into a living nightmare, she'd wandered down to Sabrosa. She hadn't been able to stand another second of being in her house and couldn't think of where else to go. She'd ordered wine, drunk glass after glass. She'd begun to rise out of her body, to float away from the strained muscles, the lack of sleep, the jagged beat of her heart, the horror. She hadn't eaten that day. She drank more. Wanting to disappear. The air around her turned thinner, her body lighter, like she really could drift off into the night. And then Carlos had sat down, solid and real. He'd looked at her face and his eyebrows had knotted and he'd asked her what she was thinking about and she dropped back into herself. She couldn't tell him the truth and the first place her mind had gone was to her father, and so she'd told Carlos the story of his short life and early death and her memories of his funeral.

She'd been back here every day since.

He sat down now and poured himself a glass from the bottle.

"Busy night?" she asked.

"We were one short in the kitchen."

"You could have called Casper."

His eyes sparkled. "But then you wouldn't have come, would you?"

She smiled into her wineglass. Took a sip. Her blood hummed through her body. Her skin prickled in the warm air.

"You seemed to be having fun. We could hear you girls all laughing from inside."

"Girls?" she scoffed. "I was telling them about my days in the Australian Ballet. Well, the nights, really."

"I'd love to see you dance." He leaned forward, elbows on the table. Her eyes grazed the dark hair on his forearms. She could smell the musk of his sweat from the kitchen dried into the white cotton of his T-shirt. She wondered if he'd taste like salt if she licked his chest.

"You'd be disappointed, I suspect," she said.

"Do you miss it?"

"Sometimes. But I wouldn't want to go back to that. I used to think I'd always dance. When we were on tour, we went to see the Royal Ballet. I got to see Sylvie Guillem live, Mademoiselle Non herself. I thought I'd be like her, that I'd keep dancing until I was middle-aged, until they had to carry me off the stage, but things change."

"What things?"

She held out her arm and squeezed the fat that hung from the muscle of her triceps, grabbed at each thigh with both hands. She guided his eyes to all her imperfections. It sent a bolt of shame and desire to her gut.

"You aren't fat, Kay. Is that what you think?"

"When you're a ballerina, you can only be muscle and bone."

"Then I'd have no hope."

But she liked the way the curve of his stomach pressed into his T-shirt. His thick arms. It was somehow more masculine than the sculpted six-packs she saw on the shirtless men in her Pilates classes.

"It was a lie anyway, what I was saying to Yolanda and Rani."

"What was the lie?"

"That leaving dance was the bravest thing I'd ever done."

"It wasn't?"

This was how it started. Carlos could always get her talking. Now he was the only person she did talk to. And this talking, this nighttime revealing, felt more and more like undressing. They hadn't so much as kissed, but somehow, this twilight intimacy was adulterous.

"Leaving ballet was brave, I guess. But I did it in the most cowardly way."

"You did?"

"I'd wanted to leave for months before I did. I would fantasize about it. I was going out more and more, trying to escape without actually committing to it. I remember it so well. It was winter in Melbourne, an especially cold one, and we were rehearsing a new production of *Giselle*. We'd just come off tour for *Swan Lake*, and now we were starting again and I couldn't bear it. Every morning I'd leave home at dawn and walk to the train station."

She could remember the walk well. Her woolen tights were not thick enough to warm her skinny legs. Her woolen hat was pulled low, her scarf high, and her hands stuffed into the pockets of her red puffer jacket. Her breath visible in the frigid morning air.

"To get to the platform, you had to go up these concrete stairs. They'd usually be wet from the night's rain. Every morning I'd consider it, how easy it would be to slip and fall. It was like a little game I had with myself, to see how much I really wanted to leave. I told myself if I really had the nerve to leave, I'd let my foot slip. But I never did, so I told myself I didn't really want it."

He listened to her and then reached over. This was what she wanted. Those few seconds of warm skin to warm skin. When she told him some intimacy and he consoled her with physical touch.

His hand brushed down her arm, across the skin she'd pinched earlier.

"That's a really sad story," he said.

"What I did instead was almost as bad for a dancer as throwing yourself down a flight of concrete stairs, and I still got to be a coward and claim it was an accident."

"What's that?"

"I got pregnant."

He leaned back in his chair, laughed. Then poured them both another glass, emptying the bottle. She took a sip and the burn began crawling up her throat. She coughed, trying to swallow it back down.

"You all right?"

"Fine. White wine always gives me heartburn."

His face scrunched up. "What do you mean? You order it every time."

"I like the taste."

It was another lie. She'd never liked the taste of white wine. But she wouldn't let herself indulge in what she'd really like. The zing of a margarita, the herbiness of a gin and tonic. All week Kay had punished herself in small ways. With bitter black coffee and car fumes and heartburn. With holding Pilates poses for so long her muscles shook and her vision blurred. With keeping her stomach empty and buckling. A foolish part of her seemed to believe that all these small harms might add up and she'd even the score. She'd make up for what they did.

She would tell Carlos all her stories, everything she had, the more personal or exposing the better. But she'd never tell him the one that mattered. The reason she was here in this courtyard drinking wine that made her sick with a man who wasn't her husband. She would never tell him that.

AS KAY WALKED up her street, she relived his touch on her arm. His fingers calloused from kitchen burns. The rasp of them on her skin. If that felt so good, she couldn't imagine how good it would be for his hands to be on her bare back, on her ass, slipping down into her underwear, pushing inside her.

When she reached her house, she was met with the smell of dog shit. She looked down to the turd left in the middle of the front lawn. What kind of person didn't clean up after their dog? She'd have to deal with it in the morning. She opened the letter box, and her skin turned cold. There was another note. She took it out and unfolded it, her sweaty fingers sticking to the paper: *20k and we're done. You have 48 hours or I'm going to the cops. Venmo: GR7219.*

She looked up at the surrounding houses. There were lights on in a few and Kay half expected to see the silhouette of someone staring down at her. But there was no one. In the block behind their house there was an apartment building. A few of the windows were lit up, but they were too far away to see inside. She folded the note in half and put it in her bag, walking up the path. As she did, she could see up the side of Rani's house. The house was mostly dark, but there was a light on in one of the bedrooms. From here, she saw the shape of a young man. It must be their son. Austin. Still awake, sitting at a desk with the curtains wide open. She gazed at him and, like he could sense it, he looked down at her. He held up a hand in a wave, but he didn't smile. She turned away and let herself into her house.

The lights had been left on downstairs, even though no one was there. The kitchen was a mess. Red dollops of sauce were dripping down the side of the bin. There was a chopping block on the bench covered in strips of carrots, and the sink was full of dirty dishes. The tray of cannelloni had barely been touched. She flicked the light off, like the dark would make the mess disappear.

The bedroom light was off, so she slipped in and went straight into the ensuite. She scrubbed her teeth and gargled the taste of wine out of her mouth. Then she went back into her bedroom. Their bedroom. The one place she couldn't avoid Janus. It was almost eleven; maybe she'd luck out.

"You're back late," he said. He was just a dark shape in the bed.

"Yeah. Sorry." But why was she apologizing? He believed that she'd been at work. "How was the cannelloni?"

"It was perfect."

She pulled off her shirt. Kicked off her pants and tried not to stagger. She tugged an old T-shirt over her head and slipped into bed.

He slid closer to her. She could smell the stink of cigarettes on him. "Who does Pilates this late?"

"It's LA. You'd be surprised."

"I guess. You're working so much, you know. You should take a break. If you ever wanted to . . . I don't know, go meet friends for drinks or anything like that, you should do it."

"What do you mean?"

"Nothing."

But he did mean something. She must have been seen there and someone had told him. Or perhaps Rani mentioned it to Brian, who repeated it to Janus. That would be preferable. Not that she'd done anything wrong, really.

She inched away from him, forcing her voice to be warm. "I actually did see Yolanda and Rani briefly when I came home for my break."

He slid closer to her, draped his arm over her so she was right on the edge, so she only had a small channel of mattress, barely enough to fit her body.

"I'll get paid soon, don't worry. I miss having you around at night. A dinner left in the oven isn't really comparable."

She bit back another apology. She wanted to elbow him in the ribs, push him off her, yell at him to give her some room so she could at least roll over. His cigarette breath was hot on the back of her head.

I can't do it, Kay. I just can't. It's too much.

She could still hear it, his voice from that night. The whine in it. It had proven the resentment that had been swelling in the back of her mind for years: that she had married a weak man.

She felt herself re-clench. Her jaw first, then the tendons of her neck. She shrank even farther away from him to the edge, trying to take up even less space.

She remembered what Rani had said that night, that marriage was a process of sanding down your edges. But Kay had kept sanding, kept scraping away at herself until she'd become this small pathetic thing. She didn't want to be small anymore.

"Do you ever think . . . you know . . . ever wish or wonder or . . ." He faltered.

"Wish what?" Was this going to be about his novel? Some more of that philosophical crap that he thought made him sound smart?

"Do you think we should have gone to the police?"

She jerked around, really looked at him. "No. Of course not."

She couldn't see his face. Only a black shadow where she knew his face was. Had he seen the note? Maybe left it in the letter box after noticing it?

"Do you think we should have?" she asked.

"No, no. I just . . . I don't know. I feel so—"

"It's not about how you feel, Janus."

"We could have gone. We could still go, explain it. Maybe this alternative is worse. Maybe the secret is worse than the truth."

"Is this a joke?"

"No."

"I know you aren't really that naive."

"I just—"

"Can you move over? I'm about to fall out of bed."

He pulled away from her and the relief was instant.

"I shouldn't have brought it up," he said.

She tried to breathe the hot anger away. When she spoke, she kept her words even and steady. "She's our daughter."

"You're right. I was . . . I shouldn't have brought it up."

He turned over so he was facing the other way, and she closed her eyes and imagined she was *there* instead. The hotel room. The crisp linen sheets. The sound of the ocean outside, Carlos in the shower and herself naked and sated in the bed. She imagined being somewhere else, as far away from her family as she could get.

Just as she drifted off to sleep, as the tug of the wine pulled her under, she heard a faint click, like their front door closing. But no. Casper and Liv's light had been out. It was her mind playing tricks on her.

TWELVE

Olivia?"

Austin was standing on the stairs, looking at Liv like she was a strange animal.

The dark room around her jolted into focus. She was by the front door. She'd been dreaming of . . . Maria. But Maria wasn't here. Austin was. He was looking at her. This was real.

"Why . . . ?" She was so confused. "Why are you in my house?"

"I'm not," he said.

She looked around. He was right. He wasn't in her house.

She was in his.

"Huh?" she said, louder this time.

He took a step down toward her, finger to his lips. "Everyone's sleeping, Liv. It's the middle of the night."

"But I'm babysitting. Maria . . . her bed . . ."

"No." He shook his head. "Not tonight."

She was sure. She was babysitting. She was putting Maria to bed.

But no. She'd babysat last night. Not tonight. She wasn't meant to be here. She wasn't meant to be babysitting tonight.

"But how did I . . . ?" she whispered, and his eyes darted down. She was holding their spare key in her hand.

He thought she'd just come in. He was thinking that she'd just let herself into his house while he was sleeping. Which was, it seemed, exactly what she'd done. For some reason, she'd used their spare key and walked into the house while everyone was sleeping.

"Oh," she said. "Oh no, I . . . I'm not sure how this happened."

She squeezed her eyes shut and opened them again. Really looked around. Austin was wearing the same outfit as this morning: jeans, black T-shirt.

"Did you just get home?" she asked.

"A couple of hours ago. I wasn't asleep."

She was wearing her vintage white lace nightdress. No shoes. No bra. She folded her arms over her chest.

"I'm so sorry," she said, which should have been her first reaction. "I think . . . I must have been sleepwalking. Shit."

He looked up again, like he was worried they were going to wake his family.

"You know . . . you look really pale. Are you hungry? Do you want to go get some food?"

It was past midnight, so she didn't think anything except bars would be open. But when they pulled into House of Pies, a diner ten minutes away in Los Feliz, the windows were lit up golden warm.

Austin had lent her his Berkeley hoodie and Rani's Chloé slides, which had been by the door and were only slightly too big. She had watched the dark houses flick by, the glowing liquor signs outside bars and petrol stations' bright white light.

They then parked in the small parking lot and made their way over to the diner, heads bowed against the night wind. It looked retro, very 1960s. But not the throwback-nostalgia vibe that some other diners had. Genuine, like it hadn't had an update since the '60s. At the counter, a man in an LA Angels cap was drinking a coffee and chatting to a middle-aged waitress. There were wooden tables and chairs in the center, and maroon booths by the windows. The only other customers were two guys who were sitting on the same side and eating their pancakes in silence. Tinny Elvis Costello played from the speakers.

Austin slid into one of the booths and she sat across from him.

"God, I missed this place," he said. "Their pumpkin pies are amazing, although they won't have them this time of year. When I was a senior, we would come here to study late sometimes, get high on sugar and keep going until one in the morning."

She couldn't believe how normal he was being. She'd effectively broken into this guy's house and he'd taken her out for pie?

"I want to say again, I'm so, so sorry. I'm not sure exactly what happened."

"What's the last thing you remember?"

"I'm doing this application for an apprenticeship, but it's due on Friday, so I . . . I was trying to stay up late and finish it." She didn't mention she'd taken one of the pills she'd stolen from his parents to keep her up, which clearly hadn't worked. "I remember Casper going to bed and then I started feeling tired and then . . . I don't know. I can't remember."

"That's creepy," he said.

"Yeah."

"You really think you were sleepwalking?"

"Maybe." It made sense—well, at least more sense than anything else. "I used to do it as a kid, but I grew out of it."

"We had a class on it. They say people repeat the stuff they do normally during the day, like your brain doesn't realize it's asleep."

"Yeah. I used to go into my parents' room, or go and lie down on the couch with all my dolls."

"You said something about Maria. Were you dreaming you were coming over to babysit?"

"Yeah. I think so."

The waitress came over, set two ice waters on the table. "What'll it be?"

"It's strawberry season, right? Have you got that amazing strawberry cream pie?" Austin asked.

"You betcha." The waitress grinned at him, then looked at her.

The menu was in front of her, a thick laminated book. There were way too many options there, and anyway, she wasn't sure if she really wanted to eat. She still felt weird and dizzy. But then her eyes settled on the men eating pancakes.

"Pancakes?"

"You want the strawberry ones, hon?"

"Sure," she said.

She pulled the ice water to her and took a long sip. She hadn't noticed how dry her mouth was. The water helped, and it made her feel more awake, made all this seem less dreamlike.

"Are you all right?" Austin said. She didn't look up at him, but she could tell from his voice he was being genuine.

"Yeah. I'm fine. I just feel . . . I mean, I'm mortified that I came into your house like that. I know you already thought I was a complete weirdo, and then now you are forced to come and sit here with me in the middle of the night when you should be at home in bed."

He reached over and squeezed her wrist. His hand was warm.

"You know you have a terrible habit of not looking at someone when you're talking to them."

She looked up. His dark eyes were fixed on hers.

"I don't think you're weird, not really."

He had a tiny black freckle right below the bottom rim of his glasses.

"Yeah, but I mean, the makeup, the saucepan . . ."

"Oh, I did think you were massively weird, but then afterward . . ." He let go of her wrist and leaned back in the booth. "You were trying to protect my sister. You were being pretty brave, if you think about it. Plus, you should hear the way she talks about you. She loves you! And Mom thinks you're the best. They'd both mentioned you on the phone before I came home. I was looking forward to meeting you."

Now she really wanted to look down at the table. "So . . . you were looking forward to meeting me, and I was so rude to you at the coffee shop this morning."

She forced herself to hold his gaze, expecting his face to close up. But instead he laughed. "Yeah, you were," he snorted. "You were a bit of an asshole actually."

She couldn't really take offense. He was right. She took a sugar packet out from the pot. Fiddled with it between her fingers.

"But now?" she said.

"Well, I don't really sleep. I'd much prefer to be in one of my favorite places having pie with a . . ." He faltered. "A rogue sleepwalker—than be lying awake in my old bedroom."

"Rogue sleepwalker, glitter-faced killer. I'm going to get a bad reputation."

"It's looking probable."

"You don't sleep?"

He pushed his glasses up his nose. "Insomniac. Don't know which one of us has it worse."

"That'd be me."

He snorted. "Yeah. It'd definitely be you. Are you feeling any better? You still look pale, but not as much as before. Thought you were the Ghost of Christmas Past for a second, your face all white in that creepy dress—"

"It's not creepy, it's vintage!"

"Yeah, well. It's creepy when you're not expecting it."

She wrapped the sweatshirt closer. It was warm in here, but the soft fleece was comforting.

"I feel . . ." She wasn't sure how to finish that. *Freaked out. Confused. Embarrassed. Nervous.* "Better than before," she went with.

"Well, good," he said.

"Here you are." The waitress was back. She deposited a huge slice of pie in front of Austin. It was covered in glazed strawberries with whipped cream and a thick crust. In front of Liv, she placed a warm plate with a stack of four pancakes, covered in icing sugar and fresh strawberries, as well as a bottle of syrup.

"Enjoy!" she said.

Austin was looking at his pie with pure delight. "Oh, how I've missed you," he said, and put a big forkful into his mouth.

She picked up her own cutlery. "You know, American food is so abundant compared to Australia. If this was Melbourne, you'd get two pancakes tops and maybe three strawberries."

She cut into the stack of pancakes, still unsure if she was going to be able to stomach it. She put a small slice into her mouth. The pancakes were light and fluffy, the sugar sweet. It zinged down into her fingers and made her head less floaty. She took another, bigger slice. This time with strawberries. They were juicy and slightly sour. Delicious. It was like she'd been spinning without realizing, and now she was grounded.

"These are so good," she said.

"Told you." He was halfway through his pie. "Hey, you forgot syrup."

"Don't like it," she said, through another mouthful.

"What do you mean? You can't have pancakes without syrup!"

She swallowed. "I can. And I will."

"You look so much better."

He was staring at her, a huge smile on his face.

"Look, you're even blushing again. That's got to be a good sign!"

"Oh, shut up," she said, and cut herself another big bite.

"So what was the dream?" he said. "With Maria? You were saying her name when you first woke up."

She stopped, holding her knife and fork just above the plate.

"I . . ." She thought about it. "I don't remember."

"Come on. We've been so honest with each other."

"I am." She leaned back in the seat. "I never really remember my nightmares."

"So it was a nightmare?"

The syrup bottle was slightly open, a globule catching the light at the top. She leaned over and pressed the lid closed.

"I remember the feeling of it. This intense fear and like . . . I had to protect someone. I dunno. But I can't remember the actual dream."

"Something to do with babysitting? That's what you were saying."

She could barely remember waking up. "Yeah, but something happened. Something that made me really scared."

He thought about that for a moment. "Maybe it was because of last night? When you thought I was breaking in? I mean, it was funny, but it was also probably scary for a while there."

"Yeah." She turned that over in her mind. "Maybe." She doubted that was enough to cause such a huge reaction.

"You know, we did a week on dream psychology as well."

"You're studying psychology?"

He nodded. "Third year. We were doing Jung and the unconscious mind—that's why we covered sleepwalking, but we also touched on dreams and nightmares and stuff."

"You're not going to try and diagnose me, are you?"

"I diagnose you as . . . a sleepwalker." He grinned.

"I don't know . . . I worry about myself, you know? I went out last week. I was meant to stay at my friend's place, but I woke up at home. I literally have no memory of what happened."

"A blackout? How drunk were you?"

"I must have been wasted. That's why my mum is so mad at me. My dad is too. He called me callous today when I said I thought they were overreacting."

"That's harsh."

"Yeah, maybe. I don't know. If I was my daughter, I would probably be pretty ashamed of me. I need to get my act together."

"But aren't your early twenties all about making mistakes and figuring yourself out in the big bad world? Rather than the easy, simple make-believe world you think exists when you're a kid."

"Maybe. I don't know. I thought I was going to succeed, you know? I thought things were going to just work out if I put enough effort in. But I didn't bank on myself being such a fuckup."

He laughed. "Yeah, I hear that. I never thought that the person who'd keep messing everything up for me would be myself."

"I just wish I wasn't making these mistakes under their roof. I never should have agreed to move back in with them. But then I guess I wouldn't be here."

"Why did you all move here?"

"My dad wrote a book that got optioned to be a movie, so they decided to come here for a bit to see what would happen."

Austin made a face.

"What?"

"I mean . . . most things that get optioned never actually get made—he knows that, right? And even the rare times when they do, they're often just buried on one of the streamers, forgotten about in a week if they even get noticed in the first place."

"Yeah, he knows that," she said, although she was fairly sure her dad didn't know that at all. "They just wanted an adventure."

"So, what's your dad's book?"

The Kind and Unkind Girls.

"Hang on . . . your dad is Janus Jansen? But I thought he was some cool Scandinavian guy. Like Knausgaard."

"Nope. Well, his parents are Dutch. They immigrated to Australia. You know the book?"

"I saw my dad's copy on the couch. I flicked through it this afternoon, but I haven't read it." He put another glazed strawberry in his mouth.

She leaned forward. "I'll tell you a secret. Neither have I."

"You haven't read it?"

"Nope. He talked about it so much, for so long, that by the time he gave me a copy, I knew the whole plot anyway, and I just . . . I couldn't read it without cringing."

"Why?"

"I mean, it's my dad putting on the voice of a woman. I don't mind the horror bits, but the parts where he's writing about sex from her perspective are too weird. I read one sentence where she's talking about her mother's breasts and calls them her 'perfect orbs' . . . What the fuck, Dad? I had to put it down after that."

He leaned back and laughed. His lips had turned slightly pink from the glaze. She wondered if they'd taste sweet if she kissed him.

"Don't tell anyone I haven't read it, all right?"

"Cross my heart."

"What about you? Berkeley must be pretty amazing."

"Yeah, I guess."

She looked down at the logo on the hoodie. "Even the name. Berkeley. Sounds so . . . I don't know. Smart."

He put his fork on the plate and rubbed his paper napkin across his mouth. "I'll tell you a secret, since you told me one."

"All right," she said, taking another bite of pancake.

"I'm failing."

That surprised her. She swallowed the pancake, and then coughed as it got stuck in her throat. She took a sip of water. "I was doing a fashion design course which I flunked out of. It was pretty humiliating."

"My parents will absolutely freak when they find out."

"Is it too hard? You must have gotten good grades to get in."

"I dunno." He gazed out the window. The parking lot looked so dark and gray out there.

She didn't know what to say. She'd heard all about the pressure of universities in America. They were so expensive, not like in Australia, where they were a quarter of the price and you were automatically given a student debt to pay off with no interest until your income hit a certain level once you were working.

"It's like, I want to study," he said. "I try to. I sit there and stare at the words, and then an hour will pass and I'll realize I'm not reading them. I'm on the same page I started with. Or I've turned the pages, but I haven't actually absorbed any of it. I was okay the first two years, but this year it's . . . impossible. I stayed on an extra few weeks, trying to do some extra-credit work, sat some makeup exams, but I'm still not sure if I passed the semester. There's no way I could do it again for next semester. I just don't have it in me."

"Why do you think that is?"

"I guess . . . I don't want to be there. That's the truth of it. I studied so hard to get in. It was my dream. I put everything into it. But this year . . . I just started feeling guilty. All I could think about was being back here. You know?"

"Guilty for what?" she said. "It's awesome you got in."

"Yeah. I guess."

They both looked out at the dark parking lot. The wind had picked up while they were inside, and the row of palm trees on the other side of the lot were being thrown about. They almost looked like those blow-up tube men out in front of car dealerships, dancing a silent manic dance.

"What are you going to do?"

"I dunno," he said. "I'm stuck. I could have gotten into a college here and lived at home. Mom would have been happy with that, I'm the first one from her side of the family to get to go to college. But I felt like I had to be, you know, the best . . . My dad's going to lose it."

She imagined Brian, with his fancy job and perfect house. He didn't seem like the kind of guy who would want his son to be a dropout. But then she thought about how he came home during the day sometimes. Maybe he'd understand better than Austin thought.

"You have to tell them. There's no point in staying if you don't want to be there."

He nodded, still looking out the window into the windy night.

"You know, most of the palm trees around here were shipped over in the early thirties," Austin said. "They only live a century at most, so we're going to watch them all die off at once over the next few years."

"They aren't native?"

"No."

She looked up at the rows of ghostly trees, their impossibly long trunks swaying in the dark.

"But . . . they're everywhere. They're all imported?"

"Every single one of them. They wanted this place to be glamorous . . . to feel like paradise, like some kind of leisure utopia. But their time is almost up."

"I didn't know trees had a lifespan."

"They do."

Now that she looked, she saw that more than a few of the trees had brown fronds and bald patches. One of them was just a long trunk with a few dead tufts on top.

"They were trying to present a certain kind of life," he said. "But it isn't real. It's bullshit." He turned back and looked down at her empty plate. "Pancakes help?"

"They really did. Thank you."

He motioned to the waitress for the check. "We should get back, I guess."

"Yeah," she agreed. Although really, she wanted to stay all night in this booth with him and watch the sun rise together over the dying palms.

THIRTEEN

From the moment she had found out she was pregnant with Olivia, Kay had worried. Every time she went to the toilet, her skin would prickle with the fear of finding blood in her underwear. She hadn't used to be a nervous person. The opposite. Sometimes it seemed like her recklessness had defined her. But this was different. She wanted this baby. She needed it. She'd started a new life when she and Janus got together. One of eating three meals instead of one; of curling up in front of a movie with a glass of wine, not dancing all night with a perfect white pill fizzing in her stomach. One of waking up in the arms of the same man every morning, not sneaking out at dawn before a stranger woke. This baby was the final part of her steady, warm new life.

Her doctor told her that bacteria could cause a miscarriage, and so food became the enemy once again. She'd stared down at the lasagna Janus had reheated, back when they were living in their first place: that tiny flat in Abbotsford. She'd only eaten around the edges, terrified it wasn't cooked all the way through. She'd gazed at the fried egg wobbling on her plate at the local café on the corner. How could it wobble if the yolk was well-done? Craving carbs on a break from a grueling day at the studio, she'd ordered a bagel with cream cheese, and sat on a bench in the sun staring at its contents. Was cream cheese counted as soft cheese? Or was it too processed to be counted as cheese at all?

Soon, she didn't have to worry about food. Her stomach swirled and buckled. Her head spun just from sitting up. She hadn't wanted to tell the studio until she was twelve weeks along, until it was definite, but the thought of being tossed in the air at rehearsal was a joke. She'd called in to tell them, breathing deep and keeping her voice steady. Her director had already taken her aside for a talk the month before about her weight gain, and she'd been looking forward to breaking the news since. But she felt so ill she wanted to cry, too sick to enjoy his shocked silence.

"You'll never come back," he'd said.

"I know."

She spent days with her cheek against the cold tiles of the bathroom floor, praying to vomit for its fleeting relief. But nothing came up. Her muscled calves turned weak. Her skin went pale. She imagined the little shrimp inside her growing thin.

But it didn't. The embryo turned into a fetus. Janus grinned as they watched it on the screen, perfect and healthy and already looking like a baby.

She had put off telling her mother. But she was starting to show and she didn't want news to reach her before she told her herself. They met at a wine bar. When she arrived, her mother was on to her second glass and halfway through a cheese platter.

"Janus and I are getting married," Kay told her.

Her mother scrunched up her brow over her chardonnay. "Which one was Janus?"

"The one I'm living with."

Her mother scraped a heap of Brie onto a cracker. "Oh, Katherine, no. Not the accountant?"

"Yes. The accountant."

"Give it a bit more time, my love. I know boring can seem endearing at first, but usually it ends in . . . well, boredom!" She pushed the whole creamy mess into her mouth and laughed, goop covering her tongue.

"Janus isn't boring. He's wonderful. My life is good now. Things are finally, I don't know . . . in order. I know what to expect. Janus is my rock. With him things will always be secure, I'll always have a steady home, and—"

"How romantic."

But for Kay, it was. For Kay, knowing what she was coming home to each day was golden.

Her mum gulped down the last of her wine and, already squinting, motioned to the waiter for another.

"We're getting married and—"

"And you want me to pay for it? I am both the father and the mother of the bride, I suppose."

Kay's dad had died in a car accident when she was seven. He'd been the only child of family money, and her mother had inherited all of it. For some people, money can be a savior. But it ruins others. Her mother had stopped working at the woman's magazine which had been her passion. Instead she'd given her all to every whim and impulse. They'd spent two years in Bali while her mother studied under a Yogi, eight months in Barcelona while she learned Spanish, four years in Sweden because she thought their socialism-informed governing was more in line with her values and she liked their style of furniture. Then, always, back to Melbourne, chasing their tails. It was Kay's mother who had pushed her into dance, and when she won a competition, she was doing it for that spark in her mother's eyes, that tight hug that was fully focused on her and no one else. She had come with Kay for two years in Paris, two glorious years where dance had been her mother's newest infatuation. And then she had found earthenware ceramics and moved on.

"I'm not asking you to pay for it," Kay said now. "We're just going to go to the registry office."

"Oh." Kay's mother stuck out her lip. "But that isn't any fun at all."

"Mum, I'm pregnant."

She waited for the spark, the focus. And it came, but there was no smile.

"No. Katherine. No. You can't. You won't be able to dance."

"I don't want—"

"Listen to me, Katherine. This isn't the answer. I'll put some money in your account so you can take some time off. You can go away, go back to Paris if you want. You liked it there, didn't you? You can recover there. Eat some good food, find a French lover."

"No, Mum, I'm—"

"You don't need to do this as some kind of . . . I don't know . . . rebellion. It's so pedestrian. Who even gets married anymore because they are pregnant? No. No, you'll go to Paris."

"We're not getting married because I'm pregnant. We wanted to anyway. And I'm happy, Mum."

The waiter put down the wine, and her mother picked it up and gulped down half.

"Katherine, trust me on this. You don't want a baby."

Kay looked at her knees. She wanted to cry. She had hoped the baby might become her mum's newest passion, like maybe she'd get really into designer onesies and bespoke cribs.

"But I'm your baby, Mum."

"This is forever, okay? Babies destroy you. Your body, your mind, your life . . . they take it all. I can't support this, Katherine. I love you too much."

Kay stood. "Okay."

"What? Are you kidding? You're leaving? Katherine, my love, you'll be calling me for money soon. I know that. I know how you are used to living. I know what kind of woman you are. And it's not a wifey, and it's definitely not a mummy. Sit down. Have a glass of wine. Have some cheese."

"I can't have cheese!" she yelled. "Or wine! Especially wine! Fuck off, Mum!"

She'd walked away, out of the wine bar and back to the little apartment in Abbotsford, and she was sure, so sure, that she was right and her mother was wrong. This would end her dark thoughts and self-starvation and fantasies of throwing herself down the wet station steps. This was what her life was meant to be: gentleness and family and stability. She'd have her baby; then she'd go to university, study choreography. She'd always admired choreographers, the power they had, the way they held themselves. She'd take a little time-out and come back stronger, her new family buoying her.

In the end, Olivia was twelve days overdue. They'd had to induce labor, using a long metal rod with a hooked end to break her waters. She'd lain on her back in the birth suite, felt the hot gush of liquid spill out of her.

The contractions started hard and fast. Every thirty seconds one would rip through her. She'd thought dancing on a fractured ankle was pain. She'd thought the ripple of yellow blisters bursting on her feet as she stood en pointe, the warmth of pus seeping into her satin shoes, she'd thought that was pain. She'd thought the audible snap of a tendon in her hip as she landed was as much as her body could hurt. But all of that was nothing compared to this.

Olivia got stuck on the way out. The crown of her head was visible for an hour before the midwives told her the baby was going to need a little help. Kay had felt the scissors, the give of her flesh under them, like cutting into thick rubber. And then the huge squirming weight was pulled out from inside her. They put her on Kay's chest: this steaming, wailing purple thing, wet with her blood. She knew it was her baby, but it felt like an organ. Like they'd torn out her liver and placed it on her bare chest.

Tears steamed up Janus's glasses.

"It's our little girl," Janus said. "You did it. She's amazing."

The baby wailed. It smelled like the inside of her body. Its face was swollen, its hair caked in blood. More and more people came into the room, looking between Kay's legs. She tried to press her thighs back together, but the midwives clamped down on her knees.

"What's happening?" she whispered. There were six people in the room now.

"You're okay," Janus said, but he was pale. She followed his eyeline. Nurses were piling towels sopped in blood on the metal table.

Janus turned back to her. "Don't worry about that. Our daughter's here."

He pulled his camera out and took a photo, the first photo of her and Olivia. She saw the print a few weeks later. Kay's skin was so pale, her lips looked bright red. Her face was blank, loveless, with the purple screaming baby on her chest. She asked him to throw it away, but he told her it was beautiful.

Kay's dancer's body was gone. Her stomach was a deflated balloon, disgustingly soft, her organs untethered inside it. She dribbled hot piss without warning. Her breasts leaked warm yellow milk, her tender nipples grating against the wet fabric of her T-shirt. Purple stretch marks clawed her thighs. Her delicate ankles were now thick stumps. She stopped sleeping. How could she sleep when her daughter wouldn't stop crying? Day and night, Olivia would wail and wail, and Kay knew Olivia hated her. She rejected her milk. She knew that Kay was a terrible mother. Sometimes Kay would lie on the couch and listen to her daughter cry and wonder if something was wrong with her baby, if maybe she was in pain, if maybe she was dying. And it would be a relief, it would be okay, because if Olivia died, Kay knew that she would too, which would be a kind of sleep. But Olivia kept on crying.

KAY SAT AT the kitchen table of their Los Angeles rental, the mid-morning heat already baking the small kitchen. She typed numbers into the calculator on her phone. The note had asked for $20,000. They had $5,500 in their bank account, which they were relying on for rent and food. Her pay would come through next week, but that would be less than $1,000. Janus wasn't due any book royalties for another month, and they'd been dwindling more and more each time. He wouldn't see another payment for his screenplay until they signed off on his new draft, which seemed like it might never happen.

Kay had another $4,000 in a savings account. Rainy-day money. But still, even with all of it together, it wouldn't be enough. She would give everything she had to this person, whoever they were, to stop them from telling anyone what they had seen on that still-dark Friday morning. But she'd never forget.

"Mum?"

Kay looked up. She hadn't noticed Olivia had come back from walking the dog. She came to stand over her at the table. Those sleepy almond eyes, that shorn hair, the spangled denim collar of her shirt hugging her long elegant neck.

Olivia put a takeaway coffee down in front of her. It would be a latte, creamy warm milk. It would probably help her hangover, work toward settling her stomach.

She sat down across from Kay at the table, sipping her own takeaway from a straw, and smiled at her. Despite everything, Kay couldn't help but smile back.

"Hot today," she said.

"Mmm," Kay agreed. "It's good you took Ginger out now—it'll be too warm for her later."

"Yeah, Rani and Austin were at the park with Rufus too. I think Ginger has a crush on him."

They both gazed down at the dog, who wagged her tail. Then Kay's eyes returned to Olivia, who, with the sunlight cast through the window onto her face at that exact angle, looked morphed into the little girl she used to be. The girl Kay saw as an extension of her own body. They had been inseparable. Kay had to make up for the bad start she'd given her daughter, so she tried to be everything for her. She was a full-time mother until Olivia started school, was there for every nappy, every tantrum, every bedtime, stroking her hair until she fell asleep. She only had to look at her daughter to know what was on her mind. On Olivia's first day, Kay had been so proud of her tiny girl in her cute new uniform, but had also ached for her during this new separation. Janus had always wanted to have another child; however, Kay had resisted, scared of a repeat of those early months. This new aimlessness made her reconsider. She'd always wished for a sibling as a child herself; it would be such a gift to give to Olivia. And so Casper was born, and the moment Kay saw him she loved him. His newborn period was nothing like Olivia's. Sure, he cried, but holding him to her body would soothe him. Kay worried she had subconsciously believed having a second baby would be a do-over, that she could fix the mistakes she made with Olivia by being a better

mother this time around. But that wasn't true; she was only failing her daughter again. Having Casper severed Olivia from her. Her
daughter seemed to need her even less, and Kay was sure she saw the
new baby as an unforgivable rejection. Her face would fall when her
eyes set on the pram when Kay picked her up from school, and she
wouldn't hold Kay's hand as they walked home. Kay felt like she was
being split in two. She'd never realized motherhood would mean
feeling guilty all the time.

Once Casper turned one, Olivia had forgiven her mother. But
Kay could no longer read her thoughts by looking at her. It was
like the scaffolding of their relationship had been demolished. She
tried to rebuild it, but there was a new fragility there that never went
away.

When Olivia had become a preteen, she'd gotten pimples and
breasts and seemed so uncomfortable in her own skin. Kay was teach-
ing classes by then, and she'd always try and help her daughter to get
in shape, to feel good about herself. She'd always imagined it would
be something they'd share, early-morning jogs and gym sessions and
maybe a mother-daughter yoga retreat one day. But Olivia became
sullen and uncommunicative, and Kay felt their bond pale and fade
even further, felt her daughter become someone she didn't understand. Olivia had started hiding bottles of vodka under her bed, going out late. Every month there seemed to be a different boy in her
life. Kay had been overbearing—she knew that—but it was only because this was part of herself she hadn't wanted to pass on to her
daughter. It horrified her to imagine Olivia living her own old life-
style. When Olivia told her she'd decided on a career in fashion, Kay
hadn't been able to cover her reaction quickly enough. It wasn't that
she didn't want her daughter to have creativity; it was just that she
knew what it meant to devote your life to an occupation that was so
unsustainable. She tried to explain this to her daughter, but couldn't

find the right words. Soon after, Olivia moved out and they'd barely spoken at all. Kay had ached for her once again. Olivia's overdose wasn't the only reason she'd wanted her to come with them to Los Angeles. Kay worried if she were left behind, maybe her daughter would untether herself from her mother completely. But perhaps that would have been better than this.

Olivia's eyes snapped away from the dog and she turned her face and the enchantment was broken. The child was gone and she looked like her adult self again.

"Hey, Mum, did you know that trees had lifespans? I had no idea."

Kay blinked. "You thought they just lived forever?"

"I guess. Yeah. I don't know."

Her daughter took a sip of her coffee, her eyes darting between Kay and the latte she'd bought for her that she still hadn't touched.

"Oh, um, I was wondering, by the way. I used to sleepwalk as a kid, right?"

"Yeah, you did. I found you standing and staring into the fridge one night like you were in a trance. A couple of other times, I came into your room and your bed was empty"—Kay could still remember the clutch of her heart in those moments—"but then I'd find you asleep on the couch or once even in your toy box."

"In the box?"

"Yeah, you looked like a little doll yourself curled up in there, covered in pink teddy bears and toy dinosaurs."

"Wait . . . do you mean Mr. Green Dinosaur?"

Kay nodded. "Yeah. I forgot about him."

"I didn't! Casper stole him and said he was Godzilla, and I knew I was too old to be annoyed, but I was." She laughed. "So what made the sleepwalking stop?"

"I can't really remember. You just grew out of it. It's really common in childhood. Why?"

"Just curious. Aren't you going to drink your coffee? I was trying to, you know, say sorry. About Thursday night."

Kay's jaw set. A coffee? Really? Kay could still feel the cold hand in hers, slippery with blood; she could still hear that labored breathing. Who was her daughter that she thought a coffee would make that okay? Who was this young woman in front of her?

"I don't want it." She glared at her daughter, watched her face fall.

Olivia pushed back the chair so it grated on the tiles and walked away.

Kay had to close her eyes; her vision was pulsing, she was so angry. She took a long lateral-style breath, like she taught her students in cooldowns. Then she went back to her calculations. They'd received a fifty percent refund on Casper's flights; the airline had refused to reimburse the full amount, so they would have a total of $12,400 to their name if she could get an advance on her pay. The rest of their savings had gone when they'd moved here. She knew it wasn't enough. She had to find more, from somewhere. There was no choice. If they didn't bankrupt themselves, this person would tell the police. They'd go to jail, all three of them, leaving Casper completely alone. But what if they just kept asking for more money? What if this kept going on and on? Her hands shook. The room spun. She needed a real drink.

A mother's terror was that she would ruin her child. Kay had never thought, not for a second, that her child would ruin her.

FOURTEEN

Casper walked down to the bus stop on Virgil Avenue. The concrete stank like piss and vomit that had been baking all day in the sun. The bridge for the 101 was above the street, and the sheltered embankment underneath was covered in colorful tents.

He'd been shocked by all the tent cities in LA when he first arrived. Now he barely noticed them. He didn't know what that said about him.

When he got to the bus stop, he leaned against the pole. His hair had still been wet from the shower when he left, but it was starting to dry in the hot late-afternoon air. The heat bore down on his shoulders through the cotton of his T-shirt.

Casper scrolled through his phone aimlessly, not even seeing the images whiz past in front of him. He realized he'd never replied to Hélène's text asking how he was, so he wrote, *How old do you have to be to emancipate yourself?*

She replied straightaway: *You'd break your parents' hearts.*

Doubt it, he replied. *I want to go back to Australia. I hate it here.*

She loved when he was dramatic. After he did a job for her, she'd always pour him a trickle of Chambord over ice, which tasted sticky and thick, but he never said anything. She'd roll off a twenty-dollar note from her stash—she didn't seem to believe in banks—and demand that he tell her some gossip.

Do you really hate Los Angeles? she wrote back.

He'd told her that before, but he didn't want to point that out. Hélène was in her eighties, and she always said her worst fear was Alzheimer's.

What's to like? he replied.

The bus pulled in and he got on, sitting by the window and looking out as it took off down the road.

God, he hated this city. Even the street signs were grimy. Everything was glaring concrete and redundant palm trees that didn't even cast any shade. There were unhoused people everywhere. Men pushing trollies filled with their possessions. People asleep on mattresses on suburban footpaths in the full sun. And then you'd see wannabe actors in their baseball hats and capped teeth step around these people like they didn't even see them. They called this place the City of Dreams, but it seemed more like all the worst parts of humanity hanging out for everyone to see.

Tye got on at the next stop.

"Hey," he said, and slipped into the seat next to him. They were going to a free lunchtime premiere of some indie movie that Tye was excited about. Casper didn't usually watch this kind of film, but he was happy for the invitation.

"How many movies do you watch every day?" he asked Tye.

"At least one," he said, "but now we are on break, I'm aiming for a minimum of two."

"What's your maximum?"

"On Tuesday I watched four."

"Four?!"

"Well, three were the *Godfather* series, so that's kind of like one big one. And then I watched *Carlito's Way* because I was in an Al Pacino mood."

"Shit," Casper said. "I don't think I've ever seen more than one in a day. Didn't you get bored?"

"I was going to do *Scarface* too, but I couldn't handle another shootout. I feel like I heard the sound of machine guns every time I closed my eyes."

"Fair. Did you get up early enough to watch something this morning?"

"Nah, I slept in. But I was thinking of watching a Denzel movie tonight. Maybe *The Bone Collector*? I don't know. I've been kind of feeling like a procedural since our stakeout yesterday."

"Yeah, so turns out that woman my dad met up with was his producer."

"Ohhhh, okay. So probably not an affair, then?"

"I don't think so," Casper said. He wasn't sure he wanted to talk about this, although it was all he could think about. He glanced at Tye, expecting him to look freaked out or uncomfortable. But actually, Tye's eyes were gleaming behind his glasses.

"Why do you look so excited?"

"Why? An affair would be the most boring possibility! It really seems like something is *actually* going on."

"And that doesn't, like . . . make you want to stay away?"

Tye raised his eyebrows at him in such a look of incredulity that Casper snorted a laugh. "You're loving this, aren't you?" Casper said.

"I know this is your family and I have to be tactful and everything. But . . . I mean, I feel like I'm the right person to help you figure this out. I even made a table while I was waiting for the bus." Tye pulled an exercise book out of his bag and opened it. "On this side we'll put what we know, on the other the stuff we still need to find out."

"There's nothing to write on this side." Casper pointed at the *What We Know* column. "We literally know nothing."

"That's not true. We know whatever went down, it had something to do with your parents and Olivia." Tye wrote that in. "We know that she went out on Thursday night, had a big night, and then . . . well, your parents were acting weird."

"And Liv had those bruises."

Tye wrote *Olivia injured* and then *broken hair clip*. Casper thought of the Home Depot bag he'd found. A claw hammer, a knife, and gloves. But no, best not to add that to the list. Tye would probably never want to set foot in his house if he told him that.

"So we know something happened that ended in Olivia getting hurt, and your parents were definitely involved. Did anything else happen that was strange? Or was there anything different from before? Like, was there anything missing?"

"I don't know. Don't think so . . ." But then he remembered the padlock. "Actually, yes. There was a mold issue in Liv's room."

Tye flicked the pen against the paper. "I don't know if that's connected, but there are no bad ideas."

"No . . ." He almost didn't want to say it. "When I got back, they'd locked up Liv's room. Like . . . with a padlock."

Tye stared at him. "A padlock?"

"Yeah. It's a legal thing apparently. Like, tenants' safety rights or something."

"Are you sure that . . ." Tye took a breath. "I mean . . . could there be someone in there?"

"No! That's crazy."

But Tye kept looking at him.

"This isn't some horrible true crime story. My dad isn't keeping women locked up in a room in our house. There aren't any sounds, for one."

He'd actually gone and listened at the door that morning, and it was completely silent. Anyway, he wasn't going to admit that; it was ridiculous.

"Okay."

"It's got something to do with Liv. I'm sure."

Tye nodded, and wrote *What happened on Thursday night?* in the *What We Don't Know* column.

"This is a good place to start," he said. "If this was a movie, we'd be going through microfilm of newspapers for that weekend."

"I guess we could search their sites—it's only last weekend."

"All right, you take the *LA Times*, I'll take the *Daily News*."

"Okay."

He pulled out his phone and typed the date in and started scrolling. There was heaps of boring politics, some big soccer match, a lot of stuff about surging house prices, lots of gun violence, and a stabbing.

"Any luck?" he asked Tye after a couple of minutes.

"I don't think so, unless she's the one who is delivering pizzas with semiautomatics on top." Tye put his phone down. "So what are we actually thinking now? Let's try and construct a plausible scenario."

"Is that what they do in movies?"

"You have to talk it out, otherwise you don't even know what you're looking for."

Casper leaned his head back onto the seat and stared out the bus window at the cafés and bars flicking past.

"So I guess I'm thinking . . . something happened when Liv went out. She got into some kind of trouble. She must have called my parents, and then they got all mixed up in it."

"What kind of trouble are you thinking? She got into a fight?"

"I can't imagine her getting physical with anyone."

"Well, someone hurt her."

"Yeah," Casper said. "I guess they did."

"It was some fashion-party thing, right?"

"Yeah. With this new friend of hers. Her name's . . ." He searched his mind. "Leilani."

Tye thought about that, then said, "Show me Liv's Instagram."

Casper took his phone out of his pocket and navigated to her feed.

"There's not much on there. She just posts pictures from old French movies and seventies fashion shoots, it's really boring."

He showed Tye, who took his phone and clicked on the tab of tagged photos. On that one, there were loads of photos of Liv. The most recent one was Liv sitting outside a bar with a girl. They both had on short dresses, their crossed legs pressed together. They were smiling, the flash of the camera making their faces bright and their hair shiny. The caption was *Goodbye, L.A.DS!* Tye pressed on the other girl. Her account was called LeiliLove.

"We found her," Casper breathed.

Tye flicked down through the photos. She posted a lot, every other day. Pictures of coffees next to Joan Didion books, pictures of her outfits in the mirror, selfies in bed where her eyes were sleepy but her skin looked perfect, pictures out with other beautiful fashiony-looking girls. Tye scrolled back. The picture of her and Liv was the most recent, from a week ago. There was nothing since then.

"Could it have been her clip? She has long hair," Tye said.

"But why would it be at my house?"

"I don't know," Tye said, and his eyes flicked away. Casper wasn't sure he wanted to know what Tye was thinking.

THE CINEMA WAS only a five-minute walk from the bus stop. As they strode along, Tye told him about the film they were seeing. The movie was shot with an iPhone in Koreatown apparently, and it was about a woman whose husband is a violent hit man, but she gets sick of it and kills him. He walked with Tye through the lobby into the half-full cinema. It was a small one, with red cushioned chairs. Tye went into the third row, his favorite, and Casper sat next to him.

The old 1950s concession ad they always played before the trailers came on. Tinny high-pitched music started. A bag of popcorn juggled. A hot dog did flips.

Tye leaned back in his chair. "You know, sometimes I see that juggling popcorn in my dreams."

"Horrible. That would be a nightmare."

"It's not a nightmare. Never."

A couple came into their aisle. Casper lifted his legs up and pulled them against his chest; Tye shifted to the side. They squeezed through and went to sit at the end.

The lights dimmed and then the slow music for the beginning of the movie began. The light from the screen set a glow over Tye's skin. His eyes reflected the movie in little gold sparks. Casper turned away and sank into the seat and tried to get into the story of the movie, not sure why his heart was beating so fast.

He watched as the tired-looking housewife finally cracked it with her crappy, cheating husband and shot him with his own gun. She went to work cleaning the house, and when it was perfect, she called Missing Persons.

"She's acting strangely. Something's wrong. Can you smell that?" the detective said to his partner when she went to bring them tea. "It smells like bleach in here."

Then Casper really was watching the movie and his heart was in his throat. Because he'd remembered something. Something that hadn't seemed even remotely important at the time: When he'd come back from swim camp, the kitchen and garage had stunk of bleach. His parents usually used some spray that claimed to be environmentally friendly and didn't even have a scent. But that day, the bleach smell had been so strong it made his eyes water.

FIFTEEN

Janus knew his wife had lied to him last night. Kay spoke to him like they were strangers, like he couldn't read all her tells. He didn't even need to see her face to know she wasn't being honest; her tone of voice was enough. Not just her voice, but her skin. The story of having one glass of wine and then returning to work wasn't true. Last night, while he was trying to sleep, he could smell the sweet scent of alcohol coming from her pores.

Janus knew she was lying, but he wasn't sure why. He was happy for her to go out with her new friends. But then there were hours between when Rani came home and when Kay did. Had she been at Sabrosa that whole time?

He pushed into the pedals of his bike harder. The sun blazed in the sky above him. He squinted into its glare. He used to have prescription sunglasses that he'd wear on hot days like this one, but he'd lost them in the move over here. He wanted to get another pair, needed to really, but they were expensive. He looked back every so often,

just in case, but he never saw the same car twice. Whoever was following him must be having a day off.

At first, Janus had been frightened to bike around Los Angeles—
the roads were so different from those in Melbourne. Now he liked
it. How sweaty he got. How long it took to get anywhere. How close
the cars got to him again and again like life and death were as pre-
carious as the thin line of his tire.

When he got to the museum, he got off his bike and wheeled it up
the wide orange pathway toward the entrance. He knew he should
be at the library finishing the script, but instead he'd opened a list of
the top ten Los Angeles attractions. The La Brea Tar Pits Museum
was number five, but was the easiest to get to by bike. It was a mono-
lith. A huge 1970s building with a low flat concrete slab of a roof. The
side walls splayed open like legs on either side of him as he made his
way down to the small dark entrance of the building.

He hadn't had sex with Kay in a long time. She used to be so as-
sertive. He'd never felt that way with a woman before, so welcomed
into her warm body. She was insatiable, guiding his hands, his mouth,
his hips. She always liked to be the one in control, and even after
more than twenty years, he could never get enough of her. Her aban-
don between the sheets was one of the few relics of the girl he'd used
to know. The dancer who had looked at him with such clear eyes
that said *I want you*. Now his wife avoided his gaze altogether.

He tried to remember the last time they'd made love, but couldn't.
He'd been so distracted with his writing that he hadn't tried to initi-
ate it very often, but when he did, she wouldn't respond to his caresses.
The last time he could recall was when they'd first moved into the
new house, packing boxes all around them, the mattress on the carpet. But that had been six months ago. Could it really have been so
long?

He remembered Kay had suggested a hike to the Bronson Caves

up in Griffith Park. They'd filmed a scene in the original *Invasion of the Body Snatchers* there. The two love interests hid in the huge cave in the orange cliff face together. The way she'd said it, with that sparkle in her eyes, made him wonder if she was really suggesting they make love in that cave. He'd liked the idea—they hadn't done anything like that in more than a decade—but they never went. He'd been so busy, and she'd stopped mentioning it.

He'd been sure if he could get his writing career back on track, then he could return his focus to Kay and to his family. He'd felt a creeping sense of shame that it wasn't panning out how he'd promised them, and so he'd spent even more time at the library, determined to make good on the reason they'd moved here. But maybe he'd been distracted for too long.

Janus wished there was someone he could talk to about all this. His usual confidant was his brother, Gerrit. But Gerrit was in Europe, on holiday with his fiancée. Gerrit had never seemed interested in love, barely mentioning even dating for the first forty years of his life. But then, last year, he'd fallen head over heels for his dog's vet. Janus was thrilled for him, of course he was. He just wished he had a working phone over there. But then again, he wouldn't be able to tell his brother about what happened anyway.

He paid the small entry fee and entered the museum. Almost instantly, he knew that coming here was a mistake. The huge, brightly lit room was full of dead things. Skeletons strung up into the shapes of the animals they'd been: the huge tusks of mammoths, the howling jaws of mastodons. All, apparently, fished out of the tar pits out the back of the museum, where they had been preserved under the thick weight of asphaltum for centuries.

He continued through the exhibit, trying to avert his eyes from the mammoth skeletons towering above him. He read about the way the pits would trap animals that wandered in, and then trap predators that came after them. Unbiased in pulling life into the ooze of thick black death.

Deeper into the belly of the building, there was a glassed-off room full of paleontologists at work, *Digging Up the Past* written above them on a sign. He stood at the glass. A woman in a white coat caught his eye for a moment and smiled. He smiled back. Then she returned to her work. He took a step closer. She was brushing the gunk from a brown-stained bone about three inches long. He watched through the glass as she swapped the brush for a tool and began scraping at a crevice. How long did it take for flesh and muscle to disintegrate? For sinew and fat to break down? For the skin of a face to slip from a skull?

He could smell it again. Old coins. That rusty copper smell of blood.

The lights were too bright and the paleontologist was staring at him through the glass and he felt like he himself was buried in this dungeon-like museum. As though the weight was real and dense on his shoulders, like that tar was pulling him down, pulling him under to suffocate him with what they had done. He didn't want to be here anymore. He strode out toward the back doors, toward the sunlight. Out of the prickle of the air-conditioning into the white-hot heat of the day. He reached into his pocket and grabbed his cigarettes and lit one, hoping there was no security around to stop him. But outside was worse. There they were, the tar pits. Stinking bubbles of sulfur oozing from the surface. There was a sculpture of a family of mammoths. An adult and child on the shore, and the other parent in the pit itself, trunk raised, mouth open in a frozen scream as it was sucked down into the swill.

He watched the tar bubble around the mammoth's legs, the sulfur stink replacing the smell of blood in his nostrils. Despair was plain to see on the statues' concrete faces. What kind of sadist had created such a disturbing scene? It would upset kids. It upset him!

Was it meant to be the father or the mother mammoth that was sinking into the bubbling tar? He looked at the little mammoth look-ing on. He imagined, for a moment, his daughter seeing this exhibit. Not Olivia now, but who she used to be. His little girl, always want-ing to hold his hand with her small sticky fingers. Creeping into their bed in the mornings and burrowing in between them, warm and sleepy and perfect. He could imagine her little hand squeezing his, looking up at him with her dark-lashed eyes and asking what was hap-pening to the elephant—why was it sinking, was it going to be okay?

He needed to talk to Olivia. Not just him, both him and Kay. This idea of never speaking about it as a way to keep the secret was suffo-cating. He was losing his wife, he couldn't ignore that anymore, and he was losing his daughter too. They needed to understand her side of it; there was no way she was acting so blasé about the whole thing without a reason. They needed to parent her again, keep her on a shorter leash, make sure she was okay. But first he needed to speak to Kay. They couldn't go on like this.

He finished his cigarette and then turned away from the scene. He was going to go to Kay's work—she couldn't avoid him there. He was sick of her lies and evasiveness. They were going to talk.

SIXTEEN

K eep holding that squat!" Kay called into the headset, the music pounding in her ears.

She was squatting herself in front of the ten people on reformer Pilates machines, punching with each hand to show them what to do with the tension ropes. Her stomach was buckling. Last night's wine was sweating down her face. She hadn't eaten anything since lunch yesterday. But she wouldn't stop this squat.

"Almost there! Feel the burn!" she called.

Even the most athletic woman in the class, who was all thin ropey muscle, was starting to sweat. The shirtless man with the *vibes* tattoo across his chest groaned. It was always men who made a show, whimpering and huffing. Women turned it inward.

"Punch it out! Punch it out! One, two, one, two."

Her vision started to blur. She needed to find $7,600. She needed to fix the floor in Olivia's room. She needed to figure this mess out. For Casper. She couldn't leave Casper. Not here, alone, in a city he didn't know. What would happen to him? Would he be put into foster care? A group home? Then sent back to Australia, where she'd never get to see him? If he knew what she'd done, would he ever look at her again with love? Or would it be gone forever?

The man in the front stood up out of his squat, groaning again and holding the side of the reformer like he was going to pass out.

"All right, stand, everyone!" she called, barely able to see through her pulsing vision. "Great work, great work! Now stretch it out!"

After class, she went looking for her boss, Tiff, the owner of the studio. She found her tacking up posters for the trauma-healing sound bath event and the new booty-twerk power yoga classes.

"Hey, Tiff!" she said. "How are you?"

Tiff turned to her and beamed. "Kay, I peeked into your class earlier. You're wonderful, you're doing such beautiful work."

She'd always thought Tiff would be a great cult leader. She had a deep throaty voice that she lowered even further in the guided meditations. She'd turned wellness into a thriving business, a one-stop shop for Pilates and yoga classes, massage, Reiki healing, forty-dollar charged crystals, and a raw-food café. She had that look that seemed like a contradiction to Kay but was very popular in this city: the purity symbol of lotus flowers tattooed up her arms, and lips and cheeks puffed up with filler.

Tiff started walking and Kay kept in step with her, trying not to show how the muscles of her thighs were trembling from the workout.

"So," she began, but Tiff cut her off.

"I got your email. I do want to help you out, Kay, I do, but it's not policy. If I give you an advance on your pay, I'll have to open that up to everyone, and I mean . . . Do you know how many people work for me? The paperwork is beyond, and I don't want to spend my time doing paperwork, you know? That's not what I need. That's not my purpose."

"That's okay." Kay tried to make her tone light and breezy with no trace of panic at all. "I totally understand."

"I'm going to have a turmeric shot, do you want one? On me?"

"No, no," Kay said. "But thank you."

She stood behind Tiff, keeping the understanding smile plastered across her face, running through the numbers in her head.

"There's your husband."

Kay turned. "What?"

"What was his name? Yannick?"

She was right; Janus was there, at her work, walking toward them. He had a plastic bag looped over one arm with take-out containers inside. There must have been some sort of soup in one. It had leaked, and she could see it welling up in one corner of the bag.

"I thought I'd surprise you," he said when he approached. She hated seeing him here, in her space, at her work. But they couldn't show cracks right now. Everything had to seem normal.

Kay put her arm around him. "That's so sweet. Thank you."

He beamed. "Do you have time for lunch?"

She couldn't lie and say she had another class; Tiff was right there. "Of course."

"Bye, Kay," Tiff said, her whitened teeth glowing yellow from the turmeric. "Nice to see you again, Yannick."

"See you tomorrow!" she called to Tiff before Janus could correct her, and steered him toward the exit. His back was drenched in sweat, clammy under her hand. She shifted away from him as soon as they reached the parking lot out front. He deflated, sitting down on one of the recycled pinewood slats that people used as benches while they waited for their Ubers.

Kay remained standing. "What's happened?"

"No, no, nothing's wrong." He took out the plastic containers, placing them one by one next to him and spilling the soup even more. "I just thought it would be nice to have lunch."

"Okay."

"I know it's not Friday, but it's been so long since we had a movie night. Maybe we could watch *Attack of the Fifty Foot Woman* tonight? Get a pizza? I'll tell Casper and Olivia that it's mandatory family time—we haven't pulled that one in a while."

"Attack of the Fifty Foot Woman?"

"I could make my signature popcorn?" He looked up at her, and for a second he was the man she fell in love with. The awkward accountant who was so good, so full of love, such a rock.

"Janus," she said, and she didn't have to say any more. They couldn't eat popcorn; it had only been a week.

"I know," he said, "I just . . . We can't go on like this. That's why I came. We need to talk properly. Without the kids around."

She sat down next to him, her trembling quads slackening as she took the weight off them.

"I think we need to talk about our daughter," he said.

Her head whipped around to make sure there was no one within earshot. "We can't—"

"No, not about . . . that. Or not that specifically. More . . . Look, I know what happened was horrible. But Liv is our child. She must be struggling so much with this."

"She doesn't seem like she is."

"No. Which is even stranger, right? But after what she did . . . I know our daughter. *We* know her. She's sensitive. She's good. It must be tearing her apart."

"She's fine."

"I know, which makes me wonder if, I don't know . . . is it possible she was so drunk she doesn't even remember? Her reaction isn't making any sense to me."

"I told her to act normally."

"That was my other thought. That maybe she's just bottling it up. But she can't do that forever. I don't want her to drown in this, Kay. We need to talk to her. Help her cope. Help her to face it in a safe way."

She couldn't think like that. Kay just needed to fix the problem, focus on making sure every loose end was tied, that all links were eradicated. She couldn't even begin to think about emotions right now; she was just trying to survive, to keep them safe. He couldn't ask any more of her, but he was.

"Come on, honey. Try to think of it from her perspective."

"No," Kay said, standing up. "Think of it from mine."

"What?"

"You left me to do it alone. Do you think about that? I'm not sure if I'll ever be able to forgive you."

His face fell. "That's why you're angry with me?"

"Angry?" she laughed. "You know, apparently marriage is sanding off your edges. But I've whittled myself so far down it's like there's nothing left."

"That's how you feel? But Kay, I like your edges. I love your edges. I fell in love with you because you were so free. So creative! This beautiful, sexy, wild thing!"

"And I thought I was marrying an accountant, not a novelist."

He blinked. "I always thought my job bored you."

"What, a steady income bored me?"

"Once I finish this draft, we'll get that big payout, you know that."

But she ignored him, kept going. "A house we could afford? A partner in life, rather than someone who is too busy contemplating the overlap of psychological and gothic horror to—"

"Giallo," he said. "It was the intersection of psychological horror and giallo I was interested in."

"Oh, I'm sorry. Too busy wanking on about *giallo* to remember to pay a bill or put their dirty plates in the dishwasher or mow the lawn?

Or, God forbid, make an appointment for their own haircut? I don't find that boring. I find it comforting. I find a secure life comforting."

Just as Janus was about to retort, the hurt raw across his face, the door to the studio swung open and shut. A young woman came out, her yoga mat slung across her back with a strap. Her nose was in her phone, but she still sensed what she was walking into. She looked up at them both and then quickly away, but stood still just a few feet from them, waiting for her car.

Everything Kay wanted to say burned in her throat. Finally, the Uber came, and the girl jumped in, casting back a pitying look at them as she flung the door shut.

"You just left me to do it," Kay whispered.

Janus took a long deep breath. "You seemed so sure it was the right thing to do, but I . . . I'm sorry, but I couldn't face it. To do that to another human. Even if she was . . . gone. It wasn't right. It was barbaric."

"It was. But the sun was going to rise and we couldn't sit around discussing it or how it made us feel. Like everything else in our family, someone had to do it or it wouldn't have gotten done. That someone is always me."

He stared at her. "When did you get so cold?"

She laughed again, and he was right; the sound was so cold, it was icy. "This is what you've turned me into."

Then she walked to her car on trembling legs, got in, and drove away.

KAY WENT HOME via the hardware store and got a mask and plastic safety glasses. She idled in the driveway and checked the mailbox. She'd assumed it would be empty; she'd only gotten the request for money last night. But there was another folded piece of paper inside. Kay's fingertips were numb as she slipped it out and opened it. This time, there was no scrawl, no demands, just a photograph printed out in black and white. It was a photo of Janus, standing by a glass sliding door. He was looking toward the camera, eyes squinting. She knew exactly where this was, exactly what Janus had been doing. He hadn't even managed that without making things worse.

She scrunched the paper up in her fist. So they were serious. Whoever they were, they weren't messing around, and they had more evidence now than just what they'd witnessed.

She pulled into the garage, barely seeing. She knew what she had to do; she'd known it as soon as she saw the number on the note last night. Even before that, when the first note had arrived. She'd known the phone call she'd have to make, and now there was no time to waste. That was what the photograph meant: that there was no more time for other options.

She parked the car, went inside, and checked every room of the house to make sure she was alone this time. She unlocked the padlock on Olivia's door and went in. It still stank of bleach.

She shook out the Home Depot bag, put on the gloves, and kept her eyes down. Squatting on her haunches in the corner of the room, she took out the knife, slicing a deep incision into the carpet a few inches from the wall. Then she used the claw hammer to pry the strip off the tacks underneath, pulled the edge. It ripped from the floor, exposing the underlay beneath. A cloud of thick gray dust came with it, straight into her face. She started coughing, her throat on fire, tears rolling from her eyes, but she didn't stop. She had to keep going, get this done. She threw all her energy at the task. Slicing strips with the knife, ripping them from the tacks, prying the metal from the untreated wood underneath. Splinters split her fingernails. Thick dust filled the air. She forced herself not to cough, which made her eyes tear more. She pulled the underlay free and piled it all up in one corner. They'd have to burn it somehow—she didn't know how—but at least they could get it out of their house. For a moment, she let the relief flood her. The stained carpet would be gone, out of her house.

But then she saw the floorboards. She'd attempted to bleach the blood out, and it had gone right through the carpet and underlay. It had blanched the wood beneath. Pulling up the carpet had been pointless.

She sat down in the corner, wrapped her arms around her knees, still in the sweaty spandex from the day, which was now covered in gray dust. They weren't going to get out of this.

It was impossible.

It was impossible.

But she had to keep trying. She had to push up against this awful, impossible thing. For Olivia. Of course for Olivia most of all, no matter how she was acting. Kay wouldn't let her daughter go to jail. Never.

And for Casper. She wouldn't let her protection of one child damn the other. No. She would sort this out, just like any other problem their family had faced. It was her job as mother to make this okay. It was her job as mother to fix things, no matter what it cost her.

She stood and opened a window. She pulled off the mask and took a breath of the hot, heavy air. Then she took her phone out of the pocket of her leggings and dialed.

"Katherine! My dear, how are you?"

"Hi, Mum," she said. "I'm glad I caught you. I wasn't sure you'd be awake."

"Yes, of course. Nell likes to go on early walks with the dogs. The sunrise is the most special part of the day and we all sleep through it."

Kay didn't know who Nell was, and she'd never known her mother to have pets, but she didn't ask.

"Are you all right, Katherine? Your voice sounds croaky. How is

Los Angeles? I didn't really take to it myself. I much preferred New York. And Chicago, I really did like Chicago."

"It's going well."

"Good, good. I'm glad to hear it. Is everything all right, my dear? It's not my birthday or Christmas. Do you need something?"

Kay gripped her hand into a fist.

"Yes. I do. I really need some help."

"I see." Her voice was so eager. "How much?"

By the time Kay hung up the phone, she knew that it would be one of those conversations that she would remember forever. That smug tone in her mother's voice would always be there, no matter how much wine Kay drank or how many years passed. Her mother had won.

But it didn't matter. They'd have the money. The problem was solved.

She took off the gloves and threw them onto the pile of carpet. She took one last look at the floor. With the sunshine coming through the window, it almost looked beautiful. The bleached stain on the floorboards looked less like a splayed-out figure and more like a glowing angel.

SEVENTEEN

The front room was dark when Casper walked up the path. As usual, no one had left the outside light on for him so he could find his keys in the dark. He banged the front door closed as he came in so they'd know he was home, not that his mum or dad had even texted to ask where he was. He'd ended up going to Tye's apartment after the film ended. It had been nice hanging out all day, an escape from being at home.

He went upstairs and into his bedroom. All the lights in their room were off except for the desk lamp. Liv was standing in the middle of the room, looking out the window.

"What are you doing?" he asked. She ignored him. She was in her nightdress, just standing there, not moving.

He went into the bathroom to brush his teeth and scour his hands. Since moving here, he'd noticed he'd always end the day with black lines of dirt under his nails. He couldn't figure it out at first, then realized it was the smog, the pollution in the air getting trapped in the ridges. He should probably start getting in the habit of washing his face too, but he was too tired right now. When he came back into the bedroom, she was still just standing there.

"Liv?"

Getting closer, he saw she was breathing rapidly. Her shoulders were jolting up and down.

"Liv?" He pressed his hand to her shoulder, her skin freezing cold. She startled, whirled around, and then came the bright flash of impact, the sharp bell-note of his ears ringing.

"Liv! What the hell!"

Hot blood dripped into his mouth. He stepped away from her, went to cover his face with his arms, but he wasn't quick enough. She whacked him again, in the jaw this time. It slammed him back and he fell on his ass on the carpet.

"Stop it!"

Liv took a step back, blinking rapidly. Then she covered her mouth with her hand.

"Casper? Oh God, are you okay?"

Her eyes were bleary, confused. And she was whirling around, as if she was looking for who had hurt him. She'd lost her mind. She'd really, completely gone insane. The pain came then, the sting strong enough to make his eyes fill. She extended her hand to him and he flinched away, but then he saw she was offering it to him, to help him up. He stood by himself, wobbling slightly. It wasn't so much the pain—although it was hurting more and more by the second—but the shock that was disorientating him. He held his nose, his face throbbing, blood dribbling between his fingers.

"Sorry . . . I thought you . . ." She trailed off, her voice still sounding confused. "I'll get some tissues."

She left the room and Casper sat down on his bed. He pulled his hand away from his face; it was slick with his blood and trembling. Liv had done this. His big sister. She'd attacked him for no reason.

The door clicked open again and she stood over him. "Here."

She was holding a wad of toilet paper. He tipped back his head and held it up to his nose, trying to stop the shakes showing.

"Are you okay?" she asked him.

The tissue under his fingers bloated with blood. His ears were still ringing. His neck hurt, his cheek throbbed, and his nose was agonizing. Had she broken his nose? Was this what a broken nose felt like?

"Well, I mean, maybe don't tip your head back like that. You're not actually meant to do that," she said.

His eyes were really watering now, but he didn't want to brush the tears away because it would look like he was crying and he wasn't.

She persisted, "All the blood will just go down your throat and make you feel sick and that's—"

"Shut up," he said.

"I'm only trying—"

He didn't want to hear it. "Just shut up."

But he could taste the tang of blood in his throat, so he tipped his head forward.

"I'm sorry," she said, her voice sounding choked.

"Yeah, I know." He pulled the tissue away, and no new blood gushed out.

"Does it feel . . . It doesn't feel broken, does it?"

"It's throbbing." He squeezed the bridge of his nose and felt a sharp jolt of pain, but it wasn't overwhelming. "I don't think it's broken. I think it'd hurt more."

"I'm really sorry," she whispered.

Casper looked down at his T-shirt. There were red splurts all down it.

"Liv." He made himself look her in the eye. "What's going on? Why did you do that?"

"I . . . I don't know. I was doing my application and I was imagining how I'd sew the pieces I was drawing. But . . ."

She trailed off, looking at her bedding, where her computer sat open. She seemed frightened and he wanted to drop it and make a joke and say it was fine. But the pain was still sharp and his jaw was starting to hurt too from where his teeth had clacked together and he couldn't get the way she'd looked at him out of his mind. Her eyes.

"Something's wrong with you," he said.

"I know that, I . . ." She swallowed. "I think maybe I was asleep? I've been sleepwalking, I think. I don't know. I know that sounds, like, super crazy, but I didn't mean to—"

"It's not just about tonight," he cut in. "What's going on with Mum and Dad? Why has everything gotten so weird? You keep dodging telling me, like it doesn't affect me too."

She stared down at her knees. "I'm sorry."

He wanted to groan. He didn't want her to apologize; he wanted to understand. He waited, hoping for an explanation. The room went silent. Was there something truly wrong with his sister? Did she need help? She looked normal right now, just like Liv, as familiar as an old worn-out T-shirt. He'd probably spent more time with her than anyone else in the world. But he didn't know her. He didn't know the Liv who had just attacked him or been involved with something so bad that it had fundamentally changed their parents.

"Don't apologize, just tell me what happened."

She looked annoyed, as if she was about to tell him to leave it alone. But then her face crumpled and she shivered, rubbing her nose with her sleeve.

"I drank too much," she said.

"Yeah, you said that."

"I had a blackout."

"You must have some idea what happened."

"I don't," she said.

"Come on. Why do you do this? Pretend everything is fine and you have no idea what's going on when you know exactly what I'm talking about? I'm your brother and I deserve—"

"Okay, okay. I just . . . I don't know . . . It was a good night. Just like I told you. We went to the gala party, my friend Leilani and I, we were going to try and network. We weren't going to drink too much, I remember that. I was meant to stay over at her place . . . but the next day I was in your bed. In between is . . . black. I don't know what happened." She looked back down at her knees. "I just want to move forward. I've been trying, Cas, I honestly have . . . I haven't been drinking or anything. I've been working on an application for this apprenticeship and I think I've got a really good shot—"

"But don't you want to know?" he interrupted.

"What?"

"Don't you want to know what happened? You obviously did something. It could have been really awful. What if you hurt someone?"

"I wouldn't have."

"Umm . . . Liv?" He pointed at his own face.

She turned away from him, putting her sketch pad on the floor and wrapping her blanket around herself. She looked like a little pathetic baby with her shorn head poking out the top like that. She was so afraid of confrontation, it was pitiful. She always had been. She'd refuse to face anything that was uncomfortable or emotional or might end in an argument. Familiar annoyance flooded him and he couldn't even look at her. Although it was also sort of a relief. He'd take annoyance over fear.

He scrunched up two little bits of tissue and put one in each nostril so he wouldn't bleed all over his sheets, and then lay down in bed. Could he trust her enough to go to sleep next to her? He stole another glance at her. She still looked like a pathetic baby, nothing like the way she'd looked before. She was staring at the carpet, her face distressed. She looked like his normal sister, not like someone who could do anything bad, let alone hurt someone.

But his face still throbbed as he lay down on the sheets, facing the wall. He pretended to go to sleep, the blood thumping in his cheek, rushing to his eye until it was swollen shut. He heard the buzz of Liv's phone, but he didn't turn around to ask her who she was texting. Then he heard her quietly get up, make her bed, and leave the room.

EIGHTEEN

A ustin opened his front door and beckoned Liv inside.

"You weren't sleeping, were you?"

"Shh."

She followed Austin up the stairs, past his parents' room and past Maria's. He pushed open the door at the end of the hallway. She'd seen inside this room once before when she was there babysitting and thought it was a spare room. A plain double bed pushed against the wall, a bookshelf, a desk. But now his stuff was on the desk, the lamp was on, the crumpled Berkeley hoodie was on the floor.

He sat her down on the bed.

"I'm sorry," she whispered. "I just remembered that you said you don't sleep and I didn't want to be by myself."

He put both hands around hers. "You're shaking."

She rubbed her hands up and down her bare arms. She hadn't noticed.

"Get into bed, you're covered in goose bumps."

She slipped between his covers. They smelled like him.

"I just don't know what's wrong with me. I hurt him. I hurt Casper. What if I hurt someone else?"

He pulled the blanket up to her chin. It was so warm under there. There was a book open on the other pillow. Austin picked it up. He must have been reading in bed; the covers were warm from his body heat.

"You think I'm insane," she said.

"Nope. I think it's kind of interesting, actually."

He rubbed her arm through the covers.

"So why did you hit him?"

"I don't know. I think I was having a nightmare. He touched me, I think, and I just turned around and hit him."

Remembering was like trying to catch smoke. The more she grasped for it, the more it faded away. Not that she wanted to remember. She didn't want to think about Casper or what he'd said. That was why she'd texted Austin.

"You know, I've been reading about sleepwalking."

"Really?" That was what she should have done. She should have gone to see a doctor or something today. Taken it seriously. But she didn't want to have to deal with it.

"Yeah. You know, it's not uncommon to hurt people in your sleep. People lash out when someone tries to wake them, that's really normal."

"Really? Or are you just trying to make me feel better?"

"People have done way worse things than that. There was this guy in Canada. He drove in his sleep to his in-laws' house and attacked them with a knife. Killed his mother-in-law. And then woke up on the freeway on his way home and went to the cops."

"That sounds like bullshit."

"He got off. Apparently it's actually possible to do all that when you sleep. There was another guy who killed his wife because he was dreaming someone was attacking her and he thought that he was defending her. How tragic is that?"

He was looking at her with bright eyes, but what he was saying was making her stomach twist.

"I don't think I want to talk about this," she said.

He blinked, then nodded. "Oh, sorry. You're right. I was coming at it from a . . . I don't know, a case study perspective."

She didn't want to be a case study. That wasn't how she wanted to be seen right now. She shifted over onto the pillow on the other side, next to the wall, to make space for him. He swallowed; Liv watched the dip of his Adam's apple.

For a moment she was sure he was going to sit on the desk chair. But instead he put the book down on the carpet, pushed the blanket aside, and climbed into the bed. Her skin hummed.

"You know," he whispered, "every time I've heard a noise downstairs, I've thought it might be you."

"Really?"

His breath was hot on her cheek. She wanted to close her eyes, just relish his warm body next to hers. She wanted to shift closer to him.

"Yep, I even went down to check."

"You must have been relieved."

He looked back up at the ceiling. "Yeah."

She could stare at the ceiling too and just let the moment pass. But that wasn't why she'd come here. She took his hand in hers. She expected him to pull away, turn to her, ask what she was doing. Or look at her pitifully, like she was a patient, a psych patient. But when he did turn to look at her, his eyes were darker, almost black.

"Austin."

"Yeah?"

"I really want to kiss you."

"You do?"

"Yeah."

He smiled at her. She closed her eyes and kissed him, just once. He rolled back onto his side, his arm circling her waist and pulling her closer so her chest was pressed against his. She looked at him, his face so close to hers. Then she kissed him again, and this time, he kissed her back.

His mouth pressed hot and wet against hers. Her hands in his hair. His glasses bumped against her cheek and, finally, her thoughts were gone completely. It was just the rhythm of his mouth, the touch of his tongue, his fingers trailing up and down her thigh. It was fire in her stomach and thrumming skin.

Her nightdress scrunched up around her waist as his hands slipped up her back. She kept kissing him, gripping his legs with her thighs, feeling the bare skin under his T-shirt. The slight softness of his stomach, the hair on his chest. He tugged his T-shirt off over his head, threw his glasses on the floor, and pulled her up on top of him. His hands slid from her thighs up onto her waist. She stared down at him. His face was so bare without his glasses. She leaned down to kiss him again, softer now. He touched the cotton of her undies, slipped one finger under the elastic on the side, and looked at her. She got off him, pulled her underwear off and tossed them on the floor, then straddled him again. She couldn't take the nightdress off or he'd see her bruise, but he didn't try. His hands went straight back to her bare hips. She could feel his hardness pushing against her through his cotton boxers.

"You're so hot," he said, "I don't know how long I'm going to last."

She put a hand over his eyes. "Then don't look."

AFTERWARD, SHE RAN her hand up his chest, trying to catch her breath. The patch of hair was rough under her fingertips. She traced the hair down to his belly button, where it turned soft.

"You're beautiful, you know?" she said.

"I'm supposed to say that to you."

She sank down to lie next to him, and he wrapped an arm around her.

"I'm so into you," he said.

She held up his hand, played with his fingers in the golden light of the lamp. "When did you decide that?"

"It's not something you decide."

"Well, when did you know?"

"Straightaway," he said, not even hesitating. "You were . . . I don't know . . . this vision in my kitchen. This hilarious, ridiculous super-hot girl who was so nice to my sister. Plus, I like it when you blush. It's sexy."

She laughed. "I hate it."

"And those first times we met, you literally were either blushing or being incredibly rude. It was confusing, but also . . . I don't know. You got in my head really fast. And then I was lying in bed, trying to read . . . I'd given up on sleep, and I kept thinking of you and how weird you were, and I couldn't help but smile. Which was good for me—I hadn't been doing a lot of smiling for a while. Then I heard this noise. I went downstairs, and there you were, and for a second it literally felt like I'd conjured you up . . . like I actually had fallen asleep and was having the best dream. I came downstairs and you were just standing there in this kind of skimpy, very slightly see-through dress like from some steamy Renaissance painting or something."

She grinned. She couldn't help it. She rested her hand on the bare skin of his chest. His heart beat against her cheek.

"I mean," he said quickly, "this time, tonight, I wasn't trying to get you into my bed to hook up with you or anything. I would have taken you out again, but you seemed so . . . freaked out. I just wanted to look after you."

She looked at him. His dark eyes and black brows and that perfect little freckle. She leaned in and rested her lips on it, just for a second. She could feel his heart rate quicken.

"Don't let me sleep," she said.

NINETEEN

C asper heard Liv sneak back in around six a.m., but he was too groggy to confront her. He had no idea where she'd been.

Now it was mid-morning and he lay on his back with a melting packet of peas on his face. He should have put it on last night when it had started swelling up. Now he had a black eye. Liv had brought the pack up for him from downstairs. Neither of them wanted to explain his face to their parents. Liv for obvious reasons, and him because he couldn't bear to make things even more strained.

She had her headphones on and was typing away on her computer, sneaking looks at him when she thought he wouldn't notice. She'd asked him a million times if he was okay until he'd told her he didn't want to talk to her anymore. The only things he did want to ask her, like where she'd gone last night, were things he knew she wouldn't answer.

His phone buzzed. He slid the peas off his face; they were melting in the hot room. He touched the skin under his eye. It was tender. He had to think up a good excuse. There was no way he was going to tell the guys at work that his sister had done this.

He opened the text; it was from Tye: *I think I might know where Leilani lives.*

Casper sat up. *How'd you find her?*

Good detective work. Should we go there?

Now it was his turn to sneak a look at Liv. She clearly wasn't going to do anything about whatever was going on, and clearly his parents weren't either. He would have to be the one to try and help her, and he couldn't do that if he only knew half the story.

Definitely, he typed back.

He got out of bed and went to have a shower. He didn't want to smell like old peas.

CASPER OPENED THE gate to Bellevue Park. He kept his head down and his sunglasses on so no one would notice the bruise. He'd already bumped into Brian and Rani and had to make up a quick story about a lacrosse injury—what a joke. He'd rather die than play such a dumbass sport.

Tye was waiting for him in a patch of shade under a tree. He pulled his headphones out as Casper sat down on the grass next to him.

"So how'd you figure out where she lives?"

"I told you, detective work."

"No, really."

Tye brought up Leilani's Instagram account again. He showed him one of the photos of Leilani posing in the mirror; then he zoomed in on the background. Out of the window behind her you could see the corner of a colorful mural.

"I know where that is. It's a coffee shop. I used to go there every weekend, it's really close to my place."

Casper beamed at him. "So you'll come with me, we'll just go knock on her door?"

Tye nodded. "Of course. You know, I used to think you were the detective and I was the assistant. But it's the other way around, isn't it?"

"What?"

"I'm the Denzel and you're the Angelina."

They'd watched *The Bone Collector* at Tye's house last night, before he'd gone home and been punched by Liv. In the movie, Denzel Washington played the detective and Angelina Jolie was the rookie cop who had to do everything he said and eventually fell in love with him for reasons that made absolutely no sense to Casper.

"Denzel was such a dick in that movie."

"Tough love, my friend. That's what people fall for."

Casper scoffed. Tye took out his notebook and added the information they'd found to the chart. Casper lay back on the grass. It was warm through his T-shirt. The sky was blue and endless, the morning sun mild. Maybe they really could figure this thing out.

"What's that?" Tye asked.

Casper looked up at him. Tye's face had gone rigid.

"What?" Casper asked, but he knew. Tye reached over and pulled off Casper's sunglasses, exposing his black eye.

"Who did that?"

"Liv was . . . She did it in her sleep, I think."

Tye touched the bruise under Casper's eye gently, with the tip of his finger. His touch made blood rush to Casper's cheeks. Tye seemed to catch himself and he shifted back.

"Sorry," he said. "Sorry, man. I just . . . That looks painful."

"It's not. It just looks worse than it is because I'm so pasty."

"I guess."

"So . . . what will we say if she's home? Don't we need a cover story?"

Tye didn't respond. His eyes were still on the bruise. Casper put his sunglasses back on.

"Seriously," he said. "Don't worry about it. I'm all right. It barely hurts."

Tye nodded. "Yeah, it just shocked me. Do you think Olivia could really be capable of . . ."

"What?"

He looked at Casper for a moment, then seemed to think better of whatever he was going to say. "Yeah, let's just go. We'll figure out a plan on the way."

THEY WALKED DOWN the hill toward Sunset Boulevard. Tye had been weirdly quiet since they'd left the park. Casper kept noticing him looking at him out of the corner of his eye. But when Casper turned to him, he'd turn away.

"So why'd you stop coming to this café?" Casper asked him.

"Huh?"

"You said you used to go here all the time."

"Oh." Tye scratched the back of his neck, looking self-conscious. "I don't know. I got sick of it, I guess."

"Okay," Casper said.

He expected Tye to say more, but he didn't, so they walked in silence. He wanted Tye to chat about movies and dumb thriller tropes to distract him. What would they do if Leilani wasn't home? What if something had happened to her, and his sister was responsible? It was better to know, he was sure of that, but that didn't mean he wasn't nervous.

They turned the corner and saw the bright pink mural. It was next to the window of the café, where you could order takeaways.

"Are you going to get a macchiato while we're here?" he asked Tye.

"I'm okay. I don't think I could deal with caffeine right now."

"That's a first!"

"Yeah, I feel a bit . . . I dunno."

"Me too," Casper said. His stomach was twisting.

They stood in front of the mural. Tye took out his phone and they both studied the image. You could see the corner of pink in the bottom left of the window frame. They looked at the building across from them. It was an old-fashioned brick apartment block, with high picture frame windows. The entrance was on the intersecting street.

"It must be the last one," Casper said, looking at the photo again. "I think you'd see a bit more of the mural if it were one of the others."

There seemed to be two windows per apartment, and there were eight in total.

"So Leilani's is apartment number four, do you think?"

The curtains of the last two windows were closed.

"Yeah," Tye said. He looked at Casper, like he was weighing up saying something. Then he nodded. "Let's do this."

They headed around toward the front of the building. It had an art deco facade with an arched entranceway with crisscrossing red and white bricks.

"What should we say?" Casper asked. "We really need to figure out a cover story."

"We could pretend that we're . . . I don't know. I don't know if she'll believe that two teenagers are anything official."

"I guess maybe we just have to tell the truth."

Tye nodded.

There were no names next to the buzzers, so Casper pressed on apartment four. They waited. Nothing. Silence.

"She must not be home," Tye said.

A weight fell on Casper's shoulders. No. She had to be home. He'd thought they'd find something out. Anything. He couldn't just go home from here, back to the constant tension and unanswered questions. He buzzed again.

Silence.

Maybe they had the apartment wrong. Maybe she didn't even live here. There could be pink walls all over this city.

"Excuse me." A stylish middle-aged woman with a bunch of flowers and a shopping bag came through behind them.

"Sorry," they both said at the same time and stepped out of the way.

"You boys okay?" she asked.

"Yeah," Tye said. "We're just trying to wake up my sister. She's late to our grandma's birthday and she's not answering her phone."

"Who's your sister?"

"Leilani."

The woman's pink-lipsticked mouth turned into a smile; she rearranged her bags and reached out a hand to shake Tye's. "Oh, how wonderful. Nice to meet you. Leilani's a lovely girl. I never knew she had family in Los Angeles, I thought they were all back in Kailua."

"We are," Tye said. "We're just down for the week for Grandma's birthday."

"Wonderful," she said, pushing the door open for them. They strode inside. The woman kept walking behind them.

Casper looked at Tye. That was incredible. He hadn't even missed a beat.

"I haven't heard much from Leilani these last few days," the woman said from behind them. "Has she been unwell?"

"Just a cold," Tye said.

They reached Leilani's door and the woman started unlocking the one next to it.

"Well, give her my love. And happy birthday to your grandma! How old is she?"

"Ninety-seven," Tye said.

The woman's eyebrows shot up. "Wow! How amazing."

Then she went through her own door and shut it behind her.

Tye looked at Casper. "I don't even know where that came from."

"Well, it was incredible."

They beamed at each other for a second; then Casper's smile fell away. He reached up to the door and knocked.

Inside, he could hear movement.

TWENTY

Janus stopped dead. He was back in her place and he was sure he'd just heard a sound. He stood completely still, listening. No. There was nothing. He was paranoid, completely paranoid. He just had to get this job done.

He opened the door of her wardrobe. It was a small wood-laminate thing that wouldn't hold much, but thank goodness, what he was looking for was right there on the top. A suitcase.

He took it down and opened it up on the bed. He threw in the crisp clothes he'd taken from her washing line and the novel from the table; then he pulled out her top drawer, emptied everything inside, and took her winter coat from the cupboard and packed that too. What else? He went into the bathroom and took her toothbrush. Then he cleared the bottle of perfume and face creams from the sink and squeezed them in as well. The suitcase was full, and there were now some clear empty spaces in her wardrobe, drawers, and bathroom. That was all he needed.

He zipped up the suitcase and took a final look around. It had to look neat, nice, like she'd known she wasn't coming back for a while.

He went back out the sliding door and around the side. He told himself not to look around, not to search the bushes for figures. As he got back onto the street, he glanced back and forth. No one was nearby. He'd done it. He scampered back onto the road, her suitcase in his hand, relieved he'd never have to set foot in her home again.

He went to two thrift stores. At the first, he emptied the suitcase into the donation bin out front. At the second, he dropped off the suitcase itself.

BACK HOME THERE was only last night's mess in the kitchen, no dinner in the oven and no placating note on the counter. After their argument, Kay had stopped pretending.

So he went outside for a cigarette instead, and after a while Brian came out too and brought them both a beer. He should be grateful to the man. The last thing he wanted was to be alone. But still, listening to Brian talk about *football* as the light drained from the day was barely preferable. The ugly plastic outdoor furniture, the patch of dying avocado plants, Ginger's incessant scratching at the back door: He couldn't think of anywhere he would less like to be.

He took a slug of his beer. The conversation with Kay was still running circles through his mind. She was so angry with him, her words sharp daggers. It was like she actually hated him. She had looked at him with an expression he knew well. It was one she wore when someone pulled out in front of her on the freeway. Or that time she saw someone hitting their dog at the park. Or, worst of all, it was the expression she wore when she spoke to her mother. He had no idea where she was right now. Los Angeles was a huge city and she could be literally anywhere. Things had deteriorated so badly. How had it taken him so long to notice?

"They don't wear helmets in Aussie League, right? Janus?" Brian was looking at him.

"I don't really follow American football. Or Australian," Janus replied.

"You don't watch it with your son?"

"No, not really."

"I used to take Austin to Inglewood to see the Rams every season. That bonding time is important for them, don't you think? Teaches them about being a man."

Janus leaned back in his chair; now he was actually focusing on Brian. Was that a dig? He wasn't sure.

"I'm afraid Casper finds ball sports as moronic as I do."

"Really?" Brian asked. "Then how'd he get that shiner?"

"What do you mean?"

"I thought he got it on the field?"

Janus just looked at him.

"Haven't you seen your son today?" Brian's brow furrowed. "He's got a black eye."

"What?" Janus pulled his phone out of his jeans pocket and brought up Casper's number.

He hit call and held it to his ear. It rang out. How had his son gotten a black eye? He hadn't had it yesterday.

"How's Olivia getting on?" Brian asked, changing the subject.

"Fine," Janus said—too fast, he knew. What if it was here? What if Olivia had hurt Casper?

Brian held his eye for a beat too long. "That's good."

Janus watched Brian as he looked down into his beer bottle and swished the liquid around, and then: "We probably won't need a baby-sitter anymore."

That wasn't what he'd expected. Something had happened, he could tell. "Why?" he asked.

"We just don't need the help." Brian was still not meeting his eye.

"Did she do something?" And then, a horrible thought. An unbearable one. "She didn't hurt Maria, did she?"

Brian looked back at him then. "Hurt her? No, of course not. We just don't need the help right now. What, you think your daughter would hurt a child?"

"No, of course not," Janus said. And it was true. He knew she wouldn't. Of course she wouldn't. There was no way.

"Well, I should get going. I'm meeting Rani and the kids for dinner on Sunset," Brian said. "Where's Kay?"

"Work," Janus said.

Brian nodded, not saying anything, but Janus knew what he was thinking.

"Okay. Well, I'll see you later, man."

Janus could barely look at him. Brian was off for a nice family dinner, and Janus didn't even know where his wife was. Brian was strong, a real man. While Janus was pathetic. Janus had left his wife to clean up the mess that he couldn't cope with. He was a deadweight dragging his whole family down. His wife couldn't even stand the sight of him. Something had happened to his son and he hadn't even noticed.

He got up and went back into the house. He needed to stop being this aimless excuse for a man. He needed to do something, anything, constructive. He thought of his character again, of Angela. What would she do? She wouldn't mope around; she'd do something active, something reckless probably.

He went into their bedroom and opened his laptop, bringing up the screenplay. Skimming through it, he saw that the Angela of his script wasn't being active or reckless; in fact, she *was* doing a lot of moping around. He'd thought it was adding depth, adding literary integrity. But Maggie was right; this was meant to be a horror story. He deleted the first scene: Angela standing on a train, sure she'd seen a monster, which turned out to be her own reflection. Instead he started with the most violent, blood-soaked image he could conjure. The flashbacks began, rolling over him, cramping his stomach, making him sweat, but he kept typing.

TWENTY-ONE

Casper went to knock again on the apartment door, but it opened before his fist made contact. Standing in the doorway was a woman wrapped in a thin dressing gown, her hair in a bun on her head and a clumpy gray facemask on.

"What?!" she said.

"Leilani?" he asked. He couldn't make out her features clearly underneath the goop.

"Yeah. What do you want? Were you buzzing me as well? I was trying to meditate."

"Oh," he said. "Sorry. I'm . . . I'm Olivia Jansen's brother. This is Tye. We wanted to talk to you. About Liv."

She looked between the two of them and then groaned. "Did Liv send you? She's getting her teenage brother to talk to her friends for her?"

"No, not at all. I'm just . . . I'm worried about her and—"

She held up a hand. "All right, all right, it's fine. Five minutes."

Leilani turned back into her apartment. Casper glanced at Tye, who looked as surprised as he was. They went into the apartment and closed the door behind them.

Inside, he recognized corners of the place from her Instagram. The big windows with their gauzy white curtains, except instead of being swept open with the sunshine flooding in, they were closed tightly. Instead of stacks of books on the coffee table, there were dirty plates and half-eaten take-out containers, and the pink velvet lounge was covered in a crumpled blanket, dotted with oily stains. It smelled weird, like stale sweat and dirty clothes mixed with a weird floral smell cloying the air. Casper noticed an expensive-looking scented candle was burning next to one of the boxes of cold noodles.

"I'll just be a moment!" Leilani called from the bathroom.

Casper and Tye moved over one of the blankets and sat next to each other on the couch.

"She seems fine," Tye whispered.

"Yeah, totally fine," Casper added.

"So what's up?" Leilani said, coming back from the bathroom. She'd washed off the mask, revealing an angry-looking pimple on her chin.

"Sorry for bothering you," Tye said to her. "We didn't mean to intrude."

"It's okay. The meditation wasn't working anyway." She sat down cross-legged on the yoga mat that was unrolled on the floor. "So what do you want?"

Tye looked at Casper. He didn't even know where to begin. It all felt kind of stupid now.

"I just . . . Liv has been acting weird since you guys went out last weekend. I just wanted . . . I guess I wondered if you could tell me what happened?"

"At the gala?"

"Yeah."

Leilani leaned over her foot, picking at the cracked blue polish on her big toenail. "It turned out to be such a shitty night. Your sister was a mess."

"She was drunk?"

"I don't know. We went there to network, you know? I was trying to cozy up to Alejandro Promadore, have you heard of him?"

They both shook their heads.

"He's a designer. Only twenty-seven, but he's insanely talented. With my help he could really bloom, you know?"

They nodded.

"Anyway, we were on a two-drink maximum. We had fun at first. It could have been a really good night. Liv said she only had two, but she was cooked. She was stumbling and slurring her words. I was worried her drink got spiked actually, so I took her back here to sleep it off. I was actually kind of out of it too. Maybe both our drinks got spiked? I don't know. I didn't even get a chance to talk to Alejandro."

Casper's phone started buzzing in his pocket. His dad was calling for some reason; he silenced it. "So then what happened?"

Leilani rolled her eyes. She grabbed a bag of weed off the table and started stuffing it into a grinder.

"I put her to bed, here on the couch. She was out like a light for like . . . maybe half an hour? Then she got up. She was acting like a complete lunatic." She looked up at Casper. "Sorry."

"It's fine, keep going."

"She was talking, but like, her words made no sense. They were all garbled like she was speaking in tongues or something. She just left without saying goodbye, and I followed her out because she almost left all her bags of clothes here. I even put them in her trunk for her, but she didn't say thanks. I was trying to help her, but to be honest, she was freaking me out. I felt really tired too. I could barely keep my eyes open. So she left and I went back to sleep. Truthfully, I think I just pushed myself too hard, you know? The Designer Showcase is nuts every year, almost as bad as Fashion Week. I've been doing self-care since then. Rethinking my direction." She tamped down the weed into a sleek black vaporizer.

"Yeah, absolutely. That makes sense," Tye said.

Leilani put the vape in her mouth and sucked on it.

"Have you heard from Liv since then?"

She nodded, holding the smoke in her lungs, then exhaled. "She texted and stuff. She mentioned that apprenticeship. I don't know. It was fun to hang out during the showcase, but she kind of scared me that night. Plus, I don't want to be just a rung on a ladder for someone, you know? It's a hard industry. I managed to work my way up on my own. She's not getting a free pass from me."

TYE AND CASPER started laughing when they were halfway down the street.

"I genuinely thought your sister had murdered her!" Tye said.

"Me too! I was so sure we'd find something horrible."

"I don't know, that smell was pretty bad."

Casper grinned at him. "Thank you. For coming with me. For being my Denzel."

Tye looked at the ground, "Stop it. You're going to embarrass me."

"So does this mean that the Boys Detective Club is over?"

"I don't know. There's still the bleach and hair clip."

Plus the weird tools in the hidden Home Depot bag, although he never had told Tye about that.

"My parents are acting strangely as well," he said instead.

"Yeah." Tye looked thoughtful. "But maybe it really was just Liv being drunk and . . . I don't know . . . puking everywhere? That would explain the bleach."

"Maybe. And maybe my parents are acting weirdly for another reason that has nothing to do with all this? Maybe they've got boring adult things going on."

"I keep telling you . . . meth."

"It's not meth!"

The sun was low in the sky, setting everything with a warm golden glow. They approached the intersection where they usually said good-bye, but Casper didn't want Tye to go. He hadn't felt this good in so long. Maybe it was just the relief, but for once things felt right.

"So, listen, I wanted to say . . . if you still want me to be in your film, I will be."

The golden light was falling across Tye's face. "Do you actually want to? Or is it just because I helped you with this stuff?"

"I want to," he said. And he did. He wanted to do something fun and silly and lighthearted. Things had been way too serious lately.

Tye beamed. "Okay, great! This is going to be awesome, Casper. I'll email you the script as soon as I get home!"

Casper wanted to tell Tye he'd come home with him, but he didn't know how to say it. So he just smiled and said, "Cool. See you later."

Tye grinned and took off down the intersecting street to his place. Casper kept walking down Maltman Avenue. He pulled out his phone and texted Hélène:

Sorry for all the dramatic messages. Do you need help with anything? Groceries?

He could swing by on his way back if she needed him. He wouldn't mind a glass of that Chambord.

She replied straightaway: *Thank you for checking on me, I'm okay. And don't stop the dramatic messages, you're more interesting than Love Island. Are you okay?*

That made him smile. The idea of Hélène watching *Love Island* was bizarre.

Yes, I think so. Today was a good day.

What happened?

I've been hanging out with someone. I dunno.

No, he was being stupid. He wasn't going to risk losing the only real friend he had.

How do you know if it's worth taking the risk with someone? Even if it might blow up everything good? he typed.

It's impossible to know. But if you really want it you won't be able to help it.

He thought about that. How funny to be getting boy advice from an old woman, but she'd probably known more passion in her life than he could imagine. She was French, after all. *How's your hip?* he wrote.

I'm hoping to improve enough to be airplane ready!

She talked about going home all the time. She'd told Casper about how they had a custom in her part of France of laying purple carnations on the graves of those who were missed, and how sad it made her not to be able to do that for her sister. She had been Hélène's last living relative, and she hadn't had the chance to see her in the decade before her death. Hélène spoke about going back to Brittany often, but Casper didn't think she'd ever actually go. Her house was filled with photographs of family who were now long dead.

Are you free to do some work for me on Sunday morning? she asked.

He wanted to see Hélène—maybe she'd be able to give him some advice—but he always worked Sunday mornings at Sabrosa, which she usually remembered. He was starting to type this as he stepped onto the road to cross over, when brakes squealed right in front of him. He looked up from his phone. Brian's car had stopped just a meter from him. Brian stuck his head out of the window.

"Jesus, Casper, you came out of nowhere!"

His heart pounded against his ribs.

"Are you all right?"

"Sorry," Casper said. "I'm fine. Sorry."

"Just be careful, okay? Look where you're walking."

"Yeah," he said, feeling stupid. "You're right."

He headed over to his house and let himself in. Then he went straight up to his room and flopped down on his bed.

His dad came and stood in the doorway.

"Casper, I tried to call you."

"Yeah. Sorry, busy day."

His father came closer and sat on the end of the bed. "What happened to your face?"

"I don't know," he said. "Lacrosse."

"Lacrosse? With those rackets on the big sticks?" They didn't have it back in Australia.

"Yeah," Casper said. "I wanted to see what the fuss was about."

His father looked at him intently, then he squeezed his foot. "If anyone hurts you, Casper, ever, you have to know you could talk to me about it."

"I know."

"I'd do anything for you, okay? I'd fight for you, I'd die for you. I'd do anything to keep you safe, and there's absolutely nothing you can't tell me."

"That's a bit dramatic."

His father smiled, but he looked sad. "That's what being a dad is all about. It's a dramatic business."

He patted Casper's foot and left the room, but Casper stayed where he was. He felt exhausted from the day. His detective work with Tye; the fear that they'd find something bad at Leilani's place; then, to top it all off, a near-death experience. If he'd stepped out just a second later, Brian's car would have hit him. Metal crushing against his flesh, a huge impossible weight thumping into him.

Something niggled at him. Tye had asked if anything was missing when he got back that weekend and he'd said no. But maybe that wasn't true. His parents hadn't come to pick him up that day, they'd texted him to get a lift with his teammate Jasper, who lived three blocks over. It had annoyed him because he'd had such a shit time already and then he'd had to endure fifteen minutes of Jasper's trite EDM. He also had a vague memory of his mum getting an Uber to work.

Not just that, but something Leilani had said. That Liv had driven home, even though she was totally out of it.

He got out of bed and made his way down into the garage. The car was there. He walked around it. Everything was totally intact; there was no damage at all. He pulled his phone out of his pocket and turned the torch on, then shone it across the car, having no idea what he was actually looking for. But there was nothing to see. The car looked normal, but as he was turning off the torch, it lit something up where the garage wall met the floor. Something glittery. He went over to it and picked it up. It was a piece of glass. A small, shattered part of a headlight.

TWENTY-TWO

Liv hit send. That was it. The application for the apprenticeship was done. The designs were compressed into PDFs, the essay was a document of one thousand heartfelt and passionate words, and it was all attached to an email and sent off into oblivion. She lay back onto the bed, exhausted.

She looked over at Casper, wanting someone to congratulate her. But he didn't look up. He had his earbuds in, and he was looking at a little piece of glass. The bruise under his eye had turned purple now, and looking at it made Liv want to throw up and apologize and cry. But instead she reached over with her foot and tapped his mattress.

"Hey," she said.

He pulled out an earbud.

"Hungry?" she asked.

"Are you going to cook?"

She snorted and held up her phone. "Yeah, I'll cook with this."

"Breakfast burrito?" he said. "The ones at Sabrosa are good."

"Don't you have one of those after every shift?"

"Yeah, that's how I know they're good. But they don't do Uber Eats."

She pushed herself up onto her feet. "Okay, fine. But only because I feel so bad for punching you in the face."

"Are we joking about that already?"

She flashed him a hopeful smile. "Yeah?"

"Okay, if it gets me a burrito." He looked back down at the glass. "What is that?"

He held it up to the light. "I don't know. I think it's part of a head-light."

She feigned interest. "Cool. All right, I'll be back soon."

As she passed her parents' door, she stuck her head in; her dad was sitting on the bed, typing away frantically at his laptop.

"Mexican?"

He startled, then looked up. "Sorry?"

"Dinner?"

"Where's your mother?"

"I don't know. Work, I guess."

"All right," he said, turning back to the screen.

God, her dad thought he was this progressive creative, but if his wife wasn't around to look after him, he turned into a petulant little boy. She hadn't noticed it when she used to live with them, but since she'd moved out and been independent, it had become so obvious. If this was what marriage was, she wouldn't ever get married. She didn't want to be tied to some man-child who needed her in order to func-tion.

She headed down the stairs and out the front door. It was possible the reason she was feeling a bit misandrist was because Austin hadn't been in touch at all today. She'd texted him hours ago with no re-sponse. Maybe to him sex wasn't a big deal. Maybe she should try and be more like that. As she let herself out the front door, she decided he was a fuckboy and she wasn't going to bother thinking about him.

Los Angeles had this glow about it. It was like a migraine aura, shimmering, beautiful, and dangerous. Not just at night, when everything sparkled limitless, but in the dusk as well. The sun low and full, sharp glare reflecting from the windows and flashing from the hoods of parked cars. Back in Melbourne, daylight had felt safe. Nighttime had felt safe! She'd walk the streets at any time without ever looking over her shoulder.

It was different here. The quiet felt hushed, the stillness like a held breath. There was always an edge to this place, even on a sunny evening.

What if you hurt someone? That was what Casper had asked her last night. Could she really say in all honesty that she knew that she hadn't? Knew for sure?

She was unconscious when she was doing these things. She really had no idea what she was capable of. She'd proved that she was out of control last night when she'd hit Casper.

Maybe it would help if she could remember the dreams, but they were all so blurry. She remembered the fear. But fear of what, she didn't know. Last night she'd had this horrible strangled feeling, like there was something around her neck and she couldn't breathe. She'd felt Casper's presence, but thought he was someone bad. Someone who wanted to hurt her.

She swallowed. Those injuries she had, they could have been from a fight. She could have attacked someone, like she had Casper, and they'd fought back.

No, she'd gotten drunk and fallen down the stairs. That was the only plausible explanation. Her parents would have told her if it was something worse than that. Plus, whoever she'd hurt would have confronted her by now. No. What she'd done to Casper was unconnected. A one-off accident that she'd make sure would never happen again.

She went into Sabrosa and ordered a feast on her credit card. She had another $500 until she maxed it out, and she was more than willing to spend it on her little brother. But she had to be careful; she was exhausted, and if she ate a big meal and then just sat around at home, there was no way she wouldn't fall asleep. She wanted to go out and forget about these nagging questions for a while. She'd finished her application; she should be celebrating. She hadn't been out since the fashion gala, which clearly hadn't gone well, but she'd be careful this time. She could go out without being reckless. She could control herself. Although now that Leilani had ghosted her, she didn't have anyone to go out with. She shot out a text to Austin.

What are you up to later?

Then she cringed and sent another one. *For wine, not sex.*

Oh God, that was worse! She stuffed her phone in her pocket before she could send a third and sat up on one of the barstools by the window and spun around, feeling like a complete fool.

Then she heard a laugh. Her mother's laugh. It was coming from the back courtyard. She jumped down off the stool and looked around. There she was. Her mother. She was sitting in the courtyard alone with a glass of wine in front of her, looking up at Carlos, who was leaning on the table and saying something to her which, apparently, her mother found really funny. Liv ducked away. Was her mother having an affair? Was that what all the weirdness at home was about? No wonder her dad was looking sad! How could she?

Her phone buzzed in her pocket and she yanked it out. But the text wasn't from Austin; it was from Brian: *Thank you for all your help with Maria, but we aren't going to need a babysitter anymore.*

THE UBER DROPPED her off at Sunset Junction. By the time she and Casper had finished a burrito each and shared a quesadilla, Austin had finally texted her back. She might have ignored him for a while out of revenge, but he'd invited her out and she was too desperate to leave the house to bother with games. She'd put some tamales on the bed next to her dad, and he'd barely looked up at her. Sneaking a look at his screen, she saw him describing some kind of lake monster slashing someone's neck with its long, algae-encrusted talons. She hesitated, unsure whether to interrupt and tell him about seeing her mother, but she didn't even know how to broach it. It was so obvious now. It hadn't been about her and the gala at all. They were having issues in their marriage. That was why her father had been weird and her mother had been distracted and cold. Misplaced anger. All this time she'd thought it was her bad behavior, her being a disappointment, her letting them down. But maybe it wasn't. There were probably things going on in this house she had no idea about.

Austin had asked her to come meet up with him and some friends on Sunset. She needed to ask him why his parents had fired her. She was fairly sure she already knew the reason: He must have told them about her late-night visits.

The glary afternoon had faded into a warm, still night. Sunset Boulevard was packed with people getting dinner and sitting outside cafés and bars. She skirted past a woman drinking a martini who hadn't noticed that her two Pomeranians were making trip lines across the sidewalk with their leashes. She looked at her map again to see where Bar Stella was, and realized she'd walked past the place a bunch of times before. It was right on the junction, with a dark pinky-red-colored wall creeping with green vines. Over the wall, she could hear the rumble of voices and music. It sounded like the place was packed.

At the door she made herself a promise. No getting messy. For real this time. She would have one drink only. She had to prove to herself that she could still go out without it ending in some big drama. Anyway, she was here on a mission: to find out what was going on with Austin's parents. And if that mission ended in sex, so be it.

She walked through the busy courtyard. It had a black-and-white-checkered floor, red cushioned seats, and lanterns hanging from small trees that cast speckled light.

The inside was huge, with marble walls and a giant painting of a toucan above the bar. Much swankier than the dingy venues with sticky floors she'd gone to back in Melbourne. She scanned the faces of the people sitting up at the bar. No Austin. She checked the groups sitting on the black leather sofas. No Austin. Could he have gone somewhere else and forgotten to tell her? Maybe he *was* a fuckboy.

In the corner she recognized a guy with dark hair leaning back on a velvet sofa drinking a margarita and talking emphatically to his date. For a moment she thought she knew him, but then she placed him. He was an actor. He was the best friend of the love interest in that movie about the woman who moves to New York to become a journalist but then is killed and becomes a ghost and solves her own murder. What was it called? She'd watched it on TV with her mum a few months ago—she'd have to tell her. Then she remembered the way her mum had looked at her when she'd bought her that coffee. All at once, the place was too loud and too obnoxious and she absolutely didn't want to be here.

She headed for the exit. But as she passed through the courtyard, she saw Austin. He was in a dimly lit corner at the back, the winks of light from the lanterns the only thing illuminating him. He was with two other people, and he was laughing, his head tipped back.

"Hey," she said, approaching.

He jumped up and grabbed her in a hug. "I can't believe you came!"

"You asked me to."

He let her go, turned. "Guys! This is my new Aussie neighbor."

"Hi."

"Hey."

His two friends smiled up at her.

He pulled her onto the bench seat next to him.

"I'm Jun," the guy said. He had short-cropped hair bleached white blond, and a glinting silver chain around his neck. He smiled and motioned to the girl next to him. "This is Sunny."

Liv smiled like she didn't know her, when really she'd already checked out Sunny's Instagram. She'd commented on a lot of Austin's posts, and Liv had wondered if she was a girlfriend. Her profile was all innuendo and meta-ironic Catholicism: A mesh top featuring the crucifixion stretched tight over her breasts. A photo of her wearing a Virgin Mary–style veil, dribbling milk out of her mouth. In her bio she'd written *Sinless Angel* over a link to her OnlyFans. Liv had clicked on it, curious, but it seemed more like performance art than smut. There was no nudity, just images of her licking various household items—a curling iron, a Perrier bottle—with a mocking glint in her eyes. In person, she seemed quite down-to-earth.

"Olivia, right?" she asked.

"Yeah. Nice to meet you."

"I love the Australian accent," Austin said. "It just sounds so relaxed, you know?"

"What do you think of Californian accents?" Jun asked.

"Yeah, do we sound superficial to you?"

"No," Liv said, embarrassed by her voice now, "not at all."

"I worry about it when I travel," Sunny went on. "Like, even in New York I feel like I sound like some airhead."

"I like it," Liv said. "There's something really warm about it."

"Do you want a drink?" Austin asked. "You can share my glass."

He pulled the bottle of wine from the ice bucket on the table. He emptied it over his glass, but only a dribble came out.

"Oh." He looked genuinely disappointed.

"Should we get another?" Jun asked, standing.

"Yeah," Austin said; then his face lit up and he put his hand in his pocket and pulled out a fifty.

"Thanks, Daddy." He giggled.

Jun raised an eyebrow and took the note from him. "Thanks, Daddy," he said.

Austin laughed again. "I'm not Daddy."

Sunny shot Liv a small smile. Liv was getting it now. Austin was drunk.

"Daddy took our family out for dinner. Everyone was very well behaved. He gave me money to have a nice evening, made sure the waitress could see all the notes in his wallet." He laughed, then flung an arm around her shoulders and squeezed her for a second. She could smell the sweetness from the wine he'd drunk, and the faintest edge of cologne.

"I'm so glad you came."

"He's been talking about you," Sunny said.

"Talking about me but not to me," Liv said back to her.

Sunny laughed. "Classic."

On closer look, Sunny's dress actually might be Ahluwalia. Liv doubted the OnlyFans account could have bought her that. She'd dressed it down with some old sneakers, like it wasn't worth thousands. If Liv owned a dress like that, she wouldn't pair it with New Balance.

Jun came back with another bottle of wine and a bottle of water.

"This is for us"—he pushed the wine into the bucket—"and this is for Daddy"—he put the water in front of Austin.

Austin ignored that, refilling his glass with wine. He gave it to Liv first. The wine was crisp and cold on her tongue, making her feel more present and awake than she had all day. For the next hour, Austin kept stealing glances at her, giddy and laughing, the glitter of the lanterns flashing in his eyes.

Eventually Sunny leaned back, stretching her arms over her head. "I've got to get home," she said. "I have an SLT class at six a.m."

"Share a Lyft?" Jun said.

"Yeah, all right."

"What do you want to do?" Austin asked Liv. "We could get another bottle?"

It would be nice to sit here, just the two of them, in the dark under the sparkling lantern. But she was terrified of another blackout.

So she smiled at him and said, "I probably should be getting back."

"Yeah, c'mon, man," Jun backed her. "You'll be tanked if you have another bottle. I'm not going to leave poor Olivia to have to try and drag your drunk ass home."

"You suck. Both of you," Austin said; then he groaned, "I don't want to go home. I don't want this night to end."

"We could walk back?" she said.

He leaned back, still sullen. "All right."

They said goodbye to Sunny and Jun out front and started the walk down Sunset. Now that it was just the two of them, she couldn't think of anything to talk about. She kept thinking back on last night. How deeply he'd kissed her, his hands on her hips, the feeling of him inside her.

There were lots of people out, despite the hour. They walked under the cold lights of a vegan cold-pressed juice bar. It was still open, a woman in crimson spandex standing, bored, behind the counter. Liv had seen a lot of places like this around; even at Trader Joe's there was an expensive juice section.

"Why do people in LA love juice so much?" she asked him, just for conversation. She expected him to say something about how people in LA were body-conscious.

"It's healthy," he said, "and easy. Kind of like fast food, you know? Easy, quick, and if you have too much, it will give you diarrhea." He laughed, but then a pained look crossed his face. "I'm sorry. That was really gross."

She kind of liked drunk Austin. He was goofy. "Well, thanks for the warning," she said.

"No problem."

They passed a red-and-blue window-serve taco stand, shut up for the night. *Best Chilaquiles in Town* painted in bold pink letters. The chefs were sitting out front on the plastic furniture, smoking cigarettes and chatting in Spanish. Up ahead was a big mural of a yellow sun and figures dancing in the sky. With the headlights from the cars on the road gliding across it, it looked like the painting was coming alive, the figures really dancing.

"Ginger didn't come to the dog park today," Austin said.

"Yeah. I was too busy."

"Rufus missed Ginger."

"Really?" she asked.

"Yeah, she's good for him."

"He's good for her as well. She missed seeing him too."

"She really gets him running around. Usually he's such a shy boy."

She laughed, looking over to catch his eye. But he didn't look at her.

They reached the corner of Maltman and cut through the empty car park of the ninety-nine-cent store.

Austin pointed over to a café with gray awnings. "We should go there sometime. Millie's Café, they have the best breakfasts. They do this one called Maynard's Special, it's incredible. Eggs over easy. Fresh spinach and goat cheese and roasted pine nuts that smell so good. Maybe tomorrow? It's great hangover food."

"I'd feel bad not going to Sabrosa. What about Carlos?"

"You can't go to the same place every day."

He was right. Ever since she'd gotten here, her life had been small. This city had so much to offer; she needed to get out there and embrace it more.

"I sent in my application."

"That's great! Congratulations." He squeezed her arm. "You should have told me before. We could have gotten champagne."

He wasn't sounding so drunk now; maybe the walk was sobering him up. She tried to catch his expression, but the streetlights were far apart now, and the light from the main drag was fading.

Above them, they heard a scuffling sound. They looked up in time to see a dried-out frond from one of the tallest palm trees on the street fall down through the night to the ground below. Now the tree looked close to death, with only a few pale bits of frond still attached.

They were getting to the hill of Maltman Avenue. Home was only about another fifteen minutes away.

"I need to ask you something," Liv said.

He scrunched his eyes shut. "I know, I know. I was meaning to text you all day. It's just, things at home are . . . I don't know how to explain it. I get so distracted and—"

"Did you tell them? Your parents? About all the stuff that's been going on with me?"

"No, course not."

She stopped. "You didn't?"

"No." He turned to her. It was too dark to see him properly; all she could see was a glint of reflected light on his glasses.

"Well, I mean . . . they fired me."

"Ah," he said. "Thought that might happen." She wished she could see his eyes.

"Why are they angry with me?"

"It doesn't matter," he said, starting up the hill again. "Seriously, just don't even worry about it."

She followed him, starting to puff with the effort. If it wasn't about her coming into their house, she had no idea what it was about.

"Tell me."

He didn't say anything. The night was silent except for their breaths, hers a little more rapid than his.

"I have to know. I really like your parents. Plus, babysitting is my only income right now, so I need—"

"Okay, okay." He took a breath. "Look, my dad says you were peeping on them. Sorry, I know that's really harsh."

"Peeping?"

"Yeah. Like, looking out through your bedroom window into theirs. He made this whole big deal of it, even though I tried to say you were probably just doing your sleepwalking thing. But he said . . . I don't know . . . it kind of seemed like it was at a . . . an inopportune time."

"Wait." She stopped. "As in . . . no."

He turned to face her, shrugged. "I don't know."

"But what you're saying is . . . maybe I was standing there watching your parents . . . have sex."

"Oh Jesus," he said, putting his hands over his face. "Don't even say it!"

"But is that what you mean?"

"I don't know! Mom was pretty uncomfortable too. It wasn't necessarily that they were . . ."

"Having sex?"

"I just think . . . well, I guess I don't know. He said you had a really weird expression on your face as well."

"Oh my God." She closed her eyes. "This is just . . . I mean, that is just . . ."

"Come on," he said. "Let me show you something cool. We can sit down for a minute."

He grabbed her hand and they kept walking up the hill. She should have made that doctor's appointment. Yes, they had no insurance right now, but clearly, she needed medical help. She was going to call first thing in the morning. She couldn't believe she had waited this long. She couldn't even wrap her head around this new information. She was a sex pest. She was some kind of creepy, deviant—

"Here," he said, "come and sit here. But we have to whisper."

They were at the top of the hill now, and he was pulling her up onto a steep incline of grass that went up to the fence of a house.

"Isn't this private property?" she whispered.

"I mean, it's just the edge. So I think it's okay."

She let him lead her up near the wooden fence. They sat down on the grass. She couldn't see the house, but she could tell just by the fence it was a new build: thin wooden beams stained honey blond. She peered through them—she was a Peeping Tom now after all—and saw the glistening surface of a pool. They wouldn't be heard.

"Look." Austin pointed.

At first, she thought he was pointing to the American flag that was flopped over a pole in the front yard of the house they were look-ing down on. She'd never seen a flag in someone's yard back home, except for maybe the Aboriginal flag once or twice. In Australia, the national flag was often banned at festivals and events because it could go hand in hand with packs of drunk, racist assholes.

But then she looked at where he was actually pointing. Not at the house with the flag and the arched entranceway, but behind and above it.

The Hollywood sign.

It was only just visible atop the huge canyon in the distance, the white letters lit up with a ghostly glow.

"Wow," she said.

"I used to come up here all the time at night when I was in high school. Just sit up by this fence and look at it. There's something . . . I don't know, mournful about it at night."

"Is there a spotlight?"

"No. It's just the lights from the city reflecting off it."

She imagined that the light was from all the screenwriters staying up rewriting their scripts. The headlights of all the wannabe actresses driving home from their bar jobs. He was right; it was sort of mournful.

"I think I'm almost sober now," he said.

"That's good, right?"

He shrugged. "I like being drunk."

"You did seem to be enjoying yourself. And your friends are really nice."

"Yeah."

She stared out at the sign. Tried not to think of that horrible word. *Peeping.* In the distance she heard a *yip-yip-yip* sound.

"I didn't want to tell you about it," he whispered. "I knew it would upset you. And it's not your fault. You must have just been asleep."

"I hope so. I mean, I must have been, right?" She laughed. "I definitely wouldn't have been doing that when I was awake."

He laughed. "I hope not."

Again, she heard it. *Yip-yip-yip.* "What is that?"

"Coyotes. They're getting braver. Coming into the suburbs looking for cats and trash."

She grimaced. "A good reminder to keep Ginger in at night."

"Yeah."

She listened, wondering if she'd hear the sound again. But there was nothing.

"It's just . . ." It felt easier to talk about this in the dark. "I don't even know what I'm doing, or what happens, when I'm asleep. If you hadn't told me, I wouldn't even know I'd been . . . looking at your parents. Like, I mean, how scary is that? I'm totally out of control and not even conscious for it."

She brushed her hand over the grass under them. It was healthy; the owners must have their gardeners water it. It would have been bright green, but in the dim, it all just looked gray. The notion that maybe the issues at home had absolutely nothing to do with her collapsed.

"I'm sort of worried I've . . . done something."

"Done what?"

"I don't know. That's the thing."

He pulled a long piece of grass out, fiddled with it between his fingers. "I'm sure you wouldn't do anything bad."

"That's what I thought. Well, that's what I wanted to think. I keep telling myself that I just got drunk and embarrassed myself, or that my parents have their own issues going on and it has nothing to do with me. But . . . I mean . . . look." She pulled her cami down the whole way, showing the bruise above her breasts. The one on her neck was basically gone now, but this one was still a dark shadow above her sternum.

"That's from that after-party where you got wasted?"

"Yeah. I was talking to Casper last night. He said he thinks I hurt someone . . . I don't want to believe it, but I think he might be right."

She stared out at the Hollywood sign. The words made her throat clench. Speaking them was corrosive, like heartburn.

"Who did you hurt?"

"I don't know. But . . . the way my parents look at me now. They look at me like there's something wrong with me. I can't keep ignoring that."

"But that doesn't mean you hurt someone. It could be anything."

"That's what I thought. That maybe I fell down the stairs or . . . something . . . and that's how I cut my head and got the bruises on my body. But I had a bruise on my throat as well, Austin. You don't get a bruise on your throat from falling down the stairs. But that's the awful thing. I can't remember any of it."

She could hear Austin breathing. He grabbed her hand, held it between his. "That's awful."

"I know."

"But it sounds like someone hurt you, not the other way around."

"Someone hurt me, that's for sure. But I did something back. I must have. Otherwise why would my parents look at me like that?"

Again, that call. *Yip-yip-yip.* Louder now. "Do coyotes bite?" she asked, attempting a laugh. But Austin just stared out at the sky, then brought her hand to his mouth and kissed it.

"If you hurt someone, you were probably just defending yourself."

"Maybe."

"Definitely."

"I don't really want to know what I did, to be honest. I just want it to stop. The blackouts, losing control and not even remembering it, the nightmares. I have to figure out how to make it stop."

"We'll figure it out. I'll do more research. I can help you."

"You want to help me?"

He shrugged, still holding her hand in both of his. "Got to use my three-quarters of a psychology degree for something. I meant what I said last night. I really like you."

"I like you too. Will you keep me awake until we figure this out?"

Even though it was dark and she couldn't see his face, she could feel that he was grinning. "I'll do my best."

She elbowed him in the ribs. "That's not what I meant."

But then he was kissing her and it didn't matter anymore.

TWENTY-THREE

Kay sat up on the window ledge. The house was totally silent. Janus had disappeared to the library first thing in the morning, and Casper was working a morning shift at Sabrosa. Olivia, who knew. Kay knew she should be keeping tabs on her after everything, making sure she wasn't getting into any more trouble, but she couldn't muster the energy.

Kay had called in sick to work and spent the last four hours working on Olivia's bedroom. At first her plan had been to put down new carpet in the room. But then the stain, that pale angel shape, would still be there underneath. If anyone ever pulled the carpet up, there it would be. No. They needed it gone, eradicated, like it had never happened.

She'd bleached the boards, trying to even out the tone. The smell had made her eyes water, but somehow it had felt good. Like she was crying, letting herself feel. The smell brought with it flashbacks of that day. Instead of blocking herself against them, she let the memories roll over her. From the moment she'd jolted awake in the early hours until that night when she'd knelt under the blasting hot shower water, vomiting into the drain.

The bleach turned the floor a pallid, uneven blond. It looked ghastly, but it was done. The stain was gone. She had to wait for the boards to dry before she could varnish them, and no doubt it would look amateur. But that was okay. If it looked like a bad attempt at home renovation rather than a crime scene, she'd take it.

She sat in the window, the sun on her back, waiting for the hot air to drink the moisture from the wood. She refreshed their bank balance again, and this time, this time, it changed. Her mother had come through, depositing $10,000 straight into their account. Kay opened Venmo and transferred $20,000 to the blackmailer, the amount of zeros feeling absurd.

It was over. She had done it. The stain was gone; the blackmail was paid. They were going to be okay.

She wanted all this weight off of her shoulders, even if it was just for a few hours. She wanted to see Carlos. She'd been there last night, but it had been busy and they'd barely had a chance to talk. She wanted to use some intimacy from her past to purge herself, to escape into a feeling of honesty, of humiliation. Maybe she'd tell him about her mother? Or no . . . that hurt was too raw after yesterday's phone call. Maybe she'd tell him about her first time? Fifteen and staying in a Paris hotel for months. Her mother passed out on the couch. She'd put on one of her mother's dresses, the dark lipstick that made her look older; then she'd gone to the hotel bar, let a Serbian businessman with thick dark hair buy her drinks. Looking back, he had been nice to her, relatively speaking, although he must have known she was underage. Still, she'd had far worse after. But she'd felt so small and stupid in his bed, and seeing that ugly plum lipstick smeared on the man's mouth was humiliating. It was all so humiliating. How much she'd wanted it, imagined it, beforehand. How quick and painful it had been in the moment. How she'd locked eyes with her mother when she'd traipsed back in the early hours and she knew that her mother had known but never asked. Yes, there was plenty in that to tell Carlos, plenty to purge.

Kay closed the window and left the room, relocking the door. She went straight upstairs, had a quick shower. Wrapped in towels, she decided she'd wear something nice. Usually she was racing around from work and had started living in spandex. Instead she pulled on a cotton dress and soft woven cardigan. Heading back downstairs, she saw Casper was in the kitchen, spreading peanut butter on some toast. He had sunglasses on.

"Sunglasses inside?"

"I've got a headache."

"Have you taken something for it?"

"Yeah. It's not that bad."

"You know, I didn't even hear you come in," she said.

"I'm quiet as a mouse."

She snorted. "Is that a joke? I always know when it's you climbing the stairs because of the way you stomp."

He looked up at her. "I do not stomp!"

"You do. Liv kind of floats around, you barely hear her. Your father scampers, all quick steps. But you, my love, you stomp."

He put down his toast. "You know who else stomps? You."

"Do I?"

"Yeah. I must have inherited it. Where are you going? You look nice."

She smiled. "Thanks, honey."

"Are you going to be around for dinner?" His tone was hopeful.

She missed her son. She'd been so distracted, it felt like she'd been somewhere else; now all she wanted was to spend time with him.

"I'm popping out for a coffee, I'll be back. Why don't you and I go

somewhere? We can drive over to Koreatown, I know you like trying new foods."

"Okay," he said, taking another bite of his toast.

"No more toast."

"Mum, I'm fifteen, I'm a bottomless pit."

"I know," she said. As she passed him, she couldn't help but put a
hand on each of his shoulders. She waited for him to groan or wrig-
gle away from her, but he didn't do either. He stayed perfectly still.

FOR ONCE, SABROSA was quiet. There was no one waiting for coffees by
the counter. She looked out to the back courtyard. There was only
one young man, sitting behind a laptop, a huge iced coffee untouched
next to him.

"Kay," Carlos said, coming out from the kitchen.

"Hi, Carlos," she said, "it's quiet today."

"Not really." He leaned against the counter. "It's always basically
empty between two thirty and three thirty. It's when the kitchen
closes so the boys can have a break before dinner. It's usually just me
this time of day."

"You and that guy." She motions to the guy sitting out the back.

"Mike? Yeah, he spends hours here. Screenwriter, you know."

"I do," she said. But she didn't want to talk about Janus.

"Americano?"

"Actually," she said, "how about a cappuccino?"

He smiled at her. "Coming right up."

She sat by the window, watching as he made her coffee. The way
his arms flexed a little as he pulled out the handles of the espresso
machine, the gentle fluidity of his movements as he steamed the milk.
She looked away.

"Here you go," he said, placing the coffee up on the counter. "Now I'm going to have to keep going with prep—sorry, Kay. You're welcome to have this in the kitchen if you want."

"Really?"

"You can't touch anything though, okay? No helping."

"I wouldn't dream of it."

She followed him into the back, holding her coffee. The room wasn't huge: It was lined with steel-top benches with an island in the middle. There was a large industrial dishwasher next to a huge square sink, parallel to a set of eight stoves on the other side of the room. Frying pans were hung from hooks, and a row of knives glinted from a magnetic band.

Carlos was set up on the island. He'd already quartered half a plastic tray of lemons, filling the room with their citrus smell. He took out some coriander—or cilantro, as they called it here—and started dicing it so finely she was worried he'd slice a finger. The smell was lovely, herby and fresh, easing the bleach burn in her nostrils.

She dipped her spoon into the froth of her coffee and then put it into her mouth. It was creamy and warm and lovely. It was so nice to feel good and free. To stop punishing herself, just for an hour. She was glad she'd come.

"You do all the kitchen prep yourself?"

"Most of the time, yes."

"Why? Shouldn't this be some kitchen hand's job? My son's probably?"

"I enjoy it. I start at six most days and don't finish until late. I like having this hour of quiet, getting everything ready and organized for tonight. You know, a moment to feel grateful for what I'm doing here."

Carlos was such a good guy. Kay basically knew nothing about him and hadn't ever asked. She wondered then if he really did fancy her. If he actually enjoyed the talks they had, or if he saw her as just another drunk customer staying past her welcome and rambling about the past.

"I'm sorry," she said, aware she was making it all about herself. "Am I intruding?"

He looked up at her and smiled. "Not at all. Now, my favorite part."

He cleared the lemons and herbs away into their white plastic containers and wiped down the benchtop. Then he took out a huge silver mixing bowl and started pouring in flour.

"The secret ingredient is lard. Don't tell anyone."

"I won't."

He put in the lard, then salt and baking soda and water, and began mixing the ingredients together with his hands. "My abuela showed me how to make tortillas when I was a kid. She used to own a bakery in San Pedro. I'd go after school every day and help her—it's a nice memory. It's something I hope to get the chance to pass along to my own kids one day."

"I hope I've passed on nice memories like that to my children. Sometimes I worry I've only passed them bad things. Like Olivia's drinking. Or Casper's flair for the dramatic!"

Carlos laughed. "He definitely takes his emotions out on my dishes, you wouldn't believe it."

"Oh, I would," she said, and took a sip of her coffee. She liked hearing these stories about her son when he was out in the world on his own. Looking at the sink, she smiled to think of Casper standing there.

"It's nice to see you smile, Kay. You seem happy today."

"Do I?"

"You do. It kills me to see so many women unhappy in their homes in this neighborhood. It's not right."

"Is it that obvious?"

He looked up at her, hands still deep in the mixture. "You never mention your husband."

"I'm angry at him. Very angry."

"Over a woman?"

She grimaced. Put the coffee cup down. "Yes," she said. Because it was over a woman, in a way. Not the way Carlos thought, but she could hardly tell him the truth.

"I think about leaving a lot," she said. "I imagine it. It's all that gets me through some days."

"What do you imagine?"

"A hotel. Somewhere near the ocean. Sheets. Crisp, clean sheets that I haven't washed myself."

"That sounds nice."

"And you," she said, without really meaning to. "Sometimes I imagine you are there."

He looked at her now, his hands leaving the dough. "You do?"

"Yes."

He took a step toward her, to where she was sitting up on the countertop. Her heart pounded. Did she really want this? He smelled different from Janus, his cologne zesty. His eyes locked to hers, such a warm, rich brown. They were lit up with desire. He wanted her. He reached her and he didn't have to touch her for her to feel the heat of his body. But she couldn't do it. She couldn't. She couldn't do this thing she'd dreamed of doing all week. She broke the gaze, turned her face away.

Silence. Then he reached for the empty coffee cup next to her, headed toward the door.

He cleared his throat. "I'm popping out now, while the dough rests. I'll walk up with you if you like. I'm going your way."

"Where are you going?"

That moment. It was there, she could have grabbed it, and now it was gone. If she'd wanted it, really wanted it, it was too late. He was walking away.

"I'm going up to call on Hélène. Haven't seen her in a while, poor thing. We don't do enough to care for our elderly around here."

He threw a tea towel over the bowl with his spare hand.

Her heart pounded against her ribs. Tingles started in her fingertips and rose up her arms.

He headed to the doorway. She couldn't let him go.

"Wait," she said, her voice small. "Carlos. Wait."

He stopped in the doorway, "Kay. It's fine. Honestly, I—"

"Come here."

He looked at her but didn't come.

"Come here. Please."

He walked over, putting the coffee cup down next to the sink. He stopped a good distance from her.

"Look, I—" he began, but she didn't let him finish.

She reached out and grabbed his white T-shirt, pulling him toward her. And then, that was it. His mouth was on hers. It was happening.

He didn't kiss like Janus. He didn't taste like Janus.

His mouth was hot, his lips slippery, and already, she couldn't help it, already she could feel her body pulsing for his. His arms wrapped around her, pulling her tight. She opened her knees to pull him closer into her, felt his soft stomach press against her hard one, his soft mouth pushing against hers. His hands were still covered in flour and it smeared against her dress, but she didn't care, couldn't think of anything but keeping him there, with her.

He pulled back, breathed deeply. "Should we not do this?"

He took a step back. But she reached under her dress, pulled her underwear down her thighs. Flicked her sandals off and tugged her underwear from her feet.

He held his hands up; they were claggy with dough. "I should wash my hands."

"I don't want your hands," she said, and slid her legs open. She could feel herself pulsing for him, pulsing for the humiliation of it. Of being splayed open on that benchtop.

He put a hand on each of her knees, pulled her legs even farther apart, and she couldn't help it: A tiny moan escaped her lips. He leaned in, and she pulled forward to kiss him, but he moved back.

Then he smiled at her and knelt down onto the kitchen floor. He pushed his head between her legs, and as the heat and wetness of his mouth encompassed her, she leaned back onto the shelves and closed her eyes.

TWENTY-FOUR

Casper sat on the back steps. He needed to get out of the house, go and do something. But he couldn't come up with anything to do. His head felt noisy; he couldn't think straight. For some reason it smelled like bleach again inside, so he'd come out here to get some fresh air, try and pull himself together. It wasn't working.

Did you get the script? Tye texted him.

It was awesome, he replied. But he hadn't even read it. He knew that made him a shit friend, but he just couldn't concentrate. This morning at work he'd kept letting plates slip out of his hands, he'd been so distracted.

He wanted to believe that nothing had happened, and it was all so easily explained away. He wanted to go out to dinner with his mum tonight and eat spicy Korean food and not have any thoughts niggling at him. But he knew that wouldn't happen. He kept thinking about the hair clip. And the piece of broken headlight when his parents had never mentioned that the car had been damaged. And Liv's bruises.

He had to let it go; he knew that. He had to move on. But all the unanswered questions made him feel paralyzed.

Ginger came out through the open door behind him. He watched as she sniffed the earth and then started digging in his dad's avocado patch, the earth flying up all around her. He was going to have to clean it up, replant the plants, fix it. Even so, he couldn't be bothered to stop her.

He had to get up. He had to let go of whatever was going on and focus on being in the world, and he had to read Tye's script.

"Get up," he said out loud, like the complete maniac he was turning into. He stood.

"Ginger, stop it!"

She ignored him.

He went over to her. "Naughty dog. No digging!"

He nudged her back legs with his foot, and she turned around and looked at him, then went back to the soil. He groaned, picked her up, and went back to the house, shutting the back door so she couldn't get out. He went over to inspect the damage. She'd pulled one plant out completely. He knelt down and grabbed it, then put his hands into the soil to make a burrow for it. His hand touched something. Something soft. Something that felt like skin.

He jerked back, looked down into the plant bed. Then he leaned down, and brushed the soil away until he couldn't doubt it anymore. Right there, poking out from the dirt, was a human hand.

TWENTY-FIVE

The blood! The gore! It's wonderful, Janus. You've really hit the mark with the horror in this draft," Maggie told him.

Janus was sitting out in front of the library, a cigarette in his hand and his phone to his ear. He'd come here even though he didn't have anything to work on while he waited to hear back on his draft; he didn't know where else to go. That was why he'd been so surprised when Maggie called him. Usually it took weeks for her to get back to him.

"Now, we just have small tweaks and then I'm going to show this to some directors—" She was interrupted by a beep. He looked at the screen. Casper was calling. He pressed decline; he'd call him back.

"What tweaks?"

"Tiny stuff. Just so it's perfect. We only get the one chance to take it out. Do you remember that Swedish film last year? *Jag välkomnar döden*? Killed it at the festivals. We'll show it to the director of that. Or there's a kid who just graduated AFI, his final short was incredible. Raw talent, you know? It's important that—"

The phone beeped again. Casper.

"Hey, Maggie, I'm so excited about this, but I'm going to have to call you right back. Sorry. Just a minute." He ended the call and accepted Casper's.

"Cas? You all right?"

"Dad," his son said. And just with that word, Janus felt a wave of panic rise up his body.

"Yes?"

"I . . . You need to come home."

"What's happened? Are you okay? Has Liv done something?"

"You tell me," Cas said.

Janus's throat went dry. He found himself standing, walking toward the bike rack, the phone still pressed to his ear.

"I'm coming," he said, and hung up.

He couldn't think as he cycled. His mind had gone blank again, filled only with that sheet of panic.

He reached his house without even processing the trip. Then he was unlocking the door, walking inside, and seeing his son, right there, sitting at the table, not looking at him.

Janus looked down and saw his son's dirty hands, the soil under his nails. The worst way, he'd found out the worst possible way.

"Cas, oh, buddy, I'm so sorry."

Janus went to him, reached out to him, but Casper flinched away. Of course he did. Of course. Janus sat down next to him at the table.

"It was an accident," Janus said. "No one meant for this to happen. No one wanted her to be hurt."

"But who is it?" Casper said, finally looking up at him. He was too young for this. His face was twisting into an expression Janus had never wanted to see on it: abject horror.

"I know I could have . . ." Casper went on. "I could have looked.

Like, I could have checked to see. Looked at . . . their face. But I couldn't . . . I . . ."

"No, no, buddy, no. I'm going to tell you the truth, okay? No more lying."

Casper nodded. "I can't deal with trying to figure it out anymore, Dad. Just tell me. Please, I need to know."

"Okay." Janus leaned back in his chair. He rubbed a hand over his face. He'd promised Kay he would never do this. But what choice did he have?

"It was the day just before you came back from swim camp."

"I figured that much out by myself."

"We . . . Okay, I'm going to start from the beginning. Your sister went out that night. She went to some after-party for her internship. She told us she'd stay at her friend's house. We weren't expecting her back. It was . . . just as the sun was starting to rise. I was in bed, awake. I . . . God, looking back, I don't even remember what was on my mind. The script, probably. I was lying there, just thinking, you know, turning some problem that felt so important around in my head. Then I heard it. A bang. A . . . thwack, from right outside the house. And from under my feet, a horrible sound. Someone was hurt. I jumped up and went to the window, but all I could see was the car disappearing into the garage."

He'd rushed downstairs. It'd been a hot night, and he'd slept in just his boxers, but that sound . . . she'd hit something. His daughter, his baby, his little girl. He'd run straight into the garage, terrified that she'd hurt herself. That the moaning sound he'd heard was Liv.

"I went into the garage . . ." He didn't know how to say it.

"And?"

"I went into the garage . . . and the car was still going. She must have had her foot on the accelerator still. She was . . . Liv was in the car. The airbag had activated and she was slumped over it. But . . ."

He leaned forward and put his head in his hands. It wasn't something he'd ever thought he'd have to say out loud.

"She'd hit her. Liv had hit Hélène with the car. She—"

"Hélène?"

"Yeah. She used to always go on those early walks, remember? Right as the sun rose, when her hip would be aching from the night? I guess she was passing the driveway, and Liv . . . Liv must not have even stopped. She plowed right through her. Hélène . . . she was . . ."

He remembered how he'd frozen. He'd just stood there, staring, not being able to believe what he was seeing. Hélène, poor sweet Hélène, she was . . .

"She was pinned against the wall of the garage. Between the car and the wall. And Olivia's foot was still on the accelerator, so the car was still going. And . . ."

Her eyes were open. She was gasping for air. Making awful, guttural sounds.

"I ran around to the driver's door. Opened it. Liv was . . . she was staring straight at Hélène. She was hurt, but the airbag had taken most of it. The seat belt had grazed her neck a bit, but . . . she was okay. She . . . she was really out of it. I put the car into reverse, then pulled the hand brake. Hélène . . ."

She'd slumped down onto the ground, her head hitting the concrete floor with a crack.

"Your mum was up by then—she must have heard the noise too, I guess. She rushed over to Hélène. I turned the car off, pulled Liv out, got her inside." Janus had kept asking Liv if she was okay, but she just closed her eyes, fell asleep on the couch. He could smell booze on her breath. He ran back into the garage. Hélène was standing up. She had her weight on Kay, but she seemed okay. Like maybe it wasn't as bad as it had looked.

"We brought Hélène into Liv's room. We were just going to lay her down on the bed and then I was going to call an ambulance. But then . . ."

Her eyes rolled back in her head. Her body began to convulse. They'd put her down on the carpet and he'd started chest compressions. But when he'd pushed on her chest, it hadn't felt right. Her sternum wasn't hard beneath his hand. It just squashed inward. He'd opened her shirt. Her rib cage was crushed. Blood started pouring out of her mouth like a tap.

"We realized then that she . . . she was injured internally."

Her breathing. The gasping breaths. The smell of old coins filling his nose. Blood gushing down around her hair. He'd never seen someone die before. He'd never known how the body tried so desperately to cling to life. Kay had held her hand the whole time, whispered that it was going to be okay. She never broke eye contact, not once.

"I went upstairs to grab my phone and I ran back down. Your mum was standing there outside Liv's room." She had blood all down the T-shirt she'd worn to bed. "I was about to call the ambulance, but I saw your mum's face and I knew that it was too late. I . . . God, how do I describe this feeling to you?"

He looked into his son's eyes, hoping for something . . . He wasn't sure what. Maybe understanding? Absolution? But Casper just stared right back at him.

"So you didn't call anyone?"

"No. I wanted to at first, but your mum . . . she said Liv would go to jail. It was drunk driving, vehicular manslaughter. That . . . that didn't seem like the answer. It was a mistake, a hideous one, but jail would ruin her. Prison wouldn't bring Hélène back, it would just take Liv away. And she would do serious time, she would never be the same."

He looked at Casper again, beseeching, and Casper nodded once.

The relief flooded through Janus. He understood, thank God he understood.

"So you covered it up?"

"We did."

He'd carried Olivia upstairs to Casper's room to sleep it off, and
they'd spent the whole morning cleaning the garage. Sweeping up
the glass, bleaching out the blood from the concrete. They'd tried to
bleach the blood out of the carpet in Olivia's room too, but that just
made its own stain. They'd needed to fix that too, but they knew
Casper would be back the next morning so they'd had to rush, just
focus on the worst parts first. He'd taken the car to an auto repair
place out in Burbank, where no one knew them, gotten a padlock for
Olivia's door from a hardware store and some supplies to rip up the
stained carpet. Then, that night, they'd started digging in the backyard. It was hard work, much harder than he'd expected. That was
why they'd decided to make a raised bed and add plants. Plus, if the
neighbors looked over the fence, it would give reason for the grave-
shaped plot. When the hole was big enough, Janus had gone upstairs.
He couldn't face actually putting her body in it and covering her with
dirt.

"But it doesn't make sense," Casper said. "She . . . Hélène . . . she
can't be dead. I've been talking to her."

"What?"

The front door opened, making Janus jump. Kay entered the room.
She looked flustered, sweaty, and there was what looked like flour on
her dress. She ran a hand across her ponytail when she saw him, an
unreadable expression on her face. Then her eyes moved to Casper.

"Honey! What happened to your eye?"

But Casper didn't respond; he just looked at her. Her eyes flicked
between the two of them; then she reached a hand over her mouth.

"Dad told me," he said.

She looked at him. "What? Why? Why would you do that?"

"He found her. In the yard."

"Ginger was digging."

"Oh, baby," she said, rushing forward. "Oh, honey, I'm sorry. I'm so sorry."

"I don't want a fucking hug or a fucking apology," Casper spat at her, and she stopped in her tracks. "What I want to know is how Hélène has been texting me when she's been dead and buried in our yard for over a week?"

TWENTY-SIX

H er phone was in her pocket," Kay told him. "The screen was
    cracked, but it was working. I had to make it seem like she was
still alive."

Casper nodded. He stood up and walked toward her. She reached
out to him, but he ducked away, heading for the front door.

"Honey!" she called after him. "You can't tell anyone! Okay? It's
not just Liv anymore, it's me and your father too. We'd all—"

"I won't."

The front door slammed behind him.

"Should I go after him?" Janus said.

She looked at her husband. For a moment, she didn't recognize
him. She expected to see the man he was. The man who'd lit up when
he came home from the office, his tie loose around his neck, his eyes
shining for her. Instead she saw a stranger in front of her. A man with
unkempt hair and shadows under his eyes, sallow skin and an exhausted slump to his shoulders. Who was this man? When had Janus
become him?

"No, give him space," she said, turning and walking up the stairs. Janus followed her as she went into their bedroom.

She pulled a gym bag out from the bottom of her wardrobe.

"Do you think he'll be okay?"

"Probably not."

"What do we do now?"

She didn't know. Why was he always asking her what to do next? She had no idea.

"We should send the email out now, right? Say that she's off visiting family, gone back to Brittany. That's the next step now, isn't it? Now her house is done? Oh, and I should check on the avo plants, right?"

Questions, questions, questions. Why couldn't he think for himself?

"I just saw Carlos," she said.

"The chef at Sabrosa?"

"He's the owner."

"What are you doing?" He'd noticed the clothes she was folding into the gym bag.

"I was just there. At Sabrosa. He said he was going to visit Hélène. He wanted to check on her. I couldn't let him go."

"Okay. But why are you packing, Kay? What's happening?"

She went to go into the ensuite; she needed her toothbrush, but he blocked her path.

"I'm leaving," she said. "I need . . . some time to think."

She took another step forward, but he blocked her again. She looked up now, right into his eyes, those perfect bottle green eyes.

"I had to stop Carlos. But also . . . I won't say I didn't enjoy it."

He blinked. "You fucked him?"

"I wouldn't say *fucked*. Not exactly. Although it depends how you define the term."

Janus took a step back, like she'd slapped him, the pain of it spreading across his face. She passed him, but didn't go to the bathroom; she'd get another toothbrush. She headed down the stairs and into the garage.

They'd pulled Hélène out of there together, brought her into Liv's room, laid her down on the carpet when the bed was too high. She'd held Hélène's hand as Janus had scampered to the door. *Stay*, she'd said, *please stay*. But it was like he didn't hear her. He walked out as Hélène coughed splatters of hot blood on Kay's T-shirt and squeezed her hand as her eyes went blank and her grip went slack.

He'd helped her dig the hole, but when it came to dragging the body out, when it came to burying her, he'd sat on the step. *I can't do it, Kay*, he'd said. *I just can't. It's too much*. He'd said he needed to lie down. He'd said he needed a moment, but then he hadn't come back down. And so she'd done it alone.

Kay opened the trunk of the car and put the gym bag in. Then she got in the driver's seat and headed for the ocean.

TWENTY-SEVEN

L iv was exhausted. They'd managed to stay up last night after they'd gotten back from the bar, but all day she'd been barely able to keep her eyes open. They'd snuck out from Austin's room that morning and gone down to Millie's Café. They'd had triple-shot espressos that made her eyes feel like peeled grapes and eaten a huge brunch; then they'd gone up to the park and lain under a dying palm. She'd rested her head on Austin's stomach and felt the rise and fall of his breath as they talked about music and books they liked and politics and what they'd do first if they were president and watched people come and go. Once the sun had faded, they'd snuck back into Austin's. She knew she should probably just go home—his parents were going to notice she was there if she stayed much longer, and interacting with them was going to be horrifically awkward—but she couldn't get an appointment with the doctor until the following day, an appointment that was going to take out a huge chunk of what was left on her credit card. She didn't want to be by herself before then. Austin had gone downstairs and had dinner with his parents and pretended he wasn't feeling well, then come back up and watched a movie with her in bed on his laptop. She'd fallen asleep just fifteen minutes in and woken with a jolt.

"I fell asleep!"

"I was right here."

"But what if you drift off too? No, I need caffeine pills," she said, rubbing her eyes.

"I could go down to the drugstore?"

She'd run out of the ones she'd pilfered from his parents a few days ago, but she didn't want to tell him where she'd gotten them from and she didn't want him to leave her in the house without him.

"It's okay. I'm going to the bathroom."

Out in the hallway she could hear the sound of the television playing downstairs. She paused outside Brian and Rani's room, making sure neither of them had come up to bed early, but it was silent, so she darted inside. She went into the ensuite and swallowed a pill from the Stay Awake container, then headed back into Austin's room and climbed back into his bed.

"Do you think the doctor will be able to help me tomorrow?"

"Yeah, I think so. They'll be able to give us some pointers at least."

She pulled off her shorts and curled back in next to him under the sheet and pressed her head into his chest. He had a psychology article up on his computer now, but the text looked blurry. She closed her eyes, listening to the rhythmic thud of his heart.

"God, I'm tired."

"You know, if you want to sleep, it's fine. I won't sleep, so I'll be here to stop you getting up."

"No, it's okay," she said, but her eyelids were so heavy. So much for the caffeine pills. They never seemed to work for her—she should have checked the use-by date.

He ran his fingers through her hair. It felt nice.

"Promise you won't drift off?" she asked.

"I promise."

Her eyelids closed, and then she was falling into dark, delicious black nothing.

SCREAMING. A WOMAN screaming.

Screaming. It was Rani.

Something heavy pushed against her.

Hands on her forearms, pushing her. Cold against her feet. Tiles.

Austin was there. Austin had his hands on her arms, pushing her into the bathroom doorway. There was red on his white T-shirt. He didn't have his glasses on, and his face was twisted with fear, his eyes wide. He slammed the door shut right in front of her face.

"Austin?"

Her voice was thick. Just a moment ago she'd been falling asleep, her head heavy on Austin's warm chest. But now she was on her feet. She was alone in Rani and Brian's ensuite.

"Austin?"

She pulled at the door handle, but it was jammed. There was a horrible sound. Brian moaning. Rani moaning. They were mixing together, making a horrible new moan.

"Austin!"

She was dreaming, she realized. Sleepwalking again. But then why could she still hear moaning? Was the blood on Austin's chest part of the dream?

Something glinted on the tiles near her foot. She looked down. Then squeezed her eyes shut. A knife, but that must be part of the nightmare. It wasn't real. She opened her eyes. It was still there. The silver glinting beneath the red.

"Austin?"

She brushed her hand under her nose and it came back crimson. A bloody nose. But there was too much. It was all down her arms, she realized. All over her hands.

She turned and looked into the bathroom mirror. Red was splattered across Austin's white T-shirt she was wearing. Smears of it were across her face and clumped in her hair. Her hands were sticky with it. She turned the tap on, rinsed her hands, tried to rub it off. It turned the sink pink.

Outside the door, she could hear crying. Guttural, gulping wheezes. "Austin?"

Sirens. Screeching around the bend and getting closer. The screaming mixing with the crying outside the room.

A bang on the door, then voices, loud and sharp, coming up the stairs. The crackle of a radio and then a man's voice that she'd never heard before. "Ten twenty-three," he said. "ETA on paramedics?"

A crackle in response and then, "Suspect detained in bathroom. Heading in now."

It was the police. The police were here.

"It's all right, it's okay," another male voice was saying. "They're almost here, hang in there."

A banging on the bathroom door. "Put down the weapon, face the wall with your hands up."

She didn't understand.

Then, shouting: "We're coming in! Face the wall with your hands up!"

It was her; they were talking to her. She turned around to the wall next to the bath, rested her hands against it. They left red smudges on the white paint.

Something grated against the door and then it opened, just an inch. She kept her cheek pressed on the wall, but she didn't touch it with her body. The T-shirt was still wet with blood. She didn't want to get it all over the paint. There was something black coming in through the door. A gun. It was a gun!

Then the door swung open and her whole body was thrown flat against the wall. Her arms were jerked down, pulled behind her back, sharp pain cracking up her bones and then something cutting around her wrists.

"You have the right to remain silent. Anything you say can and will be used against you in a court of law. You have the right to an attorney. If you cannot afford an attorney . . ."

"Austin?" she said. "Where's Austin?"

The man kept reciting the words she'd heard on TV, but she wasn't listening. She was pushed out the door into Rani and Brian's bedroom. There was blood on the walls in sprays. Paramedics crowded around someone on the floor near the bed. She was jerked out and down the stairs, tripping on them to try and look back. The two cops held her up by her arms, jerked her shoulder so it jarred with pain.

"What did I do?" she said. "What did I do?"

But she got no reply. They pulled her outside and into the back of a police car. She looked around to her house, saw Casper's light flick on.

"Assault with a deadly weapon, suspect in custody," the cop said into the radio.

The backseat of the police car was covered in plastic. It stuck to her thighs. It was rustling.

"Full name?"

Why was the plastic rustling?

"Your name?" He turned to her. The lights from the ambulance were so bright through the windscreen behind him that she couldn't see his face.

"Olivia Jansen."

Her house was right there.

She tried to get the words out. "My mum?"

She needed strength and care and someone who always fixed everything. She needed her mum.

"Age?" he said.

"Twenty-two."

He said something else to the radio and pulled out from the curb.

"But no, hang on, wait, you have to get my mum."

The car didn't slow. The plastic rustled. It was her who was making it rustle. She was shaking. She tried to still her body, tried to make it stop, but it wouldn't.

She had hurt someone.

"What happened?" she asked again. "What did I do?"

The cops didn't respond.

"Who got hurt?"

The radio crackled—they didn't pick it up.

"Please tell me."

They said nothing.

TWENTY-EIGHT

Casper woke up to the sound of commotion outside. Male voices, car doors banging. He opened his eyes, groggy. He'd gone to the cinema alone last night, watched two movies back-to-back. For a second he thought he was still in one of the movies, that he'd fallen asleep in the chair. But he was home, in his own room. Flashing red and blue lights were shining in through the window. They weren't bright enough for him to see Liv's bed.

Then, from next door, he'd heard a man yelling, "Hands behind your head! Hands behind your head!"

He sat up then. Turned the desk light on. But he already knew. In that millisecond between flicking the switch and the light turning on, as the electricity ran up the wire to the bulb, he knew. Her bed was empty.

He jumped up and ran out into the hallway. He bashed on his parents' door.

"Get up! Something's going on!"

"What?" his dad called out groggily.

"Get up! It's Liv! Quick."

He ran down the stairs, and his hand fumbled to open the front door. He jerked the lock and pulled it open and stepped out into the flashing night.

There was a cop car and an ambulance pulled up out front. Two policemen came out from next door, guiding Liv in front of them. Her hands were handcuffed behind her. She was covered in blood.

He hovered in the doorway, too shocked to move. They pushed her into the car and then the door was shut behind her and then it was too late to do anything, too late to call out or run over or try and stop this somehow. They drove away.

His father appeared next to him, his hair mussed, still in his cotton boxers.

"What's happened?" he said. "Is Liv okay?"

They watched as a stretcher was taken out from the back of the ambulance by two EMTs running toward the house next door.

"Oh my God," Janus said, and was about to run over, but Casper took his arm.

"Don't," he said. "It's not for her, Dad. The cops just took her away. She's done it again. She's hurt someone."

TWENTY-NINE

The lights were bright inside the police station. They took off the handcuffs and fingerprinted her and asked questions. Name, date of birth, address. She tried to answer. The cops took her down a corridor. Their black shoes tap-tap-tapped on the gray linoleum. They opened a door to a small room. The floor in there was white. There was a camera set up on a tripod. The cops spoke to a woman and man wearing plastic over their shoes. She itched her cheek, smearing black ink into the red. She'd wanted to scratch her face since they'd gotten here, but it was the first time no one was holding her arms. Her shoulder ached.

The door clicked shut.

The blood had turned thick and gummy. It glued her T-shirt to her stomach. Her fingers stuck together. When she moved her head, her hair would snap away from her neck.

"Olivia," one of the plastic shoe people said sharply.

"Yes?"

"Stand by the wall, please."

She did what they said.

The click and beep of a camera. Under the fluorescents, the red looked brighter. Neon splotches against the white of her T-shirt and her skin.

"Turn around, please."

She turned to face the wall. She didn't have any pants on. They'd all be able to see her purple undies.

"We're going to take some samples now."

She turned back around. The plastic shoes got closer. She looked up. It was a woman. She was the same age as Liv's mum. But she didn't look her in the eye. She stopped just a few inches from Liv and rubbed a cotton swab over her hands, across her collarbone, down her cheek.

"Do you know what happened?" Liv whispered. "Who did I hurt? Did I . . ."

She couldn't finish it. The word . . . *kill*. It was a hard and gritty lump.

"We need your clothes and we're done here."

Had she spoken? Had she asked the questions? Maybe she'd just thought them, had not even said them aloud.

"My clothes?"

"I'll come with you. You can shower."

They were back in the corridor. The woman's shoes swished on the floor. Liv's feet were bare.

A bathroom area. No windows. Just musty air and damp tiles.

"Hand me your clothes."

The woman stood there, staring at her. Liv looked back. She'd never undressed in front of anyone like this before; she'd only been naked with another person during sex, when their body was close to hers. She pulled the T-shirt up. It ripped free. Her skin smarted—it was like pulling off a Band-Aid. She yanked her underwear off. Gave the woman the lot. Her gaze didn't shift.

The water was lukewarm. But it was a relief. The blood slipped off her. She scrubbed her hair with her fingers, trying to dislodge the lumps. When the water stopped, she looked at the pink puddle at her feet. The white grouting between the tiles had turned pink too. They'd have to bleach it.

She wrapped her arms around herself and turned back around. The person was different now. A woman in uniform.

"Hi," Liv said.

The new woman gave her a rough towel. Liv dried herself, and the woman held out a gray tracksuit. On top were blue Keds.

Liv pulled the tracksuit on, relieved to be clean and covered up.

"What's going to happen now?" she asked as she hopped, pulling on the shoes.

"Holding cell until the detectives are ready for your statement." The uniformed woman grabbed her arm and they started walking. "Then you'll be transferred to Metro for booking."

"What happened?" Liv asked. "Who did I hurt?"

The policewoman looked at her for a long moment; then her grip tightened and she turned toward the door. "You'll have to ask the detectives those sorts of questions."

Liv was used to warmth from women like this. Being called *honey* or *sweetheart*. The way this woman had looked at her, the way they'd all been looking at her, wasn't like anything she'd experienced. Cold, procedural . . . but something else as well. They seemed disgusted by her.

She reached a door and waited; then a loud buzzing tone sounded and the woman pushed it open.

Down one side were three cells. The one closest was full of men.

They all turned to look at her. Liv averted her eyes, stared at the ground.

"Who ordered pink taco?" one of them said, and a bunch started laughing.

She heard shuffles from the next cell and took a quick glance. More men. One came to stand by the bars, staring at her.

"What'd she do?"

She gripped her hands into fists, praying for the last cell to be empty. Her skin turned to prickles under the tracksuit. She couldn't be locked up with all men.

"Caught kissing your boyfriend in someone else's pool? Trespass?"

"Stole some chocolate bars?"

"No, stole a lipstick! Some mascara."

Please be empty. Please be empty.

"Hey, Sandra, what did Becky do?" another male voice called out.

"None of your business," the woman holding Liv's arm said.

"Oh, come on!"

The woman opened the door to the final cell. Liv breathed in and looked up. There was someone there. Just one person, huge and half collapsed in the back corner.

"I'll be back for you soon," Sandra said. Then she locked the cell door and walked back down the corridor. The door shut with a metal crash behind her, then silence. Liv sat down. The bench was cold through the thin fleece of the tracksuit. Liv stared at the person in the corner of her cell. It was a woman, asleep or maybe passed out drunk, her head buried low in her puffy jacket. Liv could smell the rotting tang of booze coming off the woman in waves.

A loud banging from the bars. Liv looked up. There were a couple of men sleeping against the walls in the other cells, but five or six of them were at the bars dividing the cells, staring right at her.

"What'd you do?" the closest guy said. He was tall, pasty white, with a shaved head.

"Leave her," another guy said, the tats up his arm barely visible against his dark skin as he leaned back on the bench. "She don't want to talk to you."

"C'mon, Becky, give us the story," said another guy whose eye was swollen shut. "Don't get little white girls like you in here unless you really fucked up."

He had blood down his front. It looked like it had come from his nose.

"What happened?" Liv asked him.

"Traffic stop," he said. "Don't even get me started. Had it better than him."

He tilted his head toward a guy in the corner. He was probably around eighteen, skinny, with one long-fingered hand holding a wad of tissues to a bleeding scrape up the side of his face and neck.

"What did he do?" Liv asked.

"There was a call about a Black kid with a red beanie on in Los Feliz. He had a red beanie on in Echo, so . . ."

"Is he okay?"

They looked at the kid, but his eyes were closed. Liv's jarred shoulder didn't seem so bad now.

"I think I stabbed someone," Liv said, "my neighbor."

She brought her feet up onto the bench and wrapped her arms around her legs. The woman behind her snorted in her sleep.

"Why'd you do that?" the guy with the tats asked.

"I don't know," she said. "I don't even know which one of them I stabbed. I just woke up because of the screaming."

The shaved-head guy closest to the bars took a step back. "Little bitch is crazy," he said under his breath.

"What you on?" the bruised guy asked.

"Nothing. I . . . I got up and . . ." Liv swallowed. "I stabbed one of them while they slept."

The guy with the black eye let out a long whistle. "You better think of a reason quick. Or act more crazy—insanity defense."

"Just stay silent," tats guy said. "Don't say anything. Little white girl like you can probably get a good lawyer. Keep quiet."

She put her head on her knees. She wanted to scream.

"You kill 'em?"

She peered up at the shaved-head guy. He'd come back to the bars to look at her.

"I don't know."

He stared at her. She put her head back on her knees and listened to the woman next to her snore. Maybe this was all part of her dream. Maybe she was still asleep. She'd wake up in her bed and turn to Casper and tell him how vivid it had been and he'd tell her to shut up and let him sleep and she'd force herself to get up and put on Ginger's leash and go to the dog park, and Austin would be there, waiting.

THEY CUFFED HER again when they took her out of the cell hours later.

"Good luck, Becky!"

"Don't say nothin', all right? Get a lawyer."

"Bye," she said as they reached the door, but maybe it was too quiet for them to hear.

The interview room wasn't what she was expecting. She was imagining cement walls and a big mirror. Instead there were cream walls and no mirror and a long white table with a bunch of rickety chairs and, up in the corner, a video camera.

Two people in plain clothes stood up from the table. A woman with a big smile and shadows under her eyes spoke first: "Hello, Olivia, I'm Detective Sanchez, and this is Detective McGuinness. Come in and take a seat, cariña."

The door closed behind Liv, and she went over to the chair between the head of the table and the wall.

The male detective hadn't looked at her at all yet. He was flipping through a folder, eyes downcast. He was very pale, with freckles across the bridge of his nose and hair that changed from blond to ginger at the temples. His suit was a cheap knockoff Armani.

"How are you, Olivia?" Sanchez asked. "Did they treat you all right?"

She should ask for a phone call. Ask for a lawyer.

"Yes." Her voice sounded so small.

"Well, we're here to get this all straightened out for you, okay, cariño? Let's sort it out."

Cariño. She'd heard Carlos call Maria that. Maybe they didn't think she was a monster. She felt herself relax, just a little.

"Okay," she said.

"Those cuffs aren't hurting, are they? Not too tight?"

She was smiling at Liv, her hair long and shiny and parted down the middle. She had a mother's air about her.

"They're okay." Liv's hands were cuffed at the front of her body rather than the back, which hurt her shoulder a lot less.

"Do you need a glass of water?"

Actually, her throat was parched and aching, but she didn't want to be left alone with McGuinness. He still hadn't looked at her.

"I'm fine."

"Well, let's go through what happened, okay? For the record."

She looked up at the video camera.

"But I don't know," she said. "I don't know what happened. No one will tell me."

"You can just start with what you remember, all right? Start from the beginning."

"Is Austin okay?"

"Let's start from the start."

McGuinness looked up at her then; he smiled too. "You must be really tired," he said.

"Who did I hurt?" Liv whispered, holding his gaze. "Are they going to be all right?"

McGuinness's smile froze. "You don't know who you hurt?"

"We just need your statement," Sanchez cut in. "We need to hear everything from your perspective first."

"And then you'll tell me?"

Sanchez nodded once.

"I bet you can't wait to get back to your own bed," McGuinness said. "Let's get this over with so you can get home, all right?"

Home. The word was golden. So it wasn't that bad. They understood that she hadn't meant it. And if she could go home, maybe what she'd done looked worse than it was. Maybe she'd dreamed all the screaming.

"But the blood," she said out loud. "There was so much blood."

Austin's face. She remembered it. He had blood all over him too. He'd looked terrified.

"Was it Austin? Did I hurt Austin?"

Or Rani. Lovely Rani with her silk scarves and her bright paintings and her warmth. Or Brian. Kind Brian. Giving her sips from his gin and always overpaying her. Or Maria. No. That was incomprehensible.

"Olivia," Sanchez said, "start from the start."

"When is the start? I don't remember it."

She wanted to go home. To get in bed. To see Casper and her mother and father.

"Last night. You slept at the Davis house, correct?"

Her head on Austin's chest. His hands in her hair. He said he'd stay awake. He said he'd watch over her.

"Yeah. That's right."

"And what were you doing? Drinking? Did you take something?"

"What?"

McGuinness leaned forward. "You're not in trouble for that, Olivia. We just need to understand what went on."

"No. We were just watching movies."

"Okay." McGuinness leaned back. He didn't seem to believe her. It was like she'd disappointed him.

"And what is your relationship with Austin Davis?"

"Um . . ." She wanted to be honest, but she wasn't sure how to answer that. "We're friends . . ." she said, "and maybe more? We've hooked up a few times."

Sanchez wrote that down.

"He didn't want to be your boyfriend? Pretty girl like you, I'd have thought he'd want to make it official. Did that upset you?"

Sanchez was talking to her like they were gossiping at school.

"No," she said, "no, not at all. We like each other. It was . . ."

Sweet, she wanted to say. *Magical.*

Something wasn't right. They weren't treating her in a way that made any sense. But she just had to tell the story, she remembered. Tell the story and they'd fill in the gaps.

"So I stayed at Austin's. I was . . . I hadn't slept much. I've been having sleep issues. He said he'd stay awake and watch over me."

"But you got up."

"I guess."

"And you'd gone to the Davis house before in the middle of the night? You'd broken in."

"Yeah. I mean . . . I have sleep issues. I sleepwalked," she said. "I'm a sleepwalker."

They looked at each other. Just for a fraction of a second, but she caught it. That look. *Bullshit*. That's what they were thinking. *Bullshit*.

"It's true."

Sanchez smiled at her. "So you broke into the Davis house . . . sleepwalking."

"I wouldn't say I broke in. I had the key. I'm their babysitter. Well . . . I was."

"And after you broke in, you . . ." She looked at her notes. "You went to House of Pies in Los Feliz. Then you went next door again in the middle of the night after an altercation with your brother."

"Wait, how do you know that? Austin told you?"

If Austin told them, it must mean he was okay.

"This boy you like . . ." Sanchez went on. "You keep going to his house in the middle of the night. What about last night? Did he reject you?"

"What? No, no. I have these nightmares and . . . like I said, I sleepwalk . . . and last night, I don't know . . . I don't know what I did, that's what I'm trying to say. I woke up with that knife and all that blood everywhere. I didn't mean to . . . Whatever I did, I didn't mean to do it."

They stared at her, impassive. Then McGuinness leaned forward.

"How about this," he said. "You liked Austin, right? You wanted him. You watched him through your window. He's a good-looking guy, I get it. So you went to his house. Wanted to show him how much you liked him. He sleeps with you. He uses you. Then he tells you he doesn't want you. He's going back to his ritzy college and he's leaving you behind."

"What— No!"

"Last night, he drops you. That makes you angry. You feel stupid, rejected—"

"No!"

"C'mon, cariña," Sanchez said, "just tell us. We've all been there. Boys can be pricks."

It hit her then. Hard. Sometimes you felt danger in the pit of your stomach. A tightening clench. Sometimes it prickled across your skin. But right now, she could smell it. She could smell the danger in that room with those detectives smiling at her and calling her pet names and telling her she'd be going home soon. It stank.

She remembered the guy's advice: *Say nothing. Get a lawyer.* She'd watched enough cop shows to be smarter than this.

She crossed her arms over her chest.

"Let us help you," Sanchez said.

She leaned back in the chair.

"You're only making this more difficult if you don't cooperate."

Liv said nothing. They looked at each other.

"All right," Sanchez said, and her smile was gone and she didn't look like a mother anymore. "All right, if that's what you want. But you're an adult and your crime was heinous. Three stab wounds, deep ones, right in the chest. You'll be tried here in the United States. And if Brian Davis dies, you're looking at first-degree murder."

THIRTY

Janus watched the sun rise through the glass doors of the police station. He'd been waiting there with Casper since three in the morning. Casper was leaning back in the bench seat, his head resting against the wall, staring up at a flickering fluorescent light.

"I just hope she's asked for a lawyer," Janus said again. "I wish they'd let me go in there and tell her."

Janus had spent the last four hours researching American law on his phone, and now his battery was about to die. Casper kept staring at the flickering light.

"I wish I knew Morse code." It was the first time Casper had spoken to him in over an hour.

"What? Why?"

"Maybe there's someone locked away in there that's figured out how to send messages through the electricals. It's wasted on me. I don't even know SOS."

"You can go home if you need to, son. Get some rest."

"Where's Mum?" Casper said.

"I've texted her. It's still early, she probably hasn't seen it yet."

"Yesterday you said you'd be honest with me now. No more bullshit."

"I . . ." Janus took a breath. "I just want to protect you. This is . . . It's a lot."

"Bullshit won't protect me."

"Okay, all right, enough with the language. I'm being honest though, I don't know where your mother is."

"She didn't say where she was going?"

"No."

It flashed through his mind again. Kay on her knees, Carlos wrapping his hand around the back of her head. Could she be with him? Had Kay not just left him, but left him for someone else?

Casper looked at him. "Why do you think Liv would hurt Brian?"

Janus looked up at the desk sergeant, but he was too far away to hear.

"I have no idea. Maybe it was an accident."

"Do you really believe that?"

"Honestly, Cas, I don't know what to think right now. What do you think?"

Casper pulled his feet up onto the seat and wrapped his arms around his legs, turning himself into a ball of lanky teenager. "You didn't see her," he said. "I did. I saw her get into the car. She was completely soaked in blood. I can't get it out of my head."

"I wish you hadn't had to see that."

Casper rested his chin on his knees.

The sunrise was turning the sky pink above the laundromat across the road. It would be evening in Melbourne right now, a Sunday. If he hadn't dragged his family over here, Casper would be getting ready for bed. It would be the middle of winter, and he'd be curling up under his quilts, warm and safe in their boring little suburb. If they were back home, none of this would have happened.

Janus watched as a crappy-looking Honda squeaked to a stop outside. A man got out, tucking his shirt into his slacks. He looked like he'd just woken up; his dark hair was messy, and he tried to smooth it down, bending over to look at his reflection in the side mirror.

A few people had been in and out of the station while they waited. A woman who'd sat on the benches and cried silently, a mother who'd come and picked up a teenager with a black eye.

The man came in and talked to the desk sergeant. Janus noticed him nod toward them. He sat up straighter, pushed Casper's feet off the seat.

The guy walked up to them.

"Hi, you're Olivia Jansen's family?"

"Yes," Janus said, fumbling to put his phone into his pocket.

The man shook his hand. "I'm Giovanni Conti, I'll be Olivia's public defender." He shook Casper's hand next.

"I'm Janus and this is Casper." He took a breath. "I'm so relieved she's got a lawyer."

"She requested me. She's holding off answering any more questions until I get in there."

"Good girl," he said quietly.

"Now, there really is no point in you both sitting around here waiting. I can call you—"

"We'll wait," he said.

Giovanni smiled. He had dimples. Janus wasn't sure if LA-hardened lawyers should have dimples.

"Well, why don't you wait at the diner around the corner. I haven't had breakfast yet and I'm starving and you both look like you need some coffee. I'll meet you there." When neither of them moved, his dimples disappeared. "Look. Olivia's crime is serious. She won't be going anywhere until her arraignment hearing, which won't be for a while. You're not helping her by getting sore butts sitting here."

Janus looked at Casper, who did look exhausted.

"All right. What's the name of the diner?"

IT FELT STRANGE to leave the station without her. They made their way to the diner, only a five-minute walk away. It was all sky blue booths and white plastic tables. They slid into a booth, and the waiter brought them ice water.

"Hello, folks, having a great morning?"

Casper snorted a laugh. The waiter looked at him, confused.

"Fine, thanks. We're fine," Janus said. "We'll both have coffees to start with."

"Would you like to see some menus?"

"We're waiting for someone."

"All righty. No problem."

When the waiter left, it was silent. At the police station, it had felt like they should be quiet, but now, looking at each other across the table, they needed to talk. Janus needed to get his son through this as unscathed as possible.

"The lawyer," he attempted, "Giovanni. He seemed . . . competent."

"Young," Casper said.

He nodded. "Maybe that's good. You know, he's not jaded yet. He'll try."

"Yeah, hopefully."

"When he gets here, we need him to see that this is all some kind of misunderstanding."

Casper snorted again.

"Cas, he doesn't know Liv. He probably sees ugly things like this all the time. He might just assume she's . . . I don't know, on drugs or homicidal or that sort of thing. He'll assume she's a violent person."

Casper looked down at the table, and Janus knew what he was remembering. They'd watched the stretcher come out of the house. EMTs, red blood everywhere, a breathing mask over Brian's face as he was loaded into the back of the ambulance.

"He doesn't know Liv," Janus said again. "We need to make sure he understands that this was a—"

"It wasn't," Casper cut in.

"You don't know that for sure."

"I think she was sleepwalking."

Their waiter came back. He poured two coffees and then placed a silver jug of half-and-half in the middle of the table. He must have felt the tension, because he didn't try for pleasantries this time.

When he was gone, Janus leaned forward. "Sleepwalking?"

"Yes. I share a room with her, remember? I think that's what happened last time."

"No, she was drunk driving. It was an accident. This would have been intentional. It's totally different."

"Dad," Casper said slowly, "it was Liv who gave me this." He traced the shadow that was still under his eye with his fingertip.

"She hit you?" Janus asked.

He nodded. "In her sleep . . . she was having a nightmare . . . she attacked me when I surprised her."

Janus put his head in his hands. He should have pushed harder when he'd asked Cas about it. He'd known his son was lying to him. Lacrosse, what a joke.

Casper went on. "I don't think she was drunk driving last time either. I think she was asleep. Driving in her sleep."

"That's impossible."

"It's not. I've googled it."

"The internet doesn't know everything, Cas. It's . . . maybe not impossible. But implausible. Very implausible."

"Not really. I found a subreddit and heaps of sleepwalkers say they've done it. Like one girl kept going through the McDonald's drive-through. She'd wake up surrounded by burgers."

"How could you drive without seeing the road?"

"I don't know the science of it. I guess if you know the route really well?"

"But you can't anticipate hazards. What if something got in your way?"

"You'd go right through it," Casper said, raising his eyebrows. Janus remembered that blank expression on Liv's face. All this time he'd worried about that expression, about how she'd looked at Hélène like she couldn't see her. Maybe she actually couldn't.

"I went and spoke to her friend," Casper went on. "To Leilani. She said that Liv was in some sort of . . . like a fugue state, when she left her house. Leilani said she was really out of it when she got in the car."

"Drunk driving."

"No. Both Liv and Leilani said they only had two drinks."

"So . . . she doesn't even know she did it?"

"I don't think she has any idea."

A huge weight lifted from Janus. His daughter wasn't being callous; she wasn't unfeeling. But sleepwalking? Janus massaged his eye sockets. He was too tired to get his head around it. But he had to. He was the adult here. All of this lay on his shoulders. If he didn't step up, if he just let things happen, he was essentially damning his daughter. He pulled his phone out and called Kay. It went straight to voicemail again. Wherever she was, she'd turned off her phone.

He looked back up to his son. Casper was staring at him, waiting for a reaction. For him to do something.

"Why didn't you tell me and your mother this earlier?"

"Our house has hardly been a place of open communication! Anyway, I didn't even put it together until yesterday when I had all the information."

Janus's throat tightened. He took a sip of water, but it was so cold it made him cough.

"I'm getting some air," he managed, his voice strangled.

He went out to the street. The traffic had started up properly now. The air stank of exhaust. Everything looked too bright. He leaned against a wire fence that was surrounding the empty lot next to the diner and tried to breathe. But he couldn't. It was loud and the air was thick with fumes and this was too much for him. It was too much. He had no idea how to make any of this okay.

He pulled out his phone and called Kay again, clenched his eyes shut hoping it wouldn't go to voicemail. But it did. Of course it did. He lit a cigarette and took a long, slow drag. The nicotine filled his veins, and God, how had he been a nonsmoker for so long? These things were lifesavers.

For a moment he thought of his novel, of Angela. What would she do in this situation? But it didn't help. That was fiction. A world where he controlled all the variables, where things made sense. He had no control here. Taking refuge in his made-up stories wasn't going to help him now. Maybe it never had. It was just a way of hiding from the real world.

He spotted Giovanni rushing across the road while the light was red and turned away. He took another quick drag and then put out the cigarette. He imagined Liv sitting in some soulless room somewhere, alone, confused. She was relying on her father. And he was going to step up. He was going to figure this out for her.

When he made his way back into the diner, he was feeling stronger. He swung back into the booth just before Giovanni came in.

"Remember," he said to Casper. "We need this lawyer to be on her side. To know what kind of person Liv is."

Casper nodded. Finally, they were on the same page.

"What happened?" he asked Giovanni as soon as he slotted himself in next to Casper, but the lawyer was more focused on getting the attention of the waiter.

"Have you ordered food?" he asked them.

"I'm not hungry," Janus said, then looked at Casper, who also shook his head.

Once the lawyer had ordered, he looked back to Janus. "Okay, so they've charged her with attempted murder." Giovanni put a hand up. "I know that sounds bad, but it could be a lot worse. I'm going to try and plead them down to aggravated assault in the first degree."

"Oh God," whispered Casper.

"Charging her is a good thing. A very good thing," Giovanni said, and then "Thank you" to the waiter when his coffee was set down in front of him. He filled it up to the rim with half-and-half. "They might have held off a couple of days to see if Mr. Davis's condition worsened. That would mean Olivia waiting in lockup until they did."

"What if it does . . . worsen?" Janus asked him.

"You mean what if he dies? They'll add charges then. But better not to worry about that scenario just yet. For now, a prompt charge is good. I've called the judge, and I'm hoping to squeeze in her arraignment late this afternoon so that, all going well, she can sleep at home."

"That's fantastic. Truly. Thank you," Janus said. He didn't want his daughter staying another night in that place.

The waiter came back to their table with a big plate of scrambled eggs and toast for Giovanni. "Refill too please," he said, holding up his cup. "Sure you all aren't hungry?"

"We're sure," Casper said, looking unimpressed.

Giovanni shoveled eggs into his mouth. Janus and Casper watched him chew.

"So, what happens at the arraignment?" Janus asked.

"That's where they set bail." Janus could see the little bits of egg inside Giovanni's mouth as he talked. "You'll need to pull some money together, fast. It will be a lot. I'd say one, maybe one fifty."

A new wave of panic spread through Janus. "Sorry? Do you mean one hundred and fifty thousand American dollars?"

"Yep," Giovanni said, still chewing, "but you only need a ten per-cent deposit, remember."

"So fifteen thousand?" he said.

Giovanni nodded. "The other thing is to all come and look like a nice, loving, supportive family. That's what I've got to sell at this point. That Liv isn't some crazed teen who'll run off."

"She won't," Janus said. "You have to understand that Olivia is not a bad person. There will be a completely innocent explanation to all this. It will all make sense once we know the full story."

Giovanni put his fork down on his empty plate. "She says she was sleepwalking."

"It's true," Casper said immediately. "I've seen her do it."

Giovanni raised an eyebrow at him and downed his coffee. Then he stood up.

"You're leaving already?" Janus said.

"I am. It looks like I've got a bit of case law to read up on. You just focus on getting that bail together and leave the legal side of this to me."

Giovanni threw a few bills onto the table, and then he was gone.

"Do we have fifteen thousand dollars?" Casper asked.

Janus took a breath. "We have a bit of savings. And maybe my parents can pitch in a few thousand."

"And Grandma too."

Janus nodded. Kay's mother was wealthy. Janus had never gotten on well with Kay's mum—he'd even based a villain in his book off of her—but that didn't matter now. She was family. They had never asked her for money in the past; Kay had always insisted that they never could, but this was urgent. Yes, between their savings and Kay's mother, they would be able to work this out. It was going to be okay.

THIRTY-ONE

Casper poured black coffee into a mug. His dad was sitting at the dining room table, his head in his hands. The laptop was in front of him, their bank account open. Casper came around behind his dad to put the coffee down, and looked over his shoulder. Their total balance was only $1,802.

"Shit," said Casper.

Janus started, then slapped down the laptop screen. "Don't look at that."

"Too late."

Casper took a breath and then sat down next to his father at the table. "Why are we broke?"

His dad dragged his fingers over his eyelids and down his cheeks. "I don't know. Your mum withdrew a few hundred in cash last night and she transferred a hell of a lot of money out a few days ago."

"To who?"

"I don't know. It's a Venmo."

"How much?"

His dad looked at him, and Casper could tell he was weighing up whether to be honest with him or not. Casper raised his eyebrows, daring him to try and bullshit him again.

"Twenty grand."

"Whoa. Why would she do that?"

"I don't know."

His dad's phone dinged and he clutched at it. "Giovanni," he said out loud, his eyes skimming the message. "He's managed to get her an arraignment for two p.m."

Casper checked the time. "But that's in three hours!"

"I know."

His father put his face in his hands.

"I already emailed Maggie . . . she's the producer for the script. I thought it was finished and maybe that would be our Hail Mary, you know? Our deus ex machina?"

Casper looked at him blankly, but he continued anyway.

"Apparently, because there are still tweaks I . . . God, I've really messed things up. I was an accountant for over twenty years and somehow I didn't notice just how dire our finances have become. I'm so sorry, Casper. I never should have brought us here. You hate it, Liv's in much worse trouble than she ever would have gotten into back home, and turns out your mother was just trying to make me happy. I got too excited. It was selfish."

"No," Casper said. "You're allowed to have aspirations and stuff, Dad. Me and Liv . . . we wouldn't want you to give that up for us. I know I complained about coming here, but it's your dream come true, it's—"

"It really isn't. You know, I don't even like writing scripts. In fact, to be honest, I hate it. It's so regimented. I want to be able to write about the way things smell, the way things feel under your hands. Screenplays are so cold."

He smiled at Casper.

"My dream is your mother and you and Olivia. I already have my dream."

"God, that's so corny!"

"It is, isn't it? But it's true. And I'm going to take care of this. I'm going to get the money."

"How?"

"I'll call Oma and Opa. I'll call Grandma. Old friends too. I'll figure it out, Casper. You go have a shower."

"I have three hundred dollars," Casper said.

Janus nodded. "Thanks, son. See, that brings us over a thousand. We'll get there."

Casper didn't believe him, but voicing that wouldn't help right now. Ever since he'd seen that hand coming out of the dirt yesterday afternoon, things hadn't felt quite real. It was like he was floating above his body.

He went up to the bathroom, pulled off his clothes, and turned the shower on. Casper completely stank, and he needed a few minutes to himself. He stepped in and closed his eyes, letting the warm water spray straight onto his face. He wanted to get rid of this floaty feeling. He had to face what had happened, because it was real; it was the reality he was now in. His dad was facing it and he had to as well. Liv had killed Hélène. Liv might have killed Brian. His mother had buried a body. His mother had left them. His mother had drained their bank account. All of it was impossible, but it had happened. And the text messages. He should have guessed something was off; none of them sounded much like Hélène at all. She only ever sent simple messages of just a few words to organize his visits, and yet he'd believed that she was suddenly having deep and meaningful exchanges with him, when they had always reserved those for when they spoke in person. If his mother had wanted to know what he was feeling, she could have asked. Why go about it in such a weird and creepy way? He knew it was true; he'd seen her face when she'd admitted it. Still, it didn't seem possible. He couldn't get any of it to seem real. It was like his head was crammed with cotton wool.

He tried to take deep breaths, to ground himself. He had to get it together. He wanted to be strong, like his dad was being. Strong but open, ready to fight for the people who mattered. He turned the water off, pressed his hands against the tiles. Then the thought came back. The one he didn't want to be thinking. The one that had kept jamming into his cotton wool head at the police station. Liv's body count was growing. Maybe she shouldn't come home? Maybe she needed to be locked up someplace where she couldn't hurt anyone else?

He got out of the shower and toweled himself dry, then sat on the edge of the bed, trying to blink back the tiredness.

COMING BACK DOWNSTAIRS, he could hear his dad on the phone.

"And when was this? . . . Okay . . . yes, I get it. No, I didn't know that . . . No, we know you're not an ATM. This is serious though, she could go to prison, American prison, which is brutal and . . . Okay. Fine. I get it." He hung up the phone.

"Who was that?" Casper said, coming into the kitchen.

But his dad didn't reply. He was just staring at the table, his face all crumpled up.

"Dad?"

He blinked and looked up at Casper. "That was Grandma."

"And, what? She's not going to help?"

"No. She's not."

Casper didn't feel like he could push this time. His dad was pale, like he might pass out.

"Why don't you go have a shower too, Dad? Or have something to eat at least."

"We've only got two and a half hours now. It'll take half an hour to drive there. So that's two hours. We have two hours."

"What about Oma and Opa?"

"I called them first."

Casper waited, but his dad didn't elaborate. "And?!"

"And they just moved into that retirement village, remember? You can't remortgage those kinds of places, it doesn't work like that. They are going to empty their bank account. But that's only three thousand dollars. I mean, they're on a pension."

"Did you try Uncle Gerrit?"

His dad's brother was on some big trip with his fiancée around Europe. Surely that meant he had money if he was able to go traveling for a whole month.

"I've emailed him but haven't heard back. His phone isn't connected over there so I don't know how else to get through to him." His dad's eyes didn't leave the laptop screen.

"Do you think he'll come through?"

"I don't know. Maybe. Although they booked their trip all on credit cards."

"Why don't we get credit cards? Or a loan?"

"You need assets, Cas. We have no money, this house is a rental. I'm technically not even employed. I just . . . I've been so focused on the script. When they accepted the final version, it was going to be such a big payday, so I haven't been paying attention to how much our balance has been dwindling this whole time. I knew we had that savings account, so I didn't . . ."

"But Mum took that. And now we don't know where she is."

"She just needed some time to think."

"And twenty thousand dollars?"

He shook his head. "No, no, no. It makes no sense. No, she wouldn't. It's just . . . No. That's not who she is . . . There's an explanation, there has to be."

There was a knock on the door.

They looked at each other; then Casper went over to the window. He was relieved when he saw who it was.

"It's okay. It's just Tye."

He went over and opened the door. Tye smiled with relief when he saw him.

"Sorry to just barge over. I heard that something bad went down outside your place last night and then you weren't replying to my texts and . . . I got worried."

"It's fine, come in. It's good you're here."

Casper shut the door behind Tye and they looked into the kitchen.

"Go upstairs," his dad said. "I'm about to call my producer, my publisher, and just about everyone who I've ever tried to impress, and it's going to be humiliating. I don't want an audience."

"Maybe have some toast first?" Casper said.

His dad nodded, but he didn't get up from the chair. Casper climbed the stairs, Tye behind him.

He kicked his dirty clothes under his bed when they got into his room and then sat down on his unmade sheets, pushing himself up into the corner with his legs crossed. Tye sat on the edge next to him.

"Are you all right?" Tye said. "You look really . . . I don't know. Pale and strange."

Casper nodded. "It's been a . . . bad day."

"What happened? Is it something to do with those ambulances and cops?" Tye looked around. "Where's Liv? And your mum? Did they get hurt?"

"No. No, it was Liv. She did the hurting."

"Oh."

"She . . . Apparently she stabbed our next-door neighbor while he was in bed asleep. Like, a bunch of times. He's alive . . . but it's not good."

"Whoa." Tye leaned back against the wall. "Shit."

"Yep."

"Is it on the news?"

Casper hadn't even thought of that. He grabbed his phone, opened Google, and typed in Liv's name. Nothing recent came up. He loaded a news site, skimming for reports of a stabbing.

"Looks like she chose a good weekend to attack someone. See—" He showed his phone to Tye. There was hurricane in the South, a shooting on the East Coast, and a beloved sitcom actor getting me-too'd here in California.

"The American trifecta," Casper said, and flicked his phone back onto the bed.

"So she's like . . . in jail?"

"We're trying to get the bail money together."

He could hear the faint sound of his dad's voice from downstairs, but he didn't strain to listen. He didn't want to hear him beg.

Tye's brow was furrowed, and he was chewing the inside of his cheek.

"Do you . . ." Tye said slowly. "I don't know. It just . . . it makes me reconsider stuff about our mystery, you know?"

Casper was about to explain. To catch Tye up on everything, to tell him the real truth. But he stopped. He couldn't tell Tye. He couldn't tell anyone. Not ever. He trusted Tye, of course he did, but he couldn't risk sharing this secret. Plus, the weight of it, the heaviness of such an ugly truth—he didn't want to inflict that on someone else.

"Sorry," Tye said. "Is that a really rude thing to say?"

"No . . . it's just, I found out. What happened with Liv. I found the truth."

Tye looked at him, then slowly nodded. "You can't tell me, can you?"

"I don't think you want me to. It's . . . not nice. I don't think Liv is doing any of this intentionally. I think . . . well, I think she needs help. I think there is something wrong with her."

"Something that can be fixed?"

Casper thought about his sister. Of the way she'd looked after she'd hit him, all wrapped up in the blanket on the bed across from his, so upset by what she'd done and looking so pathetic and familiar.

"Yeah. I think so. She's a good person."

Tye didn't say anything at first, and then, "I have five hundred dollars. You can have it. For the bail."

"Oh, I wasn't asking you for money."

"I know you weren't. But I also know that if she really is a good person, if this isn't her fault, then she shouldn't be in jail, Cas. It's not going to help her. It'll just make everything worse."

"Are you sure?"

"Yeah. I can go home and get it now. It's just in a shoebox under my bed, all the cash from birthday cards and from feeding my neighbor's cats."

Casper imagined it. A shoebox full of cash. And then it came to him. The answer. And it was so horrible, so awful, that his throat tightened and he was terrified he was going to cry in front of Tye.

"Are you okay?"

"I just . . ." Casper said. "I thought I understood how things worked. I thought I knew what right was and what wrong was. But now it's a big ugly blur. And I'm right in the middle of it. I don't want to be a bad person. I don't want to be part of all this."

"You're not a bad person," Tye said, and he reached over and grabbed Casper's hand in his, squeezing it. He went to pull away, but Casper held on.

"They're gone. Mum is gone and Liv is gone and . . ." He was about to say Hélène was gone, Hélène was gone for good, but he couldn't. All he knew right now was that he didn't want Tye to go. He needed Tye here, with him. He interlocked his fingers with Tye's, and that feeling of their skin skimming together, of Tye's fingers coming to rest in the gaps between his own, sent sparks up his wrist. He looked up at Tye, waiting for him to pull away. Waiting for the embarrassment and the weirdness. But Tye didn't move.

"What would you do?" he asked Tye. "If it was someone you loved?"

Then, finally, Tye's eyes came up and met his. He'd never seen Tye look like that before. His face was so open, brimming over with emotion. He pulled Casper's hand toward his face and rested it against his cheek. Casper's stomach dropped and finally, finally, the cotton wool feeling left his head. He was back in his body and everything was solid.

Tye held his gaze. "If it was someone I loved, then to hell with right and wrong. I would do anything to protect them."

HÉLÈNE'S HOUSE LOOKED just like it had the last time Casper had been there. The framed photographs, the spices all lined up behind the stove, the bottles of liqueur in the glass cabinet, the laminate kitchen table, the blue woven rug on the floor. But the vase of fresh-cut flowers she always had on her table was gone, and the throw she used as a blanket was neatly folded on one arm of the couch. Already, it smelled different. It smelled stuffy and still. That smell that houses got when no one lived there anymore.

He had wanted to get in and out of her place as quickly as possible. But now he sat down at the kitchen table. Just a few weeks ago he'd sat in this very spot, laughing at one of Hélène's stories. Telling her about his life and drinking Chambord and feeling so adult. He picked up the framed picture from the table. It was old, maybe from the 1970s; the colors were all blown out. Hélène was there, young and vibrant. She was standing with three other young people. Two men in collared shirts and a woman in a brown suede vest. The woman looked a bit like Hélène, something in the eyes. It was probably her sister, the one who had died last year. Hélène had wanted to lay purple carnations on her grave. She never would now. Casper put the picture back; then he knelt down by the liquor cabinet. He moved aside the Chambord and took out the Tuica box.

Back home, his father was still at the kitchen table. He had a pad in front of him covered in numbers; his hair was sticking up on end from him running his hands through it. His face had turned gray rather than white. He probably still hadn't eaten. Neither had Casper, come to think of it.

"Dad," he said, coming into the kitchen, the box in his hands.

"I can't talk, Casper. We only have an hour. One hour. I've got to six thousand, so nowhere near enough. But I've thought of some other people to call."

Casper opened the Tuica box and emptied the rolls of cash onto the table. Janus stared.

"How?" he finally said.

"Hélène didn't like banks. And she'd say any thief who wanted to drink prune-flavored brandy was welcome to her money."

Janus looked up at his son. "No, Cas, no. You shouldn't have done that. I'd never ask you to do that."

"You didn't."

"But you're complicit now, son."

"I know," he said, and sat down to count the cash.

CASPER HAD THOUGHT everything would go slowly at the courthouse, but it was the opposite. Everything went in fast-forward. They'd barely been sitting on the wooden bench in the courthouse a few minutes when Rani and her son came in—he didn't know where Maria was. They sat on the other side with their heads down. Casper tried to glance at them, but it was hard. There were people in suits milling around, and lots of guards in khaki uniforms. Another arraignment had only just finished, and they were all still standing around, talking and looking at paperwork.

And then, within a few seconds, everything went silent. The extra people were gone and the doors at the front opened and two guards led Liv in. She was wearing a gray tracksuit that was too big for her. She looked tiny between the guards. Casper felt his dad crumple next to him when he saw her. He wasn't sure if it was from relief or from horror at seeing her like this. Liv's hands were cuffed at her front, and each guard was holding one of her arms. She looked around, lost, until she was shuffled into the seat next to Giovanni. He whispered something to her and she nodded.

The judge came in and everyone stood. He was wearing black robes, and there was a huge American flag behind his desk.

Casper kept his eyes on Liv. She stole a glance over her shoulder, straight to Rani's son. But his eyes were on the ground. The guy looked exhausted, his shirt creased and his hair messy.

"Please be seated," the judge said, and everyone sat in unison.

The judge started reading off case numbers and naming everyone who was in the room. He read the charge out: *attempted murder*. It sounded so brutal in this cold, fluorescently lit room.

Liv looked over her shoulder again. This time, the son was looking straight at her. Casper watched the glance held between them; then the son turned away back to the judge. Liv bowed her head. Giovanni put a hand on her back, but Casper could see the tiny jerk in her shoulders. She was trying to stop herself from crying.

"Mr. Conti," the judge read, "does the trial information reflect your client's correct name and other identifying information?"

Giovanni stood. "Yes, it does, Your Honor."

"Does she waive the reading of the trial information, or does she require the court to read it aloud?"

"No, Your Honor, we waive a formal reading."

"All right. Miss Olivia Jansen, how do you plead?"

Liv stood. Her voice shook as she spoke. "Not guilty."

"To all charges?"

"That's correct, Your Honor," Giovanni said for her.

"All right," the judge said. He sounded bored. He started reeling off the dates and other numbers. And then, finally, he said it.

"Miss Jansen, given your spotless record and your stable home situation, I am willing to allow conditional release until the trial date. However, your crime was extremely violent. I must take that into account. Bail is set for one hundred thousand."

Casper felt his dad go still next to him. Between the money his dad had sourced and Hélène's savings, they had scrounged $11,000. They had enough for the ten percent deposit. They'd done it.

The judge banged his gavel and then that was it. Liv was led away from the courtroom. She didn't look back this time.

People for the next case were filing in. Another family with glassy eyes—whether they were the family of the victim or the perpetrator, who knew.

CASPER SAT DOWN on the bench while his father paid the bondsman through a glass window. He felt like he was falling through the bench into the ground. Falling into the cheap green linoleum to the sewers underneath to the thick hard earth.

After a few minutes a door opened behind the glass and Liv came through with one of the men in khaki. She was still wearing the tracksuit. It wasn't like she could wear the clothes she came in with; Casper guessed they were probably in a plastic evidence bag in some back room somewhere.

Olivia didn't look up at them. Instead she stared at her hands as the guard undid her handcuffs, then she rubbed her wrists. He showed her some paperwork, which she signed. And then the guard opened the glass door for her and she came out toward them.

He waited for her to run to them, to hug them, to start crying. To smile even. But she just calmly walked over.

"Liv," his dad said. "Thank God. Are you okay?"

He wrapped his arms around her in a hug, then stood back and looked at her. Her face was pale and empty.

"I'm okay," she said, her voice so quiet Casper could barely hear her. He leaned over and hugged her too, but her body was stiff. She didn't hug him back.

His dad put a hand on her shoulder and squeezed. "Come on," he said. "Let's get you home."

She nodded. "Thanks," she said in that same quiet voice. She didn't ask where their mother was.

They walked together in silence to the Uber. She sat in the seat right behind their father and stared out the window, so she didn't see. But Casper did. His father never made a sound, but he had tears dripping down his cheeks the whole way home.

THIRTY-TWO

Day after day, Liv lay in bed, blinds pulled against all that bright-
ness outside. Her ankle was tethered to the bedpost, in case she
dozed off. She scrolled Instagram on her phone, back turned to the
room. It worked for a while. The bright colored photographs revolving against her corneas. A makeup tutorial to look like Lady Gaga, a
woman riding a horse nude, a birth announcement. It stopped her
thinking about the case against her, or her time imprisoned, or the
fact that she might go back there. It stopped her thinking about Brian
lying in a hospital room somewhere. It stopped her thinking about
Austin.

When the sun started to set on the third day, her dad seemed to
decide it was time for her to get up. Her dad came and sat on the end
of the bed and patted the tether on her ankle. She flinched away. He
pretended not to notice.

"You don't need to have that on all the time," he said. "It's really
just for sleeping."

"I don't want to risk it."

He looked at her for a moment, but didn't argue. "I just ordered pizza. Casper and I are going to watch a movie."

"I'm not hungry."

"At least just come down and sit with us. We'll watch a comedy. Something light."

"I'm really tired."

Her dad patted her ankle again, then stood. "Okay. Your call."

She stayed where she was. She didn't want to eat. She didn't want to talk to anyone, even her family. She couldn't bear for them to even look at her. She just wanted to be alone. To take the pills that the doctor gave her that would take away her dreams. Still, even with them, even with the tether, she was afraid to sleep.

A while later, her father came back in with a box of pizza.

"We saved you a half. You have to eat, Liv."

"I know."

He put the box in front of her. She took a slice of cheese pizza out and bit into it. She couldn't taste it.

"I've organized your appointment with the psychiatrist for the morning after next, okay? I think that might really help. We'll go to the station later that day for another interview, but Giovanni will be there for the whole thing, so it won't be like last time."

"Will I have to go home? Back to Australia?"

"I don't know," he said. "Maybe if you're convicted. But you'll stand trial here. That's something to ask Gio the details about, okay?"

"Okay."

"But you aren't going to be convicted, Liv. All right? That isn't going to happen."

"Have you heard from her?" She didn't need to say who. Her father knew.

"Not yet."

She nodded. Took another bite. Forced herself to chew.

"You aren't the reason why she left. It was before . . . you know. It's between me and her."

"Dad?" she said, putting the pizza slice down.

"Yes?"

"I don't believe you."

He held her gaze for a moment, and then stood. "She'll be back. She loves you."

But there was doubt in his voice, and he left her and went back downstairs. Liv stared at the ceiling. She thought of her childhood bedroom in their first house, the two-bedroom bungalow they'd lived in before Casper had been born and they'd moved somewhere bigger and farther into the suburbs. She would lie in the dark and listen to the hum of the ducted heating turning on and off, and behind that, from the slit of gold under her door, the faint whisper of the TV set in the lounge room, or her parents' voices, or the tinkle of the dishes being done. She'd feel the solid, hot weight of their cat, Leo, at her ankles, before he'd died from anaphylaxis from an insect bite years later.

Sometimes she'd wake up, and the sounds of the house would be gone; everything would be silent, the slit under her door black, the weight of the cat missing. And her aloneness would be so huge, so terrifying, she'd call out for her mother. And she'd be there, always, appearing in a triangle of light. Liv would know exactly what she'd do, and just knowing the ritual was coming would make her feel better. Her mother would sit on the end of her bed, and she'd kiss Liv's palm and then curl Liv's fingers into a fist, her mother's own bigger hand wrapping around it. *You are always safe, always,* she would say, *because you will always have my love.* And then she would push Liv's closed hand back under the covers against her chest and everything would be okay again.

Liv had never wanted her mother so much as she did right now.

But she wasn't a little girl anymore and she was not safe and things weren't going to be okay.

A few hours passed and Liv got up to use the bathroom. When she got back, she peeked around the blinds at the window directly across, Brian and Rani's room. Their curtains were closed, but she could see a dark splotchy spray on the white fabric. In this light it looked black, but she knew what color it really was.

She fished a pill out of the bottle and took it with a sip of water.

SHE WOKE BEFORE dawn the next morning. Her dad snored, it turned out. Deep rasping breaths that managed to penetrate her drug-aided sleep. He had swapped beds with Casper when they got back from the courthouse. To keep an eye on her or to guard her, she wasn't sure. But she was happy it was him and not Casper. She wouldn't trust herself to sleep at all if it were Casper.

She scrolled pet hairstyles and Lana Del Rey memes and fingernails poking through fishnet gloves. Hours passed. The sun rose. Her dad got up and left the bedroom, but she pretended to be asleep. She scrolled.

The door opened, and she could hear that it was Casper, not her dad this time. Casper's steps were more solid.

"Hey," he said.

"Hi." She didn't turn around.

"How are you feeling?"

"Fine."

"Did you sleep?"

"Yep."

He moved around the room, grabbing clothes probably. She didn't know what to say, so she said nothing, hoping he'd leave and she could go back to her screen.

"Liv?" he said.

"Yeah?"

"Why have you been going next door at night?"

She didn't answer.

"Was it because of their son? Austin?"

She kept her back to him. "Yeah."

"Okay, cool. That makes sense. I wondered."

"Does any of this really make any sense?"

All she could think was that she was bad. That there must be some violence inside her. Something nasty in her unconscious that surfaced when she was sleeping. But she didn't say this out loud.

"I mean . . . it's tricky. You know, to get your head around," he said. "But maybe sometimes it's better not to think about stuff too hard? I dunno. That's what I'm trying to do. You should have come down and watched the movie with us last night. Dad didn't do that annoying thing where he keeps pausing it to talk about the three-act structure."

"What did you watch?"

"*Nightmare on Elm Street.*"

She turned over and looked at him.

He chuckled. "Funny?"

"No."

"Too soon, I guess. We watched *Little Shop of Horrors.*"

She kept looking at him as she asked, "Cas, why did Mum leave?"

She watched his eyes slide away, and then she was sure; she was sure that it was because of her. And she knew that Casper had the answer.

"You should go for a walk or something today. Get some fresh air."

"While I still can?"

"No, that's not what I meant. I just mean . . . you're wallowing. It's not going to help. Plus, it smells in here."

She turned away from him, opened Instagram again. "Maybe," she said.

He stood there, probably staring at her back, but after a few seconds he left the room and headed back downstairs.

She scrolled, her eyes blurring. Would it be like a trial on TV? Lawyers and opening statements and witnesses and evidence. Austin on the stand. Rani. Everyone talking about her. Everyone looking at her, wondering how she could have done it, why she would have. What was inside her that was capable of such a thing.

She scrolled tanned thighs on the beaches of Malibu, of Rio, of Bali, of San Sebastián. Would it reach the papers? *Sleepwalking Maniac Murderer.* She wished someone would tell her how Brian was doing. He could be recovering. He could be dead.

She heard the sound of a car pulling in next door. She sat up, hoping it was Austin. Maybe moving back in. Or even coming to pick up some clothes. Their house had been dark and silent since Liv had gotten home. She just wanted to see him, even for a few seconds. Just see him so she knew he was okay.

Pulling the blinds to the side, she looked down to their driveway. It was a white van. Two women came out, and for a second Liv thought they must be painters. They were wearing full-body white plastic jumpsuits. They unloaded buckets and cleaning equipment from the back, pulled on masks.

They went inside the house. She imagined them climbing the stairs, reaching the corridor, and turning right. She could see their shadows reach the closed curtains. And then, so abruptly it made her gasp, they opened the curtains, pushed the window up.

There it was. Brian and Rani's bedroom.

It was worse than she'd thought. An actual crime scene. There were sprays of blood up the white walls. They had a big framed An-gelina Beloff painting above their bed that was all pale pinks and greens and now . . . crimson red, shiny on the glass. But the most horrific thing was the bed.

Liv watched as they stripped off the stained sheet. There was a huge dark red blotch on the bare mattress. That was where he was lying, asleep, when she got him. She watched them work and tried to imagine it. Her, opening their bedroom door with a knife in her hand. Her, standing above the bed as Rani and Brian slept soundly. Her, raising the knife above her head.

It made no sense at all.

She watched them take the mattress down and load it in their van; then they got to work on the room. They sprayed down every sur-face. They scrubbed the red out. Wiped it off the wooden headboard, off the glass of the painting, the carpet, the walls. They took the stained curtains down. What Liv did in just a few seconds, they undid me-thodically over the next hour.

When they were done, the room was bare and white again.

They went back downstairs, loaded up their stuff. Then they pulled off their hoods and took down their masks and leaned against the side of the van. They smiled at each other, and Liv saw that one of them had short gray hair and one of them had long dark hair in a tight ponytail. They seemed relaxed, happy to be out in the fresh air again. Like any two people who'd just finished work. The ponytailed one took a drink of water from a pink plastic bottle.

There was a knock on her bedroom door.

"Yeah?"

Her father came in. And there was something in the way he was holding himself, something in his eyes, that told her that he had news.

"What is it?" she said, pulling away from the window.

He sat down on the bed. "Gio just called to update me on Brian."

He was dead. She was sure of it. Her father was about to tell her that Brian was dead.

But her dad smiled, and she saw that it was relief that was making his eyes so intense. "He's awake. Nothing major was damaged. They've moved him out of the ICU."

He grinned at her, and she wrapped her arms around him, and he held her tight and patted her hair and told her everything was going to be okay. She wished she could believe him.

THIRTY-THREE

Janus walked down the hill to Café Sabrosa. He needed to talk to Carlos. He needed to find his wife.

Just last week, this kind of confrontation would have left him a nervous wreck. But these past days had changed him. They had changed all of them. Casper was more present, more open. There was less snark and fewer eye rolls. But there were also moments when Janus would look over to see his son's eyes glassy, some horror playing out in his thoughts. And Liv had shut down completely. She just lay in her bed all day on her phone, and he wondered if she even comprehended what was going on. She seemed to have given up. He was terrified for her.

When it had first happened, he had felt paralyzed with panic. All he'd wanted was for his wife to come back, take care of it. It made him realize how much he relied on her, how over the years she'd slowly been taking on so much of the load that he had felt like he was unable to do anything himself. But he wasn't helpless; he wasn't powerless. He'd had to step up—he hadn't had a choice. He was the one holding this family together now. He spent his days researching law and speaking to Giovanni and making appointments with various doctors for Liv, as well as cooking food and cleaning the house and doing laundry and making sure things didn't fall into complete chaos. At night, he slept lightly, listening to his daughter breathe, hoping nothing would happen. The only time he had to himself was in the shower. It was there that he thought of Kay. He imagined her with other men. On her knees, on all fours, groaning in pleasure. At first, these images made him feel sick to his stomach. But as they repeated on a loop every time he was alone for too long, he found they'd started arousing him. It was a surprise, that first time, when he'd looked down and been confronted by his own erection. He'd have thought knowing that Kay had been with someone else would have turned him off her forever, but in fact, it was the opposite. It made him want her more, made him want to blow any trace of the other man away.

He stood in the line at Sabrosa, looking at Carlos. He was there, behind the counter, chatting away to an older man who was waiting for his coffee. Carlos looked different from how Janus had imagined him. He'd met the man before, very briefly, when they'd first moved to the area. But his imagination had turned his bulk to muscle. It had made him taller, more wild-looking. Really, Carlos was a middle-aged man, shorter than him, with a slight belly. Janus's gaze must have been potent, because Carlos looked around to him. They locked eyes, and then Carlos cocked his head to the door and Janus went outside. A minute later, Carlos followed him.

"Hi," Carlos said. He wasn't even pretending, which was something. Janus didn't have time for that dance.

"Is she with you?" he asked.

"Kay? No."

"Do you know where she is?"

"She's not at home?"

"No."

"I'm sorry. I don't know. I haven't heard from her."

Janus nodded. "Okay," he said, and turned away. So she hadn't left him for someone else. That was something.

"Is Olivia all right?"

Janus looked back at him. He didn't want this man saying his daughter's name. Carlos seemed to catch the flash in his eyes, because he held up a hand.

"My brother was inside. It changed him. Irrevocably. It's no place for your daughter . . . no place for anyone. If there's anything I can do, please just ask."

Janus nodded, then walked away.

GIOVANNI CONTI SAT at their kitchen table, his laptop open and his hands skimming over the keys. They were going in for Olivia's next police interview in a few hours, so it was battle stations. Janus had asked Liv to come down twice before she appeared in the doorway. She looked so small, like a young boy with her short hair and oversized jeans and T-shirt. Still, he was relieved she was out of bed.

"Coffee?" he asked her.

"I'm fine."

She'd lost weight over the last few days, and her skin was sallow.

Giovanni jerked around to look at her, like he hadn't expected to see her.

"Oh," he said. "Good morning, Olivia! Come and sit down, all right? And yes." He swiveled back to Janus. "Yeah, a coffee would be terrific."

He looked like he had already had way too much, talking too fast and jiggling one leg under the table, but Janus didn't say anything.

Right now, this young public defender was the only thing standing between his daughter and serious jail time.

"So, Olivia, I'm working on your somnambulism defense," Giovanni said. "I studied it at law school, never thought I'd actually get to try one."

"Great." Olivia didn't meet his eye.

"We have to prove that what happened was automatistic, so, I mean, our work is cut out for us."

Giovanni laughed, then went back to tapping on the computer, his leg still jiggling. Janus put the coffee down on the table in front of him.

Olivia sat down at the table. "And what do I need to know?"

"In relation to what?" His eyes didn't leave the screen.

"I mean," she said, "don't we need to figure some stuff out beforehand or something? Have a game plan?"

"Just don't answer anything unless I tell you to."

"Okay. So what did the psychiatrist guy say? About our appointment?"

Olivia had gone to see the psychiatrist first thing that morning. Janus had waited outside in the car, but when she got back in, she didn't say anything about how it had gone.

Giovanni flapped a hand. "He's hopeless. We'll do some sleep tests, that'll be the real ticket."

"Sleep tests?"

"Yep." He took a sip of coffee. "Oh, this is nice. You Aussies always seem to know how to make good coffee."

Janus watched his daughter look Giovanni up and down. He saw her eyes go to the patch of stubble he'd forgotten to shave on his jawbone, the sauce stain on his collar, the cat hair all over his pants. Liv closed her eyes, breathed deeply in and out.

"Do I smell something?" Giovanni asked. "Janus, are you baking?"

"Blueberry-and-chocolate muffins," he said. "They'll be ready in about fifteen minutes."

He had noticed that Giovanni seemed to leave as soon as the food ran out, so he'd been prepared. He was pleased when Giovanni had said he'd be coming around to their house—he'd been worried that the lawyer would just meet them at the station right before the interview and Liv wouldn't get a chance to have a real talk with him.

"Man, you're a superstar! I had to skip breakfast this morning."

The sauce stain on Giovanni's collar must have been from the last time he wore that shirt.

"So," Liv said, her eyes open now, "the sleep tests?"

But Giovanni was still looking at Janus. "If you manage to get Camila Sanchez to eat a muffin, I won't believe my eyes. I don't think she even eats, except for maybe—"

"Hey!" Liv yelled. They both turned to her in surprise.

"Can you please explain to me what's going on? I don't know what *automatism* means. I don't know what *sambulism*, or whatever, means. I want to know what these sleep tests—"

"Okay," Giovanni said, and pulled his chair back. "Okay, I'm sorry. *Somnambulism* basically is just the medical term for sleepwalking."

She looked up at Janus, like she thought she was going to be admonished for being rude, but he smiled at her. He was glad she was sticking up for herself. She'd need to if she was going to get through this. That was one thing he couldn't do for her.

"So," Giovanni said, "when I say *automatistic*, what I mean is you weren't in control of your actions, that they weren't a conscious choice. The big issue is liability, all right? We know you did it, that's not a question. The issue is whether you can be held responsible criminally. We have to prove that you weren't aware of what you were doing, that you were performing actions with no intent, or even consciousness."

"So, what, like we plead insanity?"

"We're not at that stage yet, we're still just talking. This may never even go to trial. If we could find out what your dream was, say, or why you targeted Brian specifically, that could help. It's my understanding that there was nothing but goodwill between you?"

"Yeah," she said. "Yes, of course. I like Brian. He . . . I mean, he was just our neighbor, the guy I babysit for, Austin's dad. Do you mean . . . Are you asking me if there was something else going on? Like I wanted to stab him for some actual reason?"

"That's what they'll ask you, yes."

"No, none at all. That's why this is so"—she took another steadying breath—"confusing."

"They need to find some sort of sense in it, something to prove that you are making up the sleepwalking as a cover. So our job is to prove that you aren't."

"People have seen me do it. They could be, you know, witnesses."

He nodded, but Janus was sure it was just to placate her. She could easily have been faking it; witness testimony meant next to nothing. They needed science.

"So, what are these sleep tests?" Janus asked. He already knew, but this conversation was good for his daughter. She was finally waking up.

"I've been trying to book you in for that, they're saying they don't have time until next month, but I'm pushing, don't worry. Basically, you just sleep at a clinic for the night and they'll hook you up to an EEG to monitor your—"

"EEG?" Liv interrupted.

"Basically, they attach little disks to your head while you sleep and a machine monitors the electrical activity in your brain. It'll prove the sleepwalking one way or another."

"That sounds uncomfortable," Janus said.

"Yeah." Giovanni took a sip of his coffee. "I bet it is."

Giovanni went back to his computer and Liv sat back in her chair, a furrow between her eyebrows. Janus didn't say anything to her. She needed time to get her head around all of it.

The oven dinged, and then a wave of panic set into Janus. "Wait, hang on, what did you mean before? About that detective eating the muffins? Why would we take food to the station?"

"No, no," Giovanni said, not looking up. "They're coming here. That's why I'm here, didn't I say that in my message?"

"Here!? They want to do the interview here?"

Both Olivia and Giovanni looked up at him then. "Yes, is that a problem? I advocated for it so that Liv would feel more relaxed. They have the upper hand at the station—she'll feel like a criminal before she even sits down."

"When are they coming?"

He heard the squeak of a brake as a car pulled into the curb outside. He rushed over to the window and watched as a beautiful dark-haired woman and a stout, ginger man got out of a black car. Sanchez and McGuinness. They were here. Janus turned back; Giovanni was watching him, a question on his face. Part of him wanted to run outside, throw a blanket over the avocado plants. But no. That would make it infinitely more obvious. No. There was no reason to think they would suspect anything there. He just had to keep his cool. The doorbell rang.

FIRST, THE DETECTIVES made Liv go over what had happened again. Janus stayed in the kitchen as she spoke, pretending to tend to the muffins and stealing glances over the counter every so often. He listened to Liv explain how Austin was meant to be keeping her awake, that they'd been seeing each other. She told them about waking up with blood all over her in the bathroom and not knowing what had happened.

"What was the dream about?" Sanchez asked. Janus looked over. She was leaning an elbow on the table and staring at Liv. McGuinness was scribbling words down on a notepad even though they were recording the audio as well. He turned away to put the muffins on a plate.

"I don't remember my dreams."

"Nothing at all?"

"I remember the feelings. Fear, intense fear, and, like, this need to protect . . . like someone was in danger and I had to run to help or I wouldn't get there in time. It would be too late."

Janus approached, and as he did, he saw Sanchez's eyes slide over to McGuinness. He looked back to her, just for a flash. There was something there. Janus placed the plate of muffins on the table, and Giovanni immediately snatched one. Had their lawyer even noticed that look between the detectives? Maybe the muffins had been a bad idea.

"How is he doing?" Janus asked. "I heard that he's woken up."

McGuinness looked up at him, nodded once. "He'll be out soon."

Olivia's shoulders slumped. Her hands went over her face, like she might cry in relief. But she held herself together.

"That's great news," Janus said. "His condition can't be that bad, then."

"The family can't afford for him to be there much longer. They lost their health insurance when Brian lost his job last month."

"He lost his job?" Janus asked, but Giovanni interrupted.

"Are they planning on starting a civil suit?"

"What's that?" Olivia said.

"They might want you to pay his hospital bills," he said to her, but his eyes were on the detectives.

"We don't know. The family are being . . . less than forthcoming," Sanchez said.

Giovanni put his muffin down. "They aren't pushing for a conviction?"

McGuinness looked up from the pad. "New information has come to light about the circumstances of the family. That's all we can say at this time."

"No," Giovanni said, "you need to tell me if there is new information."

"Nothing is confirmed yet," Sanchez said.

"Still, if there is something that relates to my client's—"

"We're all still just talking . . . or not talking, on their side of things."

"That sounds significant."

"We'll update you on any new concrete evidence. Olivia, you spent a lot of time next door, didn't you?" Sanchez said.

Liv nodded. "Yeah, I guess. I mean, just babysitting and then more recently with Austin."

"And let me ask you, Olivia." Sanchez was smiling a warm fake smile. "Did you ever notice anything . . . out of the ordinary going on there?"

"What do you mean?"

"Exactly what I'm asking," she said, not breaking eye contact.

"I don't think so."

"You never noticed anything? Anything to do with Rani? Or Brian?"

"No."

"What about Austin? You two were getting very close. Did he

confide in you? You just said you felt an urge of protection. Who were you trying to protect?"

"I . . . I told you. I don't remember the dream."

"So there's nothing? Nothing at all besides a perfectly happy family that you saw next door?"

"Nothing."

"What about you?" Sanchez cut her eyes away from Olivia and looked straight at Janus.

"Me?"

"Yes. Why don't you take a seat, Mr. Jansen? We have a few questions for you as well."

"You do? About what? I haven't done anything."

Sanchez cocked her head. "What do you mean?"

Janus was sweating. He knew he was sweating. He wanted to stop. A drip inched down his forehead, but he didn't brush it away. If he did, they might notice it. Right now, no one seemed to have seen it. He sat down next to his daughter.

"Does Mr. Jansen need legal counsel?" Giovanni asked.

"I don't think so. I just have one question for him."

And Janus knew what it would be. They'd ask him if his daughter had ever done anything like this before, if he'd covered it up, if he'd ever hidden a body in their backyard.

"You look nervous, Mr. Jansen."

"I'm just a nervous person," he said.

"It's true," Liv said, but even she was looking at him intently.

"I'm a writer, you know. We writers are an anxious group of people. That's why it's always so strange when we are expected to do public speaking. I mean, who wants to see a writer sweat and stammer and get our words mixed up? You'd expect writers to be good at words, but it's easier when they are on paper, I think."

"I saw Jonathan Franzen speak at the Bovard last year. He was good. No stammering," McGuinness said.

"What's the question?" Giovanni asked Sanchez.

"The question," she said, "is why did you transfer twenty thousand dollars to Mr. Davis's bank account last week?"

They all gaped at her, and then looked at Janus. He tried to keep his face neutral while everything in his head was clicking together.

"I didn't. My wife did."

"Can we speak to your wife?"

"She's taking some time. To think."

"Think about what?"

He faked an embarrassed laugh. "We've been having some marital issues."

"So you don't know why she sent Mr. Davis that money?"

He could think of only one reason: blackmail. Brian must have seen them bury the body. That dark figure in the bush outside Hélène's house started to take shape. Hulking, tall. Brian. That prick had pretended to be his friend! He'd drunk beers with him and grinned when he knew, all that time he knew, and he was trying to take them for everything they had. But he couldn't say any of this to the police.

"Oh," he stammered, "oh, I know. Brian did some work for us recently. He helped out. And bought supplies and, you know, physical labor. She must have been paying him back."

"What kind of work did he do?"

"Gardening."

Oh God. Why did he say gardening? Literally anything else would have been better. He'd been so worried about the backyard that it had just jumped into his brain and right out his mouth.

"He was going to build a shed as well," he went on. "He'd bought the materials. I was going to use it as an office. You know, a way to spend less time at the library. He hadn't started it yet, but that was the plan."

He needed a cigarette. Could he just light one up right here?

All four of them were still staring at him. Then Giovanni grabbed the muffin he had set down before.

"Okay, you asked him your question and he answered it. If there's nothing else, I think we should leave it there."

Sanchez held Janus's gaze. Her eyes searching his. She didn't believe him—that was clear. Then she tapped her fingers on the table. "Okay."

McGuinness closed his notebook and they both stood up.

"You'll be hearing from us," Sanchez said.

Giovanni stood. "If you have any information, I really insist—"

"We will," Sanchez said, heading toward the door. But McGuinness hesitated.

"Before we go, do you mind if we see the garden?"

Janus turned cold. "The garden?"

"Yes," he said. "Just a quick look. Twenty grand is a lot of money for some yard work."

"You want to hire Brian yourself?"

Neither detective smiled at him.

"Sorry. Yes, all right. Of course. Why not."

He headed for the back door. Ginger came bounding up, eager to be let out. Janus knew why. He picked her up, held her under one arm, and opened the door for them.

McGuinness and Sanchez took a step outside. Ginger struggled in his arms. Maybe she could smell his fear, feel his heart thundering in his chest. They both looked at the avocado patch, grave-shaped. The plants wilting. Underneath the dirt, Hélène's corpse. Probably in its first stage of decay. Bloating. He'd researched it for his book.

McGuinness pointed to the patch. Janus's throat constricted.

"You got ripped off, Mr. Jansen. And avocado plants shouldn't be planted this time of year. That's why they're dying."

Ginger scrambled in his arms. "Oh, okay, that makes sense."

They turned around and headed to the front door.

"We'll be in touch." And the door snapped shut and they were gone.

THIRTY-FOUR

After Giovanni left, Liv went back to bed. Giovanni had asked her father again about the money, and he had stuck to the ridiculous gardening story. Liv knew he was lying; she'd seen the way he'd sweated as soon as they turned their attention on him. He'd been drenched in it, and got all stammery and bumbly, his eyes darting all over the place. The money, her mum's sudden departure, the comments about disharmony in Austin's family: It was all swimming around in her head, but she didn't know how to put the pieces together. Better to go back to her room and close the blinds and turn off her mind. As she climbed back into the safety of her sweaty, unwashed sheets, she heard a car pull in outside. For a moment she thought it might be her mother, finally home, finally back. She sat up to look out the window. It wasn't her mother's car. It was Rani's.

Liv held her breath.

Rani got out. Even from the window, Liv could see from the stiff way Rani moved that she was exhausted. And then the passenger door opened.

It was him. Austin. His head was bowed, so she could see that bare patch of skin on the back of his neck. She remembered running her fingers over it.

She waited for him to look up, but he didn't. Just opened the door to the backseat and took Maria's hand as she jumped down and then slung a stuffed gym bag over his shoulder. He opened the other side and Rufus jumped down. So they were back.

They headed inside their house and closed the door behind them. Liv watched as Rani went around and shut all the blinds and curtains so no one could see in. The lump rose in Liv's throat again, and she swallowed it down.

THAT NIGHT SHE didn't take the pills that the doctor had given her. She dropped in and out of sleep, memories of the conversation with the detectives coming into her head every time she surfaced.

When the morning light came bright in her eyes, she put a hand over her face. She wanted to pull out her phone, open Instagram, and disappear into it. But she didn't. She got up, pulled on some clothes, went downstairs to get Ginger.

The morning air woke her up a bit more. The sun had just risen a warm, creamy yellow. The sky was clear and blue.

At the park, a muscled man was doing reps on the equipment. Mrs. Flores from up the street walked her loops on the running track, waiting for her curlers to set. The park was just like it always was. Except there were no dogs. Not yet. She sat down anyway and waited. Maybe he would come. Maybe he would talk to her.

Ginger lay at her feet as the day got warmer and Mrs. Flores finished her loops and the muscled man shed his T-shirt. Ginger seemed more docile too. She'd lain on the end of Liv's bed for hours yesterday.

Maybe dogs really could feel their owner's emotions. If that was true, then Liv pitied her.

The muscled man took a long drink from his water bottle and then got up to leave. Liv should go too. The day was starting to heat up. She should get home before she was missed.

She stared at her knees and stroked Ginger's ears. Her eyes were getting warm, filling with tears. She tried to blink them away. But she felt them spill over, track down her cheeks. She wasn't sure how she was meant to keep going without any answers. Because there had to be answers. There had to be some sort of explanation for all this. Otherwise she really was just a monster.

The psychiatrist she'd seen had asked her all sorts of questions about her upbringing, like there might be some horror there that would explain why she'd done what she'd done. She answered his questions, but really she wanted to tell him not to bother. There was no secret trauma in her past that would account for her actions. She almost wished there were, because at least then it would all make a bit more sense.

Ginger darted out from under her hands. She trotted down toward the gate. Liv stood. If it'd been left open, Ginger might walk out into the road. But Ginger stopped, then turned around and came running back onto the grass. Bounding behind her was Rufus.

Liv watched the entrance. It was happening. Rufus was here, which meant Austin was here. But then, what if it wasn't Austin? What if it was Rani, trying to walk her dog in peace? Liv stood, frozen. She should get Ginger. She should put her on her leash. But she couldn't move.

And then there he was, closing the gate carefully behind him. Liv stared at Austin, still standing, the leash in her hand. He noticed her and hesitated, his gaze locked with hers. She'd forgotten how beautiful his eyes were.

Liv expected him to call back Rufus, to turn and head back down the hill to his house. But he didn't. He started walking toward her. She brushed her cheeks dry.

"Hey," he said. And up close she could see that little freckle under his eye.

"Hi."

He looked at Rufus and Ginger, bounding around together.

"I think he missed her," he said.

"Yeah."

Her heart was beating and her throat was clenched and her skin was all tingly, but she needed to make the most of this. She wouldn't have this moment again.

"Can we . . ." Her voice sounded strained, and she swallowed. "Do you want to sit down?"

"Okay."

They sat down on the bench. Now that he was here, she had no idea where to start. There were so many questions, so many impossible things to try and understand.

"Are you okay?" he said.

"Me? Austin, no. How can you be that nice? How can you ask if I'm okay right now?"

"I've been worried about you."

The last time he'd seen her, she was in court. And the time before that, she was covered in his father's blood.

"Are you okay?" she asked. "Is your mother? Is Maria?"

"I'm fine," he said. "Maria is confused, but she's starting to understand."

"And Rani?"

He put his hands together and squeezed them between his knees like he was cold. But it wasn't cold. "She's getting there."

Liv took a deep breath. "I'm so glad you came, Austin. I've been hoping you would. I want to say, and I know that this is nowhere near enough, but I want to say it anyway. I'm so sorry. So, so, so sorry. I don't know how it happened. I don't understand it. But it's my fault. I know that. I know I can never make it okay—"

He held up a hand. "It's okay. I know."

"It's not okay!"

"Just . . . look." He closed his eyes. The sun reflected from his glasses. "My family . . . we're not . . . I don't even know where to start."

Liv wanted to touch him. She wanted to put her arms around him, cradle his face in her hands, kiss him. But she kept her hands where they were on her lap.

"Start at the beginning. If you want to tell me, that is. You don't have to."

He nodded. "No, I . . . I think you need to know this."

He looked away from her, toward the dogs, now chasing each other in tighter and tighter circles. She watched them too. Maybe it would be easier for him to talk if her eyes weren't on him.

"You know, my mom used to live in the Bay Area. Her whole family is there actually. Tito and Tita. My cousins. We barely visit. I can only remember going once. They were the best. So warm and nice. It was . . . I don't know, before then, I never really felt like . . . properly connected with my heritage. But that weekend was the best."

"Why don't you visit very often?" She didn't know how this was connected to anything, but she was happy to listen to him talk.

"Things are weird. Between them and my parents . . . It's like . . . Okay, so you know how Mom used to be an artist? That's how she met my dad. He used to love telling the story. He was in the Bay Area for the weekend on business. He was walking back to the hotel, exhausted from this full day of meetings and getting up in the dark for his flight, he was just ready to go to bed, and then he walked past this gallery. It was super hot and the gallery was tiny with no air-conditioning, so the door was propped open. Through the doorway he saw her, my mom, on a stepladder hanging this abstract yellow-and-orange landscape. She turned and smiled at him, and told him the show wasn't open until the next day. She was only nineteen then. He was twenty-three. But he said, right away, he knew. He went back the next day and bought one of her paintings just to have an excuse to talk to her. It was the first painting she'd sold to someone she didn't know."

Liv smiled. It was like a romance movie.

"They did long distance for a while, weekends, but Dad hated it. He wanted to be with Mom all the time. He said he'd miss her like crazy during the week. He could hardly bear it. Mom was still living at home, and Dad had his own apartment, so he convinced her to move here. She didn't want to at first. And Tito didn't like him, didn't like the idea of this older rich white guy taking his youngest daughter away. But then Dad proposed. They were in love.

"He turned his second bedroom into a little art studio for her. She'd paint all day while he was at work. She said sometimes he'd come home with a bouquet of flowers, and sometimes with a bouquet of paintbrushes. But it was hard for her. She didn't know how to drive back then, and you know what the public transit is like here. I think she was pretty lonely. But then she got pregnant with me.

"I remember, when I was little, I always worried that my mom loved painting more than me. We were living here by then, and Maria's room was Mom's studio. I remember overhearing them fighting. He would say she loved her art more than she loved her family. Every time she went in there, I would cry. I thought it meant that what he was saying was true."

That didn't seem fair to Liv. But he had been a kid, and kids believed weird stuff. So Liv didn't say anything. Just let him keep talking.

"By the time I was in middle school, I genuinely believed that she wasn't a very good mom. My dad would always say she could never one hundred percent commit to us. She'd fight with him, say she just needed one day to herself a week. He always said she was too loud, too fiery. He'd say she was having one of her 'loca' moments."

He stopped then. He was shaking. Liv placed her hand on his knee without thinking, and he gripped it in his.

"She would come into my room at night and apologize to me. Say she was going to do better. Looking back, I don't know what she really could have done better. All she did was be my mom.

"It was around then that the fainting started. He said she was pushing herself too hard. Or that it was the oil paints or turpentine. Maybe she was allergic. She stopped going into her studio. Then one day I was sitting on the stairs. They didn't know I was there. I was looking down into the kitchen, you know, just being a bored middle schooler. They were sitting at the table, and she stood up to get something. And then . . . I saw it! I saw his foot jut out and she tripped and fell and then he helped her up and said, 'Have you been pushing yourself too hard again?' And he was so nice to her, and she only seemed confused for a second and then she started apologizing. If I hadn't seen it, I never, ever would have believed that he'd intentionally tripped her.

"That's when my eyes really opened. I started noticing everything. I noticed one morning my dad had scratches on his hand. I asked what it was and he made that 'loca' remark again, said something about my angry, feisty mother. I started lying awake, just listening. Waiting. Then one night, I heard it. The faintest muffled cry. I jumped up, ran into their room, smashed the door open. They were in bed, and I don't know what had happened, but something had. Mom's face was all blotchy. Dad was breathless. I hit my dad, smacked him in the face. He hit me back, twice as hard.

"He told me after that I was imagining things. That nothing like that was going on. I wanted to believe him. I started thinking maybe I was going crazy too. Everything could be explained away. Mom got

"Shit," she said. "Shit, shit, shit. But Austin . . . medications and seeing your dad hurt your mum . . . none of that adds up to what I did. None of that adds up to me going downstairs, getting a knife, coming back upstairs, and going into their room. I mean, there must be something dark inside me. There must be some horrible violence that . . ."

She trailed off. The expression on his face. It wasn't horror, but something else. He wasn't meeting her eye, and was sucking his bottom lip.

"Can you walk me through it? Can you tell me everything you remember?" she asked.

He still wasn't looking at her. "It's horrible to talk about."

"It might really help me."

"It's all a bit of a blur."

That was bullshit. That was so clearly utter bullshit. Then it clicked. The final piece. Everything clicked together.

"I didn't do it, did I?" she whispered.

His face sank into his hands.

"No," he said, voice muffled through his fingers. "No. It just . . . How can I explain it? He was hurting my mom again that night. It just . . . it just happened. And then he was bleeding everywhere and you came in and you were just standing there, eyes totally absent. You were totally malleable. And I knew you wouldn't go to jail, you know? There was a legal precedent and an explanation and—"

"Ginger!" she yelled, getting to her feet and running toward where her dog was playing with Rufus. "Ginger!"

"I'm sorry, Liv. I'm so sorry."

She knelt down to put on Ginger's leash, but she couldn't snap it into place. Her fingers kept missing the hook.

"I didn't think it through. I just panicked!"

She got the clip on and then she rushed toward the gate. Ginger kept digging her paws in; she wanted to stay. Liv half dragged her down onto the street. But soon Austin and Rufus were behind her.

"I really like you, Liv. I do. Like, I think I could have fallen in love with you. I think I might have."

She kept walking.

"It kills me to see how much this is hurting you. I didn't think it through. Clearly. I just . . . I don't know . . . acted."

"To save yourself," she snapped. "If you love someone, you put them first. You let me take the fall for you. You covered me in your dad's blood, for fuck's sake. You're sick."

He stopped talking and she thought maybe he'd leave her alone. She was almost back home now. She could see her house.

"There's something else, Liv. Something you should know."

"I don't want to talk to you."

"My dad. He had this photo of your dad. I saw it on his computer. It was like . . . he'd taken it without your dad's knowledge. I think he was spying on him, following him. He kept watching your house through the window. For hours."

"Why?" she said. "Why would he do that?"

"I honestly don't know."

She reached her front path. "Stop it, Austin. Don't follow me. Don't even look at me."

His eyes were all crumpled against the glare. She turned away from him, rushed into her house.

Her father was there at the kitchen table, Casper next to him. Her father, who'd sweated when the police had questioned him. Who'd told her never to talk about the missing time after the gala. Her father, who Brian had been following.

"You walked Ginger?" he said. "That's great. Good to get out." But then he clocked her expression and his smile fell away. "What's wrong?"

She sat down at the table. "It's time, Dad. You need to tell me everything."

"Everything about what?"

"Whatever it is I've done. I need to face it. Please."

"Face what, Liv?"

"Dad," Casper said. "She needs to know."

Her father looked between them. And then he slumped forward and started telling her the story.

THIRTY-FIVE

The motel was silent. In all her fantasies, Kay hadn't thought of that. All she'd thought of was freedom. Clean sheets, windows open to the endless ocean. She'd imagined space and sleep and escape. But the motel was cheap, and her window looked out to a brick wall. She'd tried the television, but every channel was overlaid with fuzz and hiss. She didn't want to turn her phone on, despite the promise of distraction, too worried that it would make her traceable. Plus, she couldn't bear to see missed calls or new messages. She kept reminding herself that this was what she'd wanted as she drank seven-dollar wine from a plastic cup. This was what she'd wanted.

But the wine didn't stop everything she didn't want to think about from rushing through her. Hélène's terrified face. The slap of the front door as Casper left. Janus reeling back from the impact of her words. She was a cheater. A slut. A liar. A criminal. And maybe worst of all, a bad mother. But none of these things made her break down and sob. None of them made her feel the crushing pain that they should. She was numb.

The younger version of Kay, the person she used to be, had returned. The person who could have sex with strangers but went rigid when hugged. The person who was, and always would be, alone. The person who was incapable of loving or being loved.

Kay stopped eating. She didn't deserve to eat. She had to do penance. She had to be punished for what she'd done.

So the ripe white wine filled her up until she passed out. In the morning, she'd guzzle water, endure the cracking headache, wouldn't try and soften it with ibuprofen, until it was midday and she'd walk down to the liquor store and buy more bottles.

During the day there'd be the sound of car doors closing, traffic, people talking as they walked past her room. But in the dark, nothing.

One night—her third night maybe? she'd lost count—the silence became unbearable. She tried the clock radio, spinning the knobs through white noise until a familiar song rose up and snapped into clarity. It was Stravinsky. She knew this piece. It was from the Russian ballet *The Rite of Spring*. She'd led this variation in her final year in Paris. She'd played the girl who danced herself to death in sacrifice to the seasons. She'd loved that dance; it was one of passion and fear and grief and letting go. Her toes still remembered the way the staccato notes built, her arms remembered the rising violins, her legs knew the kick of the brass. She turned up the volume, pushed the bed against the window. The horns started in chromatic waves, and she let herself dance for the first time in twenty-three years, let herself jump into the air, throw her arms, twist into jagged shapes, and leap like she was weightless, like she was gone, like her body was nothing.

It was still there, all of it. She was clumsy and imprecise, but still her muscles remembered every move. And her mind went finally, gloriously blank as her chest heaved and sweat slicked her face.

She woke up on the carpet, the radio still playing, someone

banging on the wall, vomit pooling in her hair. She pulled the cord to the clock radio out of the wall, the banging stopped, and the room was quiet again. It came back harder that day, all of it. Olivia's face crumpling when she told her she couldn't use the car to go shopping, as if she hadn't killed a woman with it just a few days before. Olivia's open smile when she pushed the takeaway coffee across the kitchen table, as if that would be enough to fix what had broken between them. Maybe Janus was right. Maybe she didn't even remember.

But Kay didn't want to think about it, any of it. The pain was right there, threatening to spill over. She couldn't let it. She stuck her fingers down her throat until she was empty again, and coherent enough to shower. Then she left the room, her hair still wet, her body shivering in the heat.

Kay walked down the main road to the liquor store. She could have taken the car. But that would have been too easy. She didn't need kindness; it would only make her loosen. The top of her hair dried quickly in the sun, while the damp ends itched against her skin. SUVs thundered down the road next to her, the glare smacking off the pavement. She was close to the parking lot of the liquor store and supermarket when she had to stop; she had to rest. She collapsed into a bench, her vision swimming, her skin cold and prickling. She did her Pilates breath. In through the nose, letting her ribs expand, exhaling through the mouth in a long slow whoosh, closing her ribs down. A shiny blue car pulled in nearby. Kay watched with squinted eyes as a woman got out. She was nicely dressed, in a silk shift dress and wedge heels. She pulled out a bunch of reusable bags from the backseat. Her tween daughter came out from the other side, teetering on her own bright green platforms. They were the kind sold to girls, cheaply made and impossible to walk in. They looked like plastic versions of her mother's.

Kay breathed as she watched them, her vision still sparkling at the edges. She didn't want to faint, not here in public. She kept breathing, focusing on her rib cage.

"Come on!" the woman called over her shoulder to her daughter. "They're coming in an hour and I still haven't made the potato salad."

Her daughter bent down, adjusting the buckle of her shoe. The mother groaned, "I told you not to wear those."

"I like them!"

"They're silly."

She turned back and strode toward the store. Her daughter straightened and took a quick step forward, but she toppled, fell hard onto her knees with a crack. She got straight back up, looked to her mum, who hadn't seen, then looked around to see if anyone else had, blinking back her tears. The girl locked eyes with Kay, and for a second her face was Kay's own younger self, and then her face was Olivia's. And then the girl followed her mother into the store and Kay made herself get up and get her bottles of cheap white wine and walk back to the motel and the silence.

But it wasn't working anymore. The pain was too close, and even after she finished her first bottle, the wine wasn't working. The sky turned black outside and the silence turned absolute and Kay couldn't stand it. She needed the ocean. That was why she'd come, wasn't it? The crashing waves, the cold, the salt. It would clear her head, wash her clean. She found her car keys, let them jingle in her hand, grabbed a fresh bottle, and stumbled out of her room. She got into the driver's seat and stabbed the keys into the ignition, missed, tried again, got it, turned the key, and heard her car roar to life.

Once she turned off the main drag, it was so dark. There were no streetlights. She could barely see the lines marking the road. She'd forgotten the headlights. She switched them on, and everything lit up.

Soon, she could see the water. Black ink roiling in the night. The silver disk of the moon casting a ghostly sheen across it.

This was why she was here.

She pulled into the lot, got out of the car, and staggered down the sandy slope. Her foot slipped out from under her, and she pitched over, slamming face-first into the sand. She laughed, a loud guffaw, and righted herself, stood back up, licked the sand from her lips, and crunched the salty grains between her teeth.

She reached the beach; the water was huge in front of her. Boundless. Here it was. That freedom. She cracked open a new bottle, drank straight from the neck. It was so beautiful. The ocean was so beautiful. She held out her arms to the sky, screamed loud and long into the night. Then she ran into the water.

It glugged into her shoes, soaked her socks, her ankles, her shins. When it reached her knees, it tugged her back, making it harder to run, but she kept going. Deeper until it reached her waist, her chest. The spray was on her face, and she felt awake, finally awake, finally free, and it was magical.

A wave rose up. She took a step backward. It was huge. Twice her height. A black cliff face. Then the wave smashed down onto her head and shoulders, heavy, so heavy. She couldn't see. She lost her feet from under her, and she was sucked deeper and deeper, spinning with nothing but blackness all around. She tried to breathe and it was cold fire down her throat and she was suffocating in this dark. She couldn't find the surface. Everywhere was black.

No. No. This wasn't what was meant to happen. She didn't want to disappear. She didn't want to be here. She wanted to be home. She wanted to hold them. Both of them. Her children. She couldn't leave her children. Not like this.

There. The silver disk. The light of the moon through the water. She pushed herself toward it, and then she broke through the surface, gasped in a breath, quick, and started to swim, sober now, totally sober, pushing herself back to the shore until her feet hit sand,

and then she ran against the water that pulled at her ankles, trying to pull her back.

Then she was on dry sand and she fell to her knees and vomited. Wine and seawater burned up her throat. She emptied her stomach, and her vision was blurred and her breaths were quick, then slower, until she was able to get to her feet and walk up to the parking lot.

She'd lost the bottle in the water, but luckily she'd left her keys in the ignition of her car. She got in, clothes sodden, took another breath, then flicked the engine on. She drove slowly this time, carefully, headlights on, the rubber of her wet shoe squeaking against the pedals. She reached the motel and turned, indicator on, into the lot. Then she got out of the car, went to her room, drew the chain. There was another bottle on the nightstand. She picked it up, opened it, and emptied it into the bathroom sink, just the smell of the wine turning her stomach. Then she peeled off her wet clothes, set the shower to hot, and got under the water. She sat down on the tiles, arms wrapped around herself, and let the tears come. The tears she'd been clenching against all this time. She wept for what might have just happened. For Hélène. For what her marriage had become. But mostly for Casper and Olivia.

No one had ever told her that watching her children grow would be so filled with grief. Baby Casper, with his squishy body, his old-man giggle. She had loved him so much and he had disappeared, gone forever. Toddler Casper, obsessed with the big slide at the playground, going down it ten times in a row but still begging to go again. Casper at primary school, beanpole lean now, his schoolbag huge on his thin frame, his little hands grasping the straps, running up to hug her at the school gates. He was gone. That was why she had sent those texts even though she knew how wrong it was. She'd used to be his world; now he wouldn't even let her in.

And Olivia. After those months of crying, when Kay had finally come back to herself, she had used to stare into her crib. She'd look down at this tiny, perfect baby, and think, *What kind of person are you? Who are you going to become?* She couldn't wait to find out. And Olivia was better than anything she could have wished for. Beautiful and creative and hilarious and kind. She should have spoken to her about what had happened. Instead she'd just dismissed her. Assumed the worst. She'd been so removed. She'd been just like her own mother.

When the water ran cold and Kay stopped crying, she got out of the shower. Her skin was pink and new. She filled a glass of water and chugged down the whole thing. Refilled it.

Tomorrow she would go to that diner on the corner. She would eat a full breakfast. She would have a cappuccino—no more of this pointless self-flagellation. What was done was done. Then she would go home. The only thing she could change now was the future. And she would. She would let go of the resentment, start talking about who she was and what she needed. She would hold the people she loved close to her, if she could. If they would still let her.

THIRTY-SIX

Since her father told her what she'd done to Hélène, Liv hadn't been able to get out of bed. It was all too horrifying. Just as she'd found out that she hadn't hurt Brian, she found that she *had* hurt someone else. An old lady. Not hurt but killed. Liv had killed Hélène. There was nothing that would ever make that okay. She scrolled political memes and gua sha transformations and nude girls in bed eating pizza.

Casper had told her he'd stay with her, that they'd spend the day watching reality TV on his laptop, but she'd told him no, so he'd gone over to his friend's place to watch a movie. She was glad he was getting out of here, doing something normal. Later, her dad checked on her. She hadn't told him what she'd found out from Austin yet. She would, eventually, but right now she wanted to scroll and disappear. He was going to run some errands, go to the supermarket and maybe get some lunch. He asked her to come with him. But she just pulled the tether onto her ankle.

"I'm fine," she told him, so he left.

About half an hour later, she heard a sound from next door. She snuck a look out the side of the blinds.

Austin. His back straight. He turned on the front step to say something to his mum or Maria inside. Then he headed toward his car. For a second she thought she saw his eyes dart up to their house and she shrank away, back into the darkness of her room.

She lay back down and grabbed her phone, focusing her attention on the bright revolving images. But then the screen went black. The battery was dead. The charger was on the other side of the desk. She couldn't reach it with the tether around her ankle. She should get up, untether herself, plug the phone in. Instead she lay there, staring at the ceiling. She could still sort of see colored squares scrolling in front of her eyes.

Time passed, and there were more sounds from next door. Doors opening and shutting, footsteps coming up and down the drive. She ignored them. But she could still hear them. All the thudding footsteps back and forth, the faint sound of Maria whining. Something was going on.

Then, clear as day, she heard Rani's voice.

"Austin! Call me back as soon as you get this! We need to go now!"

Liv looked out the window. Rani was hanging up the phone, a bag in her other hand. She threw it into the trunk, where a few others already were. She put a hand to her head for a moment; then she rushed back inside the house. The curtain was open to her room, and Liv could see the wardrobe doors were gaping wide, the drawers not closed properly. She came out again seconds later, holding Maria's arm in one hand and Maria's pink backpack in the other.

"No!" Maria yelled. "No! I want to see Daddy!"

Rani was shushing her, but didn't slow her pace. She loaded Maria into the back of the car, slammed the trunk, and then reversed out of the driveway and zoomed off down the road.

It was less than ten minutes later that the taxi pulled up. Brian got out. He was walking stiffly and a bit slower than usual, but apart from that he looked okay. Just like normal Brian. Liv stared at the back of his head as he made his way up the drive and unlocked the front door. It was so hard to believe all the things Austin had said. He still seemed so normal. Just handsome, corny, generous Brian.

Liv pulled back enough from the window that he wouldn't be able to see her in the shadows, and kept watching. He went into his room. She almost felt bad for him for a second, standing there with the gaping half-empty closet and open drawers. How could he be the person she'd known him to be, but also an abuser and a blackmailer? How could someone be both?

He sat on the bed for a moment, his head in his hands. Then she saw Austin. He got out of his car, head down. He reached his house. Stood for a moment and looked up to it. Then opened the side gate, went in, and closed it again silently. He was moving so quietly that he must know; he must have spoken to Rani. He must know his father was inside.

Liv looked up at Brian again. He was kneeling down in the wardrobe, looking at something. She moved closer. It was a small black safe. She remembered Maria had mentioned it once. She'd said that her parents had a safe in their room with jewels inside. But the safe looked too small for valuables.

Outside, Austin ducked low under the windows. He didn't know where his dad was in the house and he was trying not to be seen. Liv scanned the backyard and realized what he was doing. Rufus was still there, lying on the other side of the pool. In her rush, Rani must have forgotten him. Austin would never leave without him.

She looked back up at Brian. He'd gotten the safe open now. He was loading bullets into a small silver handgun.

Liv stared at it. She'd never seen a gun before, except on TV. Guns were illegal in Australia except for cops and farmers. The sight of it seemed absurd. Then she sprang to action. She jumped off the bed, forgetting the tether, and fell face-first on the floor. She pulled herself up, tried to yank off the tether. But her hands, clumsy with panic, couldn't unfasten the buckle. She paused, took a deep breath, then undid it and stood up. She grabbed her phone and shoved the charger plug in.

She looked back out the window. Brian had stopped loading the gun. His head was up. Like he'd heard something.

Her phone screen was still black. She pressed the side button and the battery symbol came up. There wasn't enough charge yet to turn it back on.

Brian had disappeared from her view. But she could see Austin; he was outside, his finger looped in Rufus's collar, leading him toward the side gate.

Brian reappeared in the kitchen window. He was heading outside. She looked back up at the bedroom. The gun. He'd left it behind. It was on the bed. Brian opened the back door and started running. Austin must've heard him, because he started running too, pulling Rufus along with him. But Brian was too quick. He grabbed his son from behind, ripped his hand from Rufus's collar, and pinned it behind his arm, putting him in a headlock. Austin tried to fight him, but he couldn't. Brian, even injured, was too big, too much stronger.

He was saying something to Austin, who was shaking his head. Rufus was cowering, his tail between his legs.

Her phone still hadn't turned on.

If Brian took Austin upstairs . . . She couldn't let that happen.

She didn't think. She just ran. She flew down the stairs and out the front door. She ran over to their house, grabbed the spare key, and unlocked their door. Then she was in. She was in their house.

Liv trod softly. She was just in track pants, her feet bare. Which was good—she'd be quieter this way.

Even from there, she could hear Brian's voice. His hissing whisper.

"Where is she? Call her and tell her to come back."

Liv stepped up onto the first stair. Then, with a bang of the back door, they came into the kitchen, Brian's face bright red, Austin still in a headlock. Austin saw her first; his eyes widened. She couldn't wait to see if Brian had noticed her; she took off up the stairs, around the corner, into Brian and Rani's room.

There it was. The gun, still on the bed. She grabbed it. It was so heavy. She could hear bangs on the stairs. Austin must have been trying to push Brian off. Now she held the gun and she didn't know what to do with it. It wasn't like she was going to shoot Brian with it. She needed to get rid of it. The window. She'd throw it out, let it drop in the bushes below.

She pulled at the frame, but it wouldn't budge. It was locked. She pushed open the lock, then tried again; it gave this time. She pulled the window wide open.

A hard weight smashed into her. She slammed onto the floor, the gun under her. She screamed out the last of the air in her lungs. It was Brian, and he was all hot red skin and sweat smell and panting breath.

"Dad, stop!" she heard Austin call.

Brian smashed her shoulder down so he was on her back. His nose was inches from hers. His face was twisted up, contorted with anger. He wrenched the gun from under her arm and then pushed himself to his feet. Her shoulder was sharp with pain, but she barely processed it. All she could see was the gun that was now in Brian's hand.

Behind Brian, Austin was getting to his feet. He must have been pushed over in the fight.

"Dad . . ." He was trying to keep his voice even, but she could hear the shake in it. "It's all right. It doesn't have to be like this."

But Brian was looking down at Liv. He had one hand to his chest, his eyebrows knitted together. She could see a spot of blood on his white T-shirt. It was coming from his chest. He must have ripped his stitches.

"Why are you here?" he said, the gun trained on her. "Why are you always in my house?"

"I'm sorry," she said, her voice trembling so much she could barely get the words out. She couldn't stop looking at the gun.

"Get up," he said, flicking the gun toward where Austin was standing.

She pushed herself up, her right arm screaming in pain, her fingers numb. She got up and stood by Austin. He grabbed her hand, held it in his.

"I'm sorry," she whispered. "I saw you come back, I saw the gun on the bed, I thought if I came in time, then—"

"Shut up," Brian said. "Don't do that. Don't talk between each other like I'm not even here. I'm here. I'm standing right here."

"Dad—"

"Call your mother, all right, son? Call her and tell her to come home. You don't need to say I'm here."

Austin shook his head.

"Call her!" Brian said, but then his voice changed; he sounded like he was going to cry. "I just want to talk to her. I love her. She knows that I love her."

Austin didn't say anything.

"You don't understand," Brian went on. "We always said it was me and her before everything. That we'd die together, wrinkly and old. We said we'd die together. I know she loves me."

"I'm not calling her," Austin said. "You call her if you want to talk to her."

Brian laughed, and it sounded weird, all high-pitched and frenzied. "She's got a new phone. I know that. What did she do with the other one?"

He was tracking her, Liv remembered. She must have gotten rid of it.

"Do you know what that feels like?" Brian said, and his face was turning redder. "To not have my own wife's phone number? Do you know how disrespectful that is?"

"You don't own her!" Austin yelled—she squeezed his hand to try and get him to stop. "You pushed her too far. This is your fault!"

"It's my fault? No, I don't think so." He pulled his shirt up, showing the bandages around his middle. "Look what she did to me! She's crazy!"

Liv looked to Austin. "But . . . what? I thought it was you."

Brian snorted, pulling his shirt back down. "What? He said he did it? What a joke. He would never have had the balls. No, it was my psycho bitch of a wife."

"She's leaving you!" Austin yelled. "You're never going to hurt her again!"

"If I want to hurt her, I know how, I know exactly how to hurt her the most." And he trained the gun on Austin's head and pulled back the hammer.

He wouldn't do it. He couldn't. There was no way he could actually do it. The light gleamed off the gun's silver casing. A drop of sweat inched down Brian's forehead. His finger tightened on the trigger.

"Kneel," he said. "Both of you."

They did it.

They both knelt down in front of him.

Liv bowed her head. She couldn't look.

She squeezed Austin's hand in hers.

Then something flashed past her and there was a loud thud and the gun went off and Liv looked up. The gun had been knocked out of Brian's hand and he was falling backward. His thigh connected with the window frame, and he tipped back, straight out the window. For a hideous millisecond there was just silence. Then a sickening thunk as he hit the path underneath.

Arms circled her body, pulled her close. The embrace of warmth, of safety.

"Mum?" Liv said.

Somehow, impossibly, her mum was here.

"I just got home. I came into your room to talk to you and then I saw you here through your window," she said. "I didn't think I'd get over here in time. Are you okay, Olivia? Are you all right, my baby?"

"Yes," she said, "yes, I'm okay."

She held her mother close, smelled her comforting smell.

"I'm sorry I left," her mum said. "I'm so sorry."

"I'm sorry," Liv said, "I'm sorry for what I made you do."

They heard a yell come from outside. Someone must have seen Brian fall out the window. They heard more voices.

Liv pulled away from her mother, looked around to Austin. He was still kneeling, just staring at the empty space that Brian had been in, blood blooming through the cotton of his T-shirt.

THIRTY-SEVEN

Three months later

Casper scoured the mug, scrubbing away a red lipstick stain in the shape of a crescent moon. If everyone had to work as a dish pig for a night, he was pretty sure women would never wear lipstick and people would definitely stop leaving their snotty tissues on plates and they'd never ever bring their kids along to restaurants.

Carlos came in with a stack of dishes in his hand. "Want to take your break once you've done these? Your friend is here."

Casper raced through them, then pulled off his gloves and apron. He grabbed a burrito that Xav had just wrapped in foil.

"Hey! That was for a take-out order."

"Guess you'll have to make another one."

He headed out of the kitchen toward the outdoor area, intentionally averting his eyes from the noticeboard. There, among the pictures of babies, was a postcard from "Hélène." She was loving being back in France; she didn't think she'd be home anytime soon. His father had written it, and Casper didn't want to read a word. Just hearing Carlos mentioning it to locals was enough to make his stomach turn.

His dad had convinced Uncle Gerrit to send them a blank post-card with the address written in pencil when he was in France, so that the postage stamp would look right. It meant now another member of their family was complicit in this, whether his uncle knew it or not.

Casper reached the garden and looked out at Tye. He hadn't no-ticed Casper yet; his head was bowed over his iPad, his headphones were on, and he had an empty extra-large mug of coffee next to him. He must be feeling inspired.

He and Tye had made the short film. There were some cool scenes, but it hadn't quite worked. The sound wasn't right, all muffled in some bits and blown out in others. But, surprising himself most of all, Casper had caught the bug. He loved acting. And Tye had been right. He was good at it. He was one of those Australians who moved to LA and decided to become an actor. What a cliché. He thought of something funny and sent a text to his mum before he sat down across from Tye.

"You've got a new idea, don't you?"

Tye looked up at him, and his eyes softened. "How did you know?"

"I'm getting better at reading you."

Casper pressed his knee against Tye's. It was almost winter, but it was still too warm in this seasonless city to wear long pants. But the warmth of Tye's bare skin against his own made him glad. They smiled at each other for a few moments, and then Casper unwrapped his burrito.

"Wait, wait, wait," Tye said, and pulled out his phone. "I'm going to film it this time."

"You're not putting that in a movie!"

"No, it'll just be for me."

"You're so weird," he said, but he looked into the camera as he took his first bite.

KAY WAS JUST getting ready for class when she got Casper's text: *Please ground me forever if I ever start talking about doing improv.* Kay laughed. *I promise xxx,* she wrote in reply, and then plugged her phone into the speaker dock and opened her playlist, singing along under her breath as she set up the machines.

She hadn't drunk alcohol since the night at the beach, and she found she had more energy. She didn't like to think of that night, of her driving, of that cliff of black water towering over her, but when she did, she tried to remind herself to be grateful. Maybe it was what she'd needed to stop self-destructing, to show herself how much she wanted to live. And if she hadn't come home the next morning, if she hadn't gone straight up the stairs and into Olivia's room, if she hadn't looked through the window and seen her daughter there, kneeling, then she wouldn't have stopped it.

After Brian's body was removed and Austin was taken to the hospital, the detectives took their statements. She and Olivia said the same thing: Brian was deranged. He was pacing like a maniac. He tripped over his own feet. He fell.

When Kay had collided with Brian, the gun had gone off, hitting Austin in the shoulder. But he was okay; it was a flesh wound. And when it came time to make a statement, Austin repeated the story too. His father fell.

McGuinness and Sanchez didn't seem convinced, but they didn't arrest her. They still hadn't.

Late that afternoon, with Casper still at his friend's house and Olivia having a long shower, Kay and Janus had sat in the living room, just the two of them. She turned to her husband, ready to pour her heart out, explain herself, and beg his forgiveness. But he spoke first.

"I'm sorry," he said, "for leaving you to bury Hélène. That wasn't fair."

She nodded.

"You need to start talking to me, Kay. You need to start telling me what's on your mind. I don't want you to be some put-upon wifey who looks after me."

"I've tried. You're always so distracted."

He clasped her hand. "I know. I got complacent; these past few days have shown me that. I got used to being looked after. But I'm stepping up. It's good for me."

He didn't look like the accountant she'd fallen in love with, and he didn't look like the writer she'd left either. He just looked like Janus, warm and familiar and many things all at once. She felt it then, that physical pang. She leaned in without thinking about it and he wrapped his arms around her and she curled into his chest.

"I want to see you," he whispered. "I want to see your pointy bits, the parts that aren't perfect or pretty. Those are my favorite. I mean it."

Kay had wanted to believe him; she hoped that things might change in their marriage, but didn't really think that they would. She'd been wrong. Something had shifted while she had been away. Janus *was* different. He was stronger. Not in the way she had been: rigid and cold as stone. No, his strength was emotional and open and empathetic. It reminded her of why she fell in love with him.

But that afternoon she didn't know that yet. All she knew was how good it felt to be held by her husband again, to feel close to him. And when she heard the shower turn off upstairs, she kissed him lightly, then went up to speak to her daughter. Olivia was in bed under two blankets, a towel around her head and a robe on, as though layers of material would protect her from what had just happened. She looked so pale. The fan chugged away on the desk.

Kay sat down at the end of the bed. There was so much that she wanted to say, so much they needed to speak about. She wasn't sure how to put it all into words. For a moment her daughter wasn't an adult anymore; she looked just like she did when she was a child, scared and too tender for this world.

If Kay had been just a minute later . . .

The thought was unbearable.

She took Olivia's hand and brought it to her lips, kissing her palm gently. Then she wrapped Olivia's fingers over it, just like she had when Olivia had nightmares as a child.

She meant to say she was sorry, but instead she said, "I miss you."

And Olivia held her mother's hand in hers and pressed it against her heart.

Now Kay's class began to trickle in, gossiping and claiming their machines with towels and water bottles. The guy with the *vibes* tattoo across his chest smiled at her as he stripped off his T-shirt and took his place. This time she didn't look away. She held his gaze, smiled back. Then she turned on her headset and started the class, doing the exercises along with them until sweat sheened her skin. She played the usual high-tempo pop remixes, but she ended the class with Stravinsky. She'd tried incorporating it these last few months, found her students liked it. Tiff was threatening to start a new brand of classes called Prima Pilates, promising Kay a cut. But Kay had found she just loved to move to this music again, to reconcile her past self with the woman she was now. She'd discovered that change didn't have to mean disappearance, that the past would always be there. Olivia was an adult, but she'd always need her mother. Casper was becoming a man, but he'd also always be Kay's baby boy. She had to loosen her grip, give in to the duality of the present, the unpredictability of the future. Stravinsky helped her do that.

When the class ended and Kay was fizzing from the workout and the music, everyone had begun to leave, but the man with the *vibes* tattoo lingered. Kay took her phone off the dock and sent a text message. When she got her reply, she looked up at the guy again, bit her lip suggestively. She'd found it was best to be obvious. Then she went into the equipment storeroom and left the door open.

JANUS HAD BEEN preparing dinner when he got Kay's text message: *Six-foot, early 30s, covered in bad tattoos?* His stomach lurched the way it always did. That sting of violent jealousy that then, almost immediately, twisted into desire. *Yes*, he replied. He'd never known lust so potent before. That first night, he and Kay hadn't spoken as they got ready for bed. She'd brushed her teeth and put her pajamas on in the bathroom; he'd lain under their sheets waiting for her. Finally, she put on her hand cream and came to bed. She turned the light off and lay down, and Janus didn't roll to her, didn't hold her.

"The thing with Carlos," she'd said, "it wasn't . . . I don't really know how to—"

"I want you to tell me about it," he said.

"No, Janus, no. That will just make you feel worse."

He'd rolled over and slipped his hand up her pajama top, the silk just as soft as her skin. "Tell me about it. Every detail."

Janus shook the memory off and started setting the table. He almost set a fourth place. He was still getting used to Olivia not living with them anymore. It would take time to adjust. A lot of things had changed in these last few months. He'd taken on three days a week of accounting work for a bioscience company in Glendale. There hadn't been a choice; they needed the cash. But, in another surprise, he found it suited him. He felt like he had balance back in his life, and he was good at accounting. There were no perspectives, or notes, or "trying different angles." It was just numbers. On the two other weekdays he'd slowly been working on his next novel. He was done with the script. The director they'd found, the twenty-three-year-old with the short film that had made a splash on the festival circuit, had wanted to do his own rewrite, and Janus was relieved to hand it over and get his payment. He didn't think the film would ever be made, but that didn't seem so bad now. His family weren't living on that knife's edge of poverty anymore. Their well-being, and his identity, were no longer bound so tightly with the ups and downs of his writing career. That felt good.

The next morning, Janus was woken by his phone buzzing. Kay was wrapped in his arms, naked, and he breathed in her hair, then shifted over to look at the message. It was from Olivia: *Casper and I want to do the thing this afternoon, just checking if it's still okay?*

He looked at the time, only just past seven. Amazing for her to be up this early. He replied, then turned his phone off and lay back next to his wife.

OLIVIA LOOKED DOWN at her father's message: *That's fine. I think it's a nice idea xx.* She slipped her phone back into her pocket and took another drink from her water bottle. Then she pulled her mask back on, zipped up her fluorescent vest, plugged her earphones in, and went back to the wall. The paint stripper stank, but she was starting to get used to it. She grabbed a broom and submerged it in the steaming bucket. On the wall in front of her, among the rainbow tags, was a stenciling of a moon with a lasso around it. Or maybe it was a noose. She wasn't sure, but it rang a vague bell. It was probably from a movie, knowing this town. Olivia scrubbed it, watching the paint run and the image turn to sopping water.

It was the fourth weekend of her community service, and so far she'd been on time every day. She'd been nervous about it, wary of the workers, worried it would be too hard, that people walking past would stare. But she didn't mind the hard work, and she was too busy to notice anyone staring. The others were fine too. Everyone seemed to just want to get it done. Plus, after five days a week working her apprenticeship, engrossed in sleeve lengths and drapery and scrimping to make her clothes and hair look chicer than they really were, it was sort of nice to put on her shittiest old T-shirt and her crappy jeans and just work.

Anyway, it didn't matter if she liked it or not. She wanted to do it. Giovanni had pleaded her down to just misdemeanor assault. She was *repaying her debt to society* now with six hundred hours of cleaning graffiti and picking up trash and whatever else they threw at her. Her parents had begged her to tell the truth, to tell the police that it was Rani who had stabbed her husband and Austin had set Liv up. But she'd refused because she *was* guilty, just not of that. She had killed Hélène. She needed to pay for it, somehow, or she'd never be able to live with herself. She deserved to live with a conviction next to her name. Luckily, she'd gotten approved for the apprenticeship before her conviction. But whatever job she had next, they'd likely do a background check and she'd have to explain. For the rest of her life, she'd have this stamp on her record. She was okay with that. She turned her music up louder, kept scrubbing.

They'd had the remaining pills in the Stay Awake bottle in Rani and Brian's medicine cabinet tested. Turned out he'd swapped them with a high dosage of Ambien. No wonder they hadn't made her stay awake; they were meant to help insomniacs fall asleep. She'd done some research and found case studies of the active ingredient, zolpidem, causing sleepwalking episodes. Not just that, but sleep-driving, sleep-talking, and sleep-eating apparently. It was a rare side effect, but it had happened before, and she hadn't gotten out of bed again since the last time she took one, the night Brian was stabbed. Still, it wasn't something that could ever be proven definitively, which meant there was always that nudge of fear every time she laid her head on her pillow. She'd always wonder if she'd wake up somewhere else, if something terrible would happen that she wouldn't understand.

Later, when she picked up Casper, they didn't talk. They just blasted TLC and sang along all the way to the garden center and then to the house on Maltman Avenue.

Out in the garden, they built up the sides of the patch with dark brown bricks. Then they poured more soil right on top of the avocado plants, which were now long dead. When they were sure they had at least four inches and that they wouldn't disturb her, they started planting.

Once it was done, Liv and Casper took a step back, hands dirty, shoulders aching, and looked at what they had created. The patch was now covered in carnations, in the darkest shade of purple.

"It looks like a bruise," Casper said.

She stared at the grave. "Maybe it should."

Liv didn't stay for dinner, but promised she'd be back on Friday for *Cat People*. They'd started up their weekly movie nights again, now that Liv had moved out. She'd also started going on regular dog walks with her mum. They'd meet to get a coffee at Millie's Café—her mum never wanted to go to Sabrosa anymore—and they'd go for an early stroll together. The first few times it had been strained, but now she found she really enjoyed it. She was getting to know her mother in a different way, as a person rather than just her mum. They were both being more honest, letting each other in. It was nice.

But tonight, after planting those flowers, she needed escape. She met Austin, Jun, and Sunny at a club on Sunset. She did tequila shots, but only three, and she danced, heat rising through her limbs, sweat clinging to her skin. She closed her eyes and focused on the thump of the music and her body. She was alive and so she had to live; she wasn't going to drown in guilt and sadness.

She dragged Austin home before he got too drunk. She'd spent too many nights sitting with him in the gutter waiting for his head to stop spinning. Hearing him revolving through all his regrets, all the things he should have done differently. Stayed at Berkeley. Told someone about his dad when he first figured out what was happening. And that night . . . she didn't like to hear him talk about that night.

It wasn't far to walk. Their apartment was above a shop. It was a tiny studio, just a bed, bathroom, and kitchenette. It was all they needed.

She stripped off her sweaty clothes and lay down on the mattress. The sign from the pizza shop across the street shone directly into their window, bathing everything in red. Austin got into bed next to her, his bare skin glowing and his breath hot. The light bumped over the scar his father's bullet had left on his shoulder.

They stared at each other. With one finger, he stroked down the bridge of her nose, along her cheekbone, down her neck, like he was committing her to memory. Then he bent down and pulled the tether onto her ankle.

ACKNOWLEDGMENTS

Writing a novel is fun but hard. There are so many people who helped me to get here, but I'll do my best to keep this brief.

Stephanie Rostan, you're incredible. Thank you for being my literary agent and my voice of reason. Thank you for believing in me in the dire moments when I stopped believing in myself!

I am so lucky to have not one but *three* editors who have helped me shape this story into something better: Lexy Cassola, Lindsey Rose, and Robert Watkins, you all pushed me to go deeper and to be braver. Thank you. My hugest appreciation to the whole team at both Dutton and Ultimo Press, especially Lashanda Anakwah, Sarah Oberrender, Andrea Johnson, Charlotte Peters, and copy editor Mary Beth Constant.

Thank you so much to Jon Cassir and Whilhelmina Ross at CAA. Thank you to Courtney Paganelli and Mark Nardullo at LGR, and Anna Carmichael at Abner Stein.

Thank you to Amy Snoekstra, Martina Hoffmann, and Roz Campbell. You all read different drafts of this novel and led me away from the urge to rip it up into pieces and start a little fire. Your insight and wisdom helped me to make this into the novel it is now. Thank you to all my wonderful friends. Especially Isobel Hutton, Phoebe Baker, and Lou James, who never let me get away with selling myself short; and to Tegan Crowley and Heather Lighton, who read everything I write and make me feel like this whole author business is worthwhile. To Lucy Roleff, who inspires me with her art and kindness, and to my writers' group: Jemma van Loenan, Bec Carter-Stokes, and Claire Stone. We're still going strong after a decade!

Ella Baxter and Susie Thatcher, I don't know how I would have gotten through these last years without you both. You are wonderful writers and incredible mothers. I'm so lucky to have met you.

To everyone who befriended me in Los Angeles, especially Joe Osbourne. I often reflect on the time I spent there and it was a big reason why I wrote this book.

This story has made me think hard about family. I know how lucky I am to have one that never makes me feel like I have to be anything but myself. Thank you to my mother, Liz; my father, Ruurd; and my sister, Amy. Thank you to my Lamb family across the seas.

To Marlow, Sadie, and Ryan, there are so many clichés about love and you make all of them feel true, but I'll just say this: My heart is three times bigger because of you.

ABOUT THE AUTHOR

Anna Snoekstra is the author of *Only Daughter*, *Little Secrets*, and *The Spite Game*. Her novels have been published in more than twenty countries and sixteen languages. She has written for *The Guardian*, *Meanjin*, *Lindsay*, *Lit Hub*, and *Griffith Review*. She is a profile writer for *The Saturday Paper*. In 2023 she released her first audio drama, *This Isn't Happening*.

Follow her author journey on Instagram @snoekstra.